Praise for *The Secrets We Keep*

"An immensely powerful, and ultimately uplifting, debut novel."
—bestselling author Katie Fforde

"I thoroughly enjoyed this. I was completely immersed to the point it no longer seemed like I was reading but discovering the truth and lies of these brilliant characters."
—Louise Douglas, author of *The Secrets Between Us*

"A moving exploration of grief and love and the darker depths that lie beneath the surface of a seemingly idyllic marriage."
—Tamar Cohen, author of *The Mistress's Revenge*

"I read *The Secrets We Keep* last night in one big gulp...It's beautiful and sad, the characters so well-drawn, and the writing is gorgeous. I had to take a deep breath and let out a big sigh when I'd finished."
—Julie Cohen, author of *Where Love Lies*

the

secrets

we

keep

the

secrets

we

keep

Stephanie Butland

sourcebooks
landmark

Published by Sourcebooks Landmark, an imprint of Sourcebooks, Inc.
P.O. Box 4410, Naperville, Illinois 60567-4410
(630) 961-3900
Fax: (630) 961-2168
www.sourcebooks.com

Originally published as *Surrounded by Water* in 2014 in the United Kingdom by Bantam Press, an imprint of Transworld Publishers.

Library of Congress Cataloging-in-Publication data is on file with the publisher.

Printed and bound in the United States of America.
VP 10 9 8 7 6 5 4 3 2 1

For my grandmothers,
Isabel and Ursula,
who always knew I was a writer

Hey, Mike.

This is stupid. It's 4 a.m. and I'm sitting downstairs in the dark, writing a letter to you by flashlight. I don't want to put the light on. I don't know why not. I don't know anything. I don't know what day it is. I don't know where you are, but I know you're somewhere. You can't just be nowhere. Not all of that you. You can't have just gone.

Blake was in tears and in uniform when he came to the door, and all I could think of was that you were hurt, that something had happened to you, that you'd gotten in the way of some idiot drunk driver or waded into an argument that had gotten nasty. I remember thinking, Murphy's law that you've gotten hurt walking the dog when it's your job that's supposed to be dangerous. I was already thinking about how we would all tease you for getting into trouble walking a West Highland terrier. I didn't want to look at Blake's face. It wasn't a face that looked as though it was planning to do any teasing, so I didn't look. I couldn't.

I took my coat from the hook and I started to put it on over my pj's because I assumed he was going to take me to the hospital to see you. And then I started to think about it all more seriously. How sad it would be if it was something that meant you couldn't do your job anymore—if you were going to be in a wheelchair, if you had lost your sight—and of how we would get through it, whatever it was, because—well, because what else would we do? It would be you and me, our world inside the big world, a yolk in an egg. It would work. We would make it. It wouldn't have been the first time things didn't go according to plan. I was so ready to be strong.

But my fingers struggled with the zip, and I couldn't see properly, and Blake still wasn't saying anything, even though I was asking, asking, what's happened to him, where is he, was it a car crash, did someone hit him, why can't he ever learn that off duty means off duty. He was just crying, and then he put his hands over my hands and took them away from my coat, and he said my name, twice, once gently, and then again firmly so I had to look into his face, and then I knew.

Blake caught me as I fell. The next thing I knew, I was on the sofa and he was trying to make me drink bloody tea. I think I screamed. I might have thrown the cup—there's a mark on the wall, anyway—and I was shaking, shaking, and he was sitting next to me and talking, but I couldn't hear a thing. Nothing. The newspaper was on the floor. We'd been halfway through the crossword when you took Pepper out. And suddenly I got the one that we were really stuck on. 3 across, Geg (9,3). Scrambled egg. Of course. How often have we said how, once you get it, it's impossible to see how you ever couldn't? And I opened my mouth to tell you. And you weren't there. And just for a split second I saw the world in which you'd never be there again. I think I pulled out some of my hair.

I don't know why I wasn't worried when you were gone so long. I suppose I assumed you'd found some old lady to help across the road. Maybe I didn't think about it at all. Already I look back at that me, happy and unaware, and barely recognize her. Another world. A better world.

Andy came—I suppose Blake had called him—and he took my hand, and he cried, but I didn't. I just felt sick at the thought of how many hands would touch mine in my life, but never yours again. I felt as though I was underwater too, with you, although of course I knew they'd gotten you out. Pepper jumped up onto my lap, and he was still a bit damp—Blake said it was him standing barking on the bank, then swimming around in circles, that drew attention to where you were—and his wet fur felt like the only real thing in this whole horrible world.

And I've been blundering around in the blackest blackness ever since. It hasn't even been two days and already this terrible place feels as though it will be my home forever. I could never have imagined how dark, flat, endless this place would be. Maybe that's why I've stopped putting the lights on: they're pointless. They don't stop the dark.

Oh God, Mike. I can't bear it here, but at the same time I can't be anywhere else. I can't believe that it's true. You wouldn't do this to me. You wouldn't. You promised. You're the person who's supposed to protect me, so you can't be the cause of this.

And anyway, there is so much of you. You can't be nowhere. Where are you?

Come home.

E xxx

B LAKE AND ANDY HADN'T talked about what they would do when they left Elizabeth with her mother-in-law, eight hours after the emergency call from another late-night dog walker reported a young woman, soaked and unconscious, on the bank of Butler's Pond and whipped their world into chaos. They'd obeyed Patricia's stoical instructions—"You know there's nothing you can do for us, so just let us be for a bit"—and gone, leaving the two women side by side on the sofa. Elizabeth was no longer sobbing but making a strange, sad hum of a keening, as though her body had already forgotten how to breathe without also making a cry. Patricia stared straight ahead, eyes glassy, something throbbing in the jut of her jaw.

Even though there's been no discussion, it feels as though there is only one option for the two men. At the gate, Blake says, "Shall we go and have a look?" A question that's not really a question, and they walk the short mile to Butler's Pond in silence as Throckton starts to wake around them.

Andy pulls out his phone. Dials, waits, wonders whether the sound of his wife, sleep-soft and stretching, will be something he can bear. "It's me," he says when she answers, then, after a pause, "Not really. Michael died. Michael drowned." His voice is flat and tight: locked down, for now, until it's safe to start thinking about what's happened. It's too soon to glance at the death of his best friend since childhood for more than a second. Blake matches Andy's steps and listens as he answers Lucy's questions: "I'm with Blake… It looks like an accident… No, I'll go to work… I don't really know, to be honest… OK. Will do." He ends the call and says, "She says I have to make sure I have something to eat before I go to work. She says to say she's thinking of you." Blake nods. Andy redials. He is surprised that his hands are steady. "Me again. I meant to say I love you." He is not the only one, as the news makes its way around Throckton this morning, who will tell someone he loves them. Who will think, *There, but for the grace of God, go any of us.*

It's still dark, so the floodlit place where Michael drowned and Kate Micklethwaite was saved seems more strange than sad. Kate is in the hospital, vomiting water from her lungs and guts, shivering and unable to speak or focus or do anything but submit to needles and lines and wires, something she will have no memory of. Michael, his body identified by Blake earlier, is already in the morgue, where a pathologist will later confirm what Elizabeth has already been told, that he drowned. Alive when he went into the water, dead when he came out. As simple as that.

So Blake and Andy stand and watch as the grass, the mud, the water are photographed and scrutinized. Although Butler's Pond is generally accepted as a beauty spot, a place for Sunday strolls and dog walking and picnics, this corner of it isn't the prettiest. It's one of those places where rubbish blows to and breeds. The duty officer, recognizing the watchers, offers to lift the tape, but Blake waves him away. They are close enough.

"Unbelievable," Andy says after a while.

"You should never underestimate the water," Blake says.

"He was a bloody idiot to go in there," Andy mutters. They both think of the time six months earlier when Michael, one of the first on the scene of a house fire, had walked into the building and emerged with a mother and baby. Everyone had raged at him—firefighters, senior officers, Elizabeth, Patricia—but he had remained steadfast: someone had to save those people and the fire trucks were six minutes away, which Michael knew was long enough for a toddler to die of smoke inhalation. So he'd gone in.

Blake had been working with Michael that day. He remembered how they had both raised their faces to the wind, asked each other if they smelled smoke, just before the call came in. They both knew the drill: get the neighbors out, keep people away, and wait for the fire department. Never, ever go into anywhere full of smoke unless you are absolutely sure you can get out again. But Michael had gone in, and then there was nothing to do but wait, and hope. The hope had run out just a second before the first fire engine had pulled up. Turning toward the firefighters, he had told them what had happened; turning back, he had seen Michael running up the path, blackened and hacking, propelling a young woman who was herself screaming, every line of her body a prayer as she held forward a child who was silent and still in her arms.

And then the controlled chaos began, the hoses and the water and the aching, burning smoke.

It had been months until Michael had admitted to Andy—it was late, and drunken, and deniable—that there was a moment when he thought he was going to die, and he'd been terrified, and life had never been quite the same since, but he couldn't say exactly why. Andy had put him in a taxi home and they'd never spoken about it again. Now, he wishes that he'd asked more questions.

"I don't think he will have felt anything," Blake says, a catch in his voice.

Andy doesn't know whether he's being asked for a medical opinion or a word of comfort, but he agrees with a nod. And then they turn and walk back to the village, avoiding the eyes of the first curious runners and dog walkers as the light starts to make some real headway into the sky. They make a strange pair—or at least they would, were the overall impression that they gave not one of two men walking home after being up all night, united by something outside themselves. Blake is tall and broad, straight and strong. Only close inspection would show that his uniform is not as crisp as it was when he put it on before walking to work sixteen hours ago. His cap hides his receding hairline and so he looks younger than his forty-seven years when he's wearing it. The shadow of the peak hides the shadows under, and in, his eyes. Next to him, Andy seems slight and short, although there's only four inches' height difference, but the doctor is walking with his head down, letting his tiredness show, wearing mismatched clothes, his pale skin made paler by his thick eyebrows and dark brown hair.

He'd gotten dressed in a hurry in the dark, fumbling for quietness and struggling to make the words he'd just heard make sense. "I'm asking you as their friend," Blake had said, "but your medical eye might help. I don't want an on-call doctor if I can have someone she knows here. Just in case. Come and see what you think."

Lucy had sat up in bed and switched on the light as he was searching the bottom of the wardrobe for his shoes. "So the boys sleep, for once, and now you're the one who is waking me up," she'd said, and he'd told her, more simply and quickly than he would have liked to, his own shock speaking, what had happened. Michael, their best man, godfather to their twins, here one minute, dead in the dark water the next. Lucy's eyes, rounding as she listened. Her pushing him away—"go, go to Elizabeth, see what you can do, tell her"—and then she'd hesitated, because, well, tell

The Secrets We Keep

her what? Andy had kissed the top of her head and gone, sat for a moment longer than he needed to on the top stair, fastening his laces, finding what he needed for what would come next, realizing he was just going to have to do it anyway.

"I have to go back to the station," Blake says when they reach the market square. "You?"

"I don't know." There's time for Andy to go home, take a shower, watch cartoons with the boys, and tell Lucy he's all right: there's time to touch them, all three of them, just the simplest stroke of hair or brush of hand that might help. But he's not sure he trusts himself. "I think I'll go have half an hour at the office before I start." The bed in the consulting room will be too narrow to be properly comfortable; the staff shower will run out of hot water before he has finished washing. Better, safer, for now.

"I'll look in on Elizabeth later," Blake says. "I can take Pepper out when I walk Hope."

"I'll call on my way home," Andy says. And, even though they see each other often, they shake hands as they part.

❋

"It's terrible that we have to be practical, but we do," Patricia says later. Elizabeth nods but doesn't agree. She's barely moved from the place Blake steered her to when he brought the news. Every now and then Patricia picks up the balled tissues that lie around her daughter-in-law. Every now and then she stops to have a few tears herself, caught unawares by something she comes across: her son's handwriting on the notepad in the kitchen, his muddy sneakers by the back door. Early on the first day, the phone had rung, and neither she nor Elizabeth had gone to answer it. Instead they'd sat, transfixed by the sound of Michael's recorded voice, cheerfully telling the caller that they'd get back to him or her as soon as they could. It was the only time that Patricia had been comforted by Elizabeth: what seemed horrifying to the newly childless mother gladdened the widow who afterward, during the night, would switch the answering machine on again, sit on the bottom step, and call the number from her cell phone over and over, until her husband's voice became like a blanket, the words heard so often that they became meaningless, but the sound warm and soothing.

Less than forty-eight hours from the knock on the door that would always mark the Before and After of Elizabeth's adult life, she's had conversations about identifying Michael (which Blake has done), the inquest (opened and adjourned), the funeral (a week away), visiting the funeral home (which everyone seems to think she should do), her sister coming over from Australia (which everyone seems to think Mel should do), and the girl Michael saved (hospitalized, shocked, and distressed, but not in any physical danger). She has agreed to meet the vicar, the funeral director, and Michael's boss. She has flinched from every mention of death, or body, or even any use of the past tense as far as Michael is concerned. She feels as though she is being asked to do an awful lot of adult things at a time when she has never been less able to do them. When she looks in the desk for the envelope Michael had put there—*If Michael dies first* written across it in large letters, next to the one marked *If Elizabeth dies first* and which she runs her hands over, wishing, wishing that it had been her, so she didn't have to bear any of this—she cries again. But these tears are not grief: they are gratitude. Elizabeth remembers the afternoon Michael had sat them down and suggested they do this.

It was not long after they'd married, and she'd laughed at him, but when she'd seen the look on his face, when he'd said,

"Elizabeth, you and I of all people know how suddenly people can be lost," she'd felt ashamed of herself and taken the job seriously. They'd both already lost a parent. They'd each put a copy of their will in the envelopes. Then Michael had photocopied the details of their burial plot so they each had a copy of that.

"Seriously?" Elizabeth had asked when he'd bought the plot. "We could have a great weekend away for that money."

"Yes," he'd said, "but a space in a graveyard is forever." They'd written lists of who they wanted to have their possessions. They'd chosen hymns and poems and laughed about how Elizabeth's choice of "All Things Bright and Beautiful" would go down in Throckton. "It will make you smile," she'd said, "and Mel and I used to sing it every Sunday at church. We chose it for our mother's funeral. It's our theme song. Throckton will just have to lump it." When it was done, they'd sealed the envelopes and gone to bed with a bottle of wine.

Elizabeth is so glad of the envelope. Instead of making decisions she can brandish sheets of paper at people. No to medical research, no to an official police funeral, no to cremation. Yes to "Abide with Me" and "The Lord's My Shepherd" and being buried in his uniform. She decides that if it isn't in the envelope, it doesn't matter, and lets Patricia choose caterers and cars and go through her wardrobe and pick out something for her to wear for the funeral. Between conversations, she sits, mostly quiet, and waits. Waits for this not to be true.

❖

Elizabeth has never been to a funeral home before. She and Patricia enter the building together and then take turns going into the room. Patricia goes first and comes out swollen-faced and silent, nodding and clasping Elizabeth's hands. So, still unsure, she rises and faces the oak-effect door.

It's a smaller room than she thinks it will be. The light is low, and the smell of flowers, from a complex arrangement in which some of the smaller blooms are dying, is a mixture of sweetness and must. There's a cross. And there's a seat, next to the coffin. Because there's a coffin. There's a coffin. Elizabeth closes her eyes and tries to make herself breathe. She looks again. Yes, there's a coffin. Mike's coffin. Her soul winces. The top part is open, the rest closed.

Experimentally, Elizabeth puts her hand on the wood near the bottom, where she would imagine Mike's feet to be, were she able to think about his cold, dead feet in a box. She checks her heart and feels nothing new, nothing worse. She takes a step farther up. Her hand is where his knees would be. The wood is smooth. Her palm runs up thigh, over stomach, rests on chest, in a horrible pantomime of what she's done so often in life. Her mind is saying, *Well, if Mike was gone, this is how it would be, yes, but he can't be gone. He can't be.*

Elizabeth knows what needs to come next. So she takes another step, and she looks down.

Mike's face is swollen, only slightly, and an odd color, although that might be the light. Blake had driven them the short distance, neither of them ready for the walk, or the people, or the light of an ordinary day. He had told them in the car that Mike would look as though he was sleeping, but this face, solemn and enclosed, bears no resemblance to her sprawling, duvet-hogging, snoring husband, liable at any moment to throw out an arm and pull her in to him, even though he was fast asleep.

Elizabeth realizes she is holding her breath as she fights to recognize what's in front of her. Cautious, she reaches out her left hand, her own skin dull in this dull light. She touches his face. Her thumb strokes the indentation to the left of his right cheekbone. He is cold, and his skin is powdery, and she watches, waiting for him to open his eyes. Tears fall from hers and gather on his face, and she wipes them away gently with the thumb that wears his wedding ring, and just for a moment these are his tears, and they are crying together.

Elizabeth bends down and whispers, "You can pretend all you like, but I know you haven't left me. I know you wouldn't leave me."

She whispers, "I want to hold your hand." Her own hands, free to rake through her hair and twist around each other and catch at tears falling from her chin, tingle at the horrible thought of being contained in the way his are.

She whispers, "Show me that you haven't gone," and she sits, and she waits, her hand on the coffin where she thinks Michael's hand must be. She closes her eyes. "You promised you would never leave me," she says, trying a different tack, thinking a prod might work where a plea has failed. Time stops, and the world stops, and even the tears stop for a while, as Elizabeth strains for a sign, all of her senses ready and oh so willing. But no sign comes.

TRAGIC DEATH AS MAN SAVES TEEN

Local policeman Michael Gray, 37, drowned in Butler's Pond late Sunday night. It is believed he was walking his dog when he spotted 19-year-old Kate Micklethwaite in trouble in the water and dived into the freezing lake to save her. Michael's dog, Pepper, raised the alarm and passersby found Kate soaked through and unconscious on the bank. Pepper was identified by the attending police officer, Blake Osbourne, who said, "I didn't take a lot of notice of the dog at first. Then when the casualty had been taken away in the ambulance, I realized the dog was still barking. When I went over to it, it jumped into the water and was swimming in circles. When I recognized Pepper, my heart sank. Michael was a brave police officer and an important member of our community. We will all miss him terribly, as a colleague and as a friend."

Michael was well-known in Throckton, where he grew up. He leaves a widow, Elizabeth, whom he met while traveling around Australia. His mother, Patricia, head librarian in Throckton, speaking through a family friend, said, "We cannot believe this has happened. Michael was a good, kind man, a loving son and husband, and I don't know what we will do without him. We are in shock. It is typical of Michael that he would die saving someone else."

Kate Micklethwaite is expected to leave the hospital in the next few days. She has regained consciousness, and her condition is said to be stable. Her father, Rufus

Micklethwaite, owner of architectural practice Light and Shade, broke down as he said, "Kate is a determined girl, and we are sure she will make a full recovery. Her mother and I are so grateful to Mr. Gray and so devastated by this tragedy. We cannot believe this has happened. It feels like a nightmare."

An inquest into the death of Mr. Gray was opened and adjourned until April, pending the postmortem report.

P ATRICIA MAKES HER FIRST foray into Throckton proper on the day before the funeral. For the past week she's walked swiftly, head down, to Michael and Elizabeth's house and back, but it's not far, and she's been coming and going at odd times—before eight in the morning, after nine at night—when she's less likely to be stopped and sympathized with by people she knows. She's bypassed the town square and the streets where her friends live. It's not that she doesn't appreciate their support; it's that, for now, everything needs to be controlled, appointments made, so she can be ready. There has been no spare energy in Patricia, no space for an unplanned conversation. The funeral director, the police officers, the vicar have all come to them, knowing how grief immobilizes and restricts the heart's ability to stray far from the hearth.

But Patricia knows that difficulties don't get less difficult for being left unfaced. And so she is walking from her house into the town, ready and not ready.

Silence washes in front of her as she walks. The familiar streets, curving and banking down to the square, feel the same as they always have. The pavements are broad enough for two strollers to pass; most people keep their hedges nicely trimmed. Patricia has lived here all her life, and she doesn't think there's anyone in this small town she doesn't know by sight. The market square is more of a triangle, and Patricia can tell you the history of every shop that's there: why the family who owns the butcher's shop settled here, how much nicer the bookshop was before it started selling gifts as well, why the baker is closing down. She hasn't gotten as far as the crossroads before the first person has stopped her, with tearful eyes, with kind words to say about her son.

The day is both frosty and bright, and the air spears her as she takes deep breaths and looks firmly ahead, trying to see who is looking at her before deciding whether to accept the proffered eye contact. Of course, for everyone who seeks her eye, there are others who turn away, embarrassed and unsure, as though the death of a child could be catching. Patricia has no time for such people. She has spent the last six days holding Elizabeth's hand as they planned a funeral for a man who neither of them can believe is dead.

A part of her wonders whether she is up to this, but as she said to Elizabeth—who refuses to take off Michael's sweater and who, after three days of crying and vomiting, had to be coaxed into a bath like a child—she's always gotten on with what life has dealt her. She didn't ask to be a widow, but when she became one she got on with it. "You had Mike," Elizabeth had said, without malice but with a shuddering sadness that had made Patricia pause, before agreeing that, yes, having a seven-year-old boy to look after when she lost her husband did make a difference. Privately, she thought that she never would have let herself go, regardless. John had always admired her smartness, and she considered it a point of honor to maintain those standards. Which is why she is walking through Throckton today. Monday is her day for the hairdresser. The library, where she works, is closed on Mondays, and so she's had a wash and blow-dry at the hairdresser's every

Monday for the last forty years, with a cut every two months. When she realized this morning what day it was, she decided she'd go anyway. "We have to start somewhere," she'd said to Elizabeth on the phone, and Elizabeth had said yes in a way that meant no, and Patricia had checked that Andy would be with her, and then she'd put on her black dress and her green scarf and she'd buttoned up her coat and she'd stepped out onto the streets that had been the backdrop to her life. Her always-neat hair, still chestnut like her eyes, is as much a part of Patricia's identity as her low-heeled court shoes and the fact that she never wears makeup or trousers. Now that her identity as a mother is lost, she clings to what she has.

❋

Andy has been a regular visitor at Elizabeth's house since Michael died, calling in at lunchtime or on his way to or from work before returning to the warm sweet chaos of his own home. (He is making an effort, in his mind, not to call it "Michael and Elizabeth's," but he did it just this morning, telling Lucy he was going around during his lunch break but not in the evening, and Lucy said gently, "It's just her house now.") He's not sure that Elizabeth registers his presence a lot of the time, as she sleeps and gazes, rubbing, rubbing at her collarbone without noticing that she is doing it, but needing to do something. This morning, though, Elizabeth is talking.

"I don't know how she can do it," she says for perhaps the fifteenth time. "How can she have her hair done? How can she go and have her hair done when Mike's—when this has happened? How can she care what she looks like?"

"I don't think she does care about her hair, so much as needing to do normal things," Andy says. "I think it's just her coping strategy."

"Coping strategy? Christ, Andy, we don't need a strategy. We need…" And Elizabeth is crying again, her body rounding in on itself, her breath coming spiked and harsh from a broken place. "We need Mike. You have a strategy for marketing, for chrissakes. For selling your house. You don't have a strategy for this."

"I'm sorry," Andy says, thinking, *I've said one thing, one thing, and I've made it worse.*

"No, I'm sorry," she says. "It's not you. I just—I don't know how she can. I feel like I'm having to force myself to keep my throat open every time I try to eat something. I can't imagine how I used to be able to do the things I used to do. And her son has—and she's lost her son—and she's not even going to miss her hair appointment."

"Elizabeth—"

She holds up a hand. "I know, Andy; each to their own." And then her hand falls, with it her shoulder, the straightness that her spine had had for that outraged minute or two. "She'll be sitting at the hairdresser's, won't she, saying, 'That daughter-in-law of mine, not having her hair done for the funeral—what would Mike say at her letting herself go?'"

Andy smiles a smile that says, *Yes, but I'm not going to say so.* "This is the hardest thing either of you will ever go through," he offers instead.

"That's assuming we'll get through it," Elizabeth says.

❧

Throckton is, as Patricia's mother used to say, big enough to get up to something but small enough that everyone will know about it. Patricia had married a man who drove local buses all his working life and was as content in his job and his hometown as any man could be. He borrowed library books about natural history, and it was only when his mother told Patricia's mother that he'd taken a shine to her that Patricia started to notice him: the way he was often there as she was closing the library, his hesitating smile, his clean fingernails. Patricia has often thought about how proud John would have been to see their son, straight and strong as a country oak, serving their community in the way he did. It would have been better if Michael had married a local girl, of course; there seemed no sense in bringing a wife back from Australia when there were so many here who would have snapped him up, but still. Even so. She had a son to be proud of. Patricia pauses for a moment, pretending to look in her handbag to avoid the next well-wisher. John always told her how strong she was—she often wonders whether he had a sense that he didn't have long, that he was trying to make her ready—but she isn't sure she is strong enough to think of her son in the past tense yet.

✱

Anyone watching Elizabeth—and there are plenty of people, a seemingly endless churn of concerned faces, all with the same questions and touches above the elbow and tears and apologies, all with different memories of Michael, each of which sticks a little shard of hurt into a place that she doesn't expect—anyone watching sees the moments when she starts to realize the enormity of what's happening to her.

She pushes her hair back. She holds her breath and her eyes grow bigger, or appear to, although it's actually just the effect of the tears filming before they start to tumble. Her lips pull tightly in, then vanish from sight. She opens her hands, palms wide to the world, an unconscious begging. These are the moments when Michael's death starts to seem real. Even though she cries almost constantly, thinks about Michael constantly, talks only about Michael, winds her wedding ring around and around her finger and Michael's around and around her thumb—even though she is a picture of grief, the moments when Elizabeth starts to truly get what her life is about now make the people around her move toward her, touch her, just fingertips on her shoulder, an arm looping around her back. Just a touch to say, *Remember, I am here. This will not be the end of you, although, at this moment, you feel ended.*

Although Andy feels hopeless, helpless, barely in control himself, he is the best at these moments. During his years as a doctor he's watched a lot of deaths and he's seen a lot of grief. He's told a lot of bereaved people that, yes, he can prescribe sleeping pills and antidepressants, but the fact is that grief is a long road. It's a process, and it takes time. So, he tells his bereft patients and friends and relations: "What you need more than anything is time, and the expectation that this is going to take time. Let yourself be sad. You've loved; you've lost. Let there be time to heal." Of course, people agree with him, but he knows that most of them are disappointed. They want someone, somehow, to take the pain away.

But Elizabeth is different. She doesn't want him to take the pain away. She's almost translucent with misery. She bats away suggestions about sleeping pills; she ignores fruit and cookies and other morsels Patricia tries to get her to eat; she lets tea go old and cold at her elbow. Andy watches her, and he wishes for a cure for grief. Either that or a cure for drowning. Or one for bloody stupid heroics. He wishes for his best friend back.

When Patricia gets back from the hairdresser's, Elizabeth says, "They've done a good job today, Patricia," and Patricia says,

"They said they would come here to do yours, if you wanted," and Andy takes Pepper for a walk around the block because the weight of the effort in the room is crushing his chest.

Mike,

I think it's starting to dawn on me. The fact that you're not here and you're not coming back. Even though I feel like all I do is cry, even though you are all that people come and talk to me about, even though I've looked at you lying in a box with your name on it and tomorrow I'm somehow supposed to watch as they put it in the ground—it's all still unreal.

When I wake up and you're not there, it takes me a minute or two to realize that your side of the bed is empty forever, not just because you're on an early shift. When Susan next door brought in the shopping I'd asked for, I'd gotten some fig rolls, even though you were the only one who ever ate the things. I ironed all of your shirts yesterday because not ironing them felt like giving up; I didn't know what else to do with them. I hung them in the wardrobe, and the smell of your leather coat burst out at me when I opened the door. It was like a punch in the stomach.

People keep offering to "clear things out" for me. They mean, "Let me throw away Mike's toothbrush, because I understand that you don't want to. Let me get rid of the half-used shaving foam and the nearly gone shower gel and the new shower gel ready for when that one runs out, because it will be easier for me to remove these reminders than it would be for you to do it." But I say, "No, thank you." I don't understand why a half-empty bathroom cabinet is better than one with all of your half-used stuff in it. I can shower in the smells you showered in. I can open your aftershave and let lime scent the air while I have a bath, although it doesn't smell the same when it's not on your skin, and when I wear it, it seems too sharp. I can put the blade of the razor that you ran down your face against my fingertip. Why would I want your things taken away?

Yesterday I took Pepper into the garden—Blake has been walking him for me—and stood with my bare feet on the cold stones and felt frightened by how big the world is. Nothing seems to make sense anymore. Sometimes I want to go to bed and it's only 10 a.m.; sometimes a whole day goes by and I haven't even gotten dressed. I can't eat, and then I'm standing in front of the fridge eating cheese out of the packet while your mother hovers and offers to make me an omelet.

I keep trying to work out what happened. I don't know how you ended up in there, in that cold water. I don't know why you couldn't get out. I don't know why I thought it was a better idea to sit on the sofa when I could have put my coat on and come with you, and then there would have been two of us, and between us we could have saved that girl without losing you. I don't even remember when my evening bath became such a habit that the evening walk became your job. I don't know why I didn't realize you were late, or ring you, or do something. There are so many places where things could have taken a different turn, but they didn't.

So I don't think this is the real version. I've just slipped into the wrong scenario somehow. Every time I hear the door open, I wait for it to be you, and you'll smile your normal homecoming smile, and I'll say, "God, Mike, I was just having the most awful dream."

E xxx

B LAKE'S FIRST ACT, ON the morning after Michael died, was to
ask whether someone else could be family liaison officer for
the Micklethwaite family. He wasn't surprised by the answer he
got. He said, very calmly, "You are asking me to be compassionate
to the person whose actions resulted in the death of the man who
has been my friend and colleague for more than fifteen years. You
want me to support people who have not lost their daughter, while
I also support a widow so shell-shocked that she barely remembers
her own name. I'm not sure I can."

"You can, Blake," had come the answer, "and I'm afraid
you must."

He looked at his shoes while he heard how he is the best, the most
experienced officer available, and was reminded that family liaison
wasn't so much about drying tears as looking out for something that
has been missed. "We owe it to Michael to make sure that we have
the full story." He listens to the part about how, although obviously this was a difficult time for them all, losing a colleague and
friend, the powers that be have every faith in his professional capa-
bilities; we must be strong for our fallen colleague. After a while
he stopped listening and just waited for the noise to stop. When it
did, he went straight to the hospital and found Kate Micklethwaite.

Even surrounded by tubes and wires, tucked under a faded puce blanket and seen through a mist of grief and resentment, she is a beautiful girl. Her mother, Richenda, wan and almost worn through, has a certain grace as she gets up to greet him; her fingernails are the pink of the inside of shells, her hand small in his. Kate's father Rufus's handshake is gruff and wary. Kate doesn't move, but the atmosphere in the room, and the conversation he's just had with the doctor on duty, tell Blake that she is doing nothing more worrying than sleeping. Richenda offers him a chair and he sits. Rufus says, "We've already had some of your people around. She doesn't remember anything, apart from slipping on the bank. She's in shock." His voice breaks. "She could have died." Blake holds Rufus's gaze for long enough for Rufus to understand what Blake isn't saying—*your daughter could have died, but my colleague did die*—before he sits and introduces himself as their family liaison officer.

Rufus wants to know why they need him. Blake takes a deep breath. *You're good at your job*, he tells himself, *you can do this*, and he selects the candor card. "You might not need me at all, Mr. Micklethwaite," he says, "but I'm here if you do. I'll keep you informed about matters relating to Michael Gray." He pauses as Richenda's whole body seems to flutter at him.

She indicates her sleeping child. "We haven't talked about Michael with Kate yet," she says, her eyes pleading for understanding and her hands, unconscious, making a prayer, "and your colleagues only asked what she could remember; they didn't tell her anything."

"Ah." Blake plays the caution card alongside candor. "Well, I'll keep you informed of developments regarding Michael. We'll need to talk to Kate again about what happened, and my colleagues will be in touch about that. If Kate or any of you want extra support or help, I can point you in the right direction. That's what I'm here to do. You've been through a difficult time"—Rufus barks his agreement, a what-would-you-know laugh Blake ignores, concentrating on Richenda—"and you may find that there are all sorts of repercussions as you go through the next few months. I'm here to help, and to keep you informed of any—developments."

Rufus walks to the window and looks out over the parking lot, his back to Blake, unwilling to admit that he is in a place where a police family liaison might be appropriate.

Richenda nods her understanding. Carefully, holding Blake's gaze then flicking her glance to Kate to make sure he understands, she asks, "How is Michael's family?"

"Struggling," he says. Tears stand ready to ambush him and he stands, too suddenly, the scrape of the chair making Kate stir. They all freeze, a tableau of tension watching to see whether she will wake or sleep on.

She sleeps.

Blake leaves. He's gotten as far as the elevator when Richenda catches up with him, interrupting as he swipes at his eyes.

"Thank you," she says, then, "I'm so sorry. About your colleague. We are so grateful to him."

"He was more than a colleague," Blake says. "He was a great friend."

"I'm so sorry," Richenda says again. She means it, he can tell.

The elevator doors open before Blake has time to see whether he has a grace card. Not this time. He steps in and almost says, *I can do my job better than this.* But he doesn't trust his voice to get the words out, and he isn't sure that Richenda deserves to hear them.

Blake goes straight home. He drinks whiskey until he can barely move. Had there been anyone to talk to, he couldn't have spoken, his tongue too slow to form so much as a word, his thoughts too fast to catch. He wonders what on earth he could have done differently, what he could have said to Michael to change the equation that had this result. There seem to be an infinite number of possibilities, spiraling away from him like mirrors reflected in mirrors, as useful as shadows.

In the end, he sleeps in his chair.

❀

It is five days after the accident when Kate is allowed home. What she remembers is not enough for anyone, but it's all there is: after leaving a friend's house, realizing she'd had too much to drink, she'd decided to take a walk around Butler's Pond to clear her head. She hadn't known how close to the water she was walking until she lost her footing. She remembers the slip, the fall, the cold. She has no recollection of anything else, until the hospital. She had no idea that Michael was even there, something that makes Elizabeth blanch when Blake tells her. The doctors cannot say whether or when any other memories of that night will return, but she is recovering well in all other respects. She knows her family, the month and year, that she has a place at Oxford to study geography. She can tell her mother where to find her iPod and the book she's reading and the clothes she would like her to bring in for when she is allowed to get up and dress. Her temperature, pulse, heart, lungs, bowels, pupils are all behaving as they should. So Rufus and Richenda have been permitted to maneuver her into the car and bring her home.

As Richenda locks the car and follows Rufus and Kate up the path—wretched, wretched squeaking gate—she thinks about the time she has spent sitting by her daughter's bedside in the intensive care unit: about how those first twelve hours had been like twelve months of waiting for bad news to open its mouth, and the time since filled with a mix of fear, relief, and fresh guilt. Her shoulders ache, her eyes feel scratchy, her hips are knotted from too long in bad chairs, her bowels blocked with cheap sandwiches and more coffee than she wanted. But the pain in her body is nothing, really. Her heart has been shriveled by watching her daughter struggle and sob, sleep and ebb. There's been nothing for her to do for Kate but dampen her lips with a flannel and watch the monitors as though it's the watching that makes them give the readings that make the nurses smile and the doctors nod. Her mind hurts from thinking about what could have happened to her girl, nineteen years old, but still as precious and vulnerable to Richenda as she was on the day she was born, a miracle of blood and squalling. Her mind hurts even more from the effort of avoiding thoughts of what did happen to that poor policeman.

During the hell of the Accident & Emergency Unit, Rufus and Richenda had stood truly together for the first time in twenty years, answering questions with one voice, holding one breath. As soon as Kate was declared out of danger, they had filled the time at her bedside with round after round of Who's to Blame? It's a game they are both good at, with an easy seventeen years of practice under each of their belts—nearer twenty-two, if you go back to the First Mistress incident, although the birth of Kate is tacitly acknowledged by both parties to have been a wiping clean of the slate.

But the stakes of Who's to Blame? had never been as high as they were in the bleak, bleeping hospital room, and for once the deck was not loaded in Richenda's favor. Rufus blamed Richenda for not knowing where Kate was going. Richenda retaliated by reminding her husband of two facts: their daughter was nineteen, and he was her father and equally entitled to know where she was, especially as they were both in the house when she went out. Rufus scored extra points for being the first one to wonder when Kate might be home; Richenda drew level by trying to call her and, finding her phone switched off, leaving a message. Both of them admitted to having no idea why she was anywhere near Butler's Pond. Both were guilty of going to bed still wondering where Kate was, but Rufus claimed a bonus for not having yet gone to sleep when the hammering at the door began. Richenda was the one who had interrogated each of Kate's friends—not that there were many, most being off on gap-year adventures—as they arrived at the hospital full of tears and exclamations. In what his wife considered to be a rare show of backbone, Rufus had refused to leave his daughter's side when the police came to her hospital room, and sent them away when he judged that Kate had had enough of them.

In the end, they'd called it a draw. "So long as she's all right, it doesn't matter, does it?" Rufus had asked. "No, it doesn't," Richenda had replied and had patted him on the leg—knee rather than thigh—and found a feeble smile from somewhere.

And now they are coming home, the words *out of danger* dancing in front of their tired eyes, permission at last to admit that for a moment, just a moment, they wondered whether Kate would live beyond the night that she, for no good reason they can imagine, had to be rescued from January-cold water by a man she didn't know.

Someone has left flowers for Kate on the doorstep. Rufus has stepped himself and Kate around them, but Richenda picks them up. "I'll put these in your room, Kate, if you like," she says, and Kate nods as she starts to make her way slowly upstairs. Their home, all shades of cream and green, feels cold. The stainless steel of the kitchen, plates and pans and wine glasses neglected since the midnight sprint to the hospital, couldn't be less welcoming.

Richenda knows that her husband doesn't like the flowers—she can feel him sneer, without turning around to see it—but the burst of too-sweet scent and too-frilly petals as she cuts through the cellophane makes her smile.

"Carnations aren't illegal," she says, "and you should be glad that people are thinking of her."

Rufus doesn't reply. He is cutting bread to go in the toaster. She can see it's too thick, but she doesn't say anything. He always cuts it too thick. It always burns. He always grumbles as he scrapes the black crumbs away. She no longer points out the dial that controls the temperature, but she thinks about it, every single time.

"Do you want some toast?" Rufus asks.

We are both tired, Richenda reminds herself. *We have both had a terrible few days. He has done worse things than forget that in twenty-five years of marriage he has never seen me ask for, make, or eat toast.* "No, thank you," she says, and she takes the vase upstairs.

❀

Richenda is on a damage-limitation dash to see a client and then on to the supermarket that afternoon when Kate comes downstairs. Rufus, sure the danger is over, is trying to salvage something from a missed deadline; he makes "won't be a minute" faces at his daughter while he talks to a client on the phone.

"Jeez," she says when he hangs up. "That woman wants a summerhouse really badly."

Rufus laughs more than he needs to. "I've had to say I'll drive the plans over to her later," he says. "Do you want to come? You don't have to come in."

"No," she says as she settles herself into the corner of the sofa. "I'd like to know how Michael is, though."

"Michael?" Rufus has a moment of genuine perplexity. The man who saved Kate's life has been so thoroughly rebranded, under this roof, as "that poor policeman," that he has to work out who she means. When Michael doesn't have a name his death is fractionally easier to bear: it becomes generic, sad but acceptable, a policeman sacrificing himself for the community he served.

"Michael Gray," she says. "I keep asking how he is, but no one's telling me. I'm not stupid, Dad. I'm getting better. You can tell me. Is he hurt?" Her words are braver than her eyes.

Rufus thinks about the conversations that he and Richenda, and he and Richenda and Blake, have had about this. Blake has told them that there's a limit to how long his colleagues will be able to avoid the issue of Michael's death when they talk to Kate. Although no one's in any doubt that what happened was an accident, a dreadful accident, Kate will almost certainly be required to appear at the inquest.

"And anyway," Blake reminded them—in a rather patronizing fashion, in Rufus's view—"this is Throckton, and this is all anyone is talking about. And as soon as she's home and back on Facebook, there'll be nothing you can do."

"Yes, yes," Rufus had said. "We get the picture. She needs to know. We need to find the right time."

And he and Richenda had agreed they would tell her carefully, together, when they thought that time had come. But looking at his daughter, he sees that it will never be the right time. He sits down next to her, settling one leg underneath him so he can face her, takes her hands.

"Michael Gray died," he says, looking straight into her eyes. "He drowned. The police need to talk to you some more, when you're up to it, but they think he got you out of the water and then couldn't get out himself."

"No," she says. Rufus watches her, helpless as she turns the color of a lime-washed wall, anxious as the hands he holds go from warm to cold to chill.

"No." The shaking seems to start at her heart and ripple out, more violent at her fingers and toes.

"It was a terrible accident," Rufus offers, although he can see how inadequate his offering is. "A terrible accident, Kate. But accidents happen. And you have to think that you could have both been dead."

"No." And Kate pulls away from him and lies back, and she closes her eyes, and Rufus sits with her cold feet in his lap and wills the heat from his hands into them. He's still there when Richenda gets home. He's still thinking about the weight of what has happened: of how a death on your behalf might make you bow or buckle, or force you to be strong. Neither option is what he wants for his daughter. But they are the only options Kate has.

Mike,

I'm going to the F word in the morning. I've become one of those people I used to despise, who say "passed on" and "gone" instead of the real word for the thing that you've done, except now I understand why they did it, because when you hear the real word it's like being taken back to that first horrible moment, every single time.

Apart from the funeral home, the only times I've been outside until now are when I've stood on the paving stones by the back door while Pepper frolics around the garden. (I'm sure he's looking for you. He thinks you're hiding, or playing. I don't know how to explain it to a dog.) Even this pathetic winter light is too much for me. Your mother opens the curtains every morning when she comes. I leave the bedroom ones drawn all the time.

I miss the little things. I miss smiling with you about nothing much, like Pepper squeaking and growling in his sleep, or your mother plumping the cushions when she thinks I'm not looking. I miss you getting into bed in the middle of the night and wrapping yourself around me. I miss eating pizza out of the box and drinking champagne out of the flutes that were the first thing we bought together. I miss the smell of Deep Heat in the bathroom when you've had a shower after a run.

I miss you.

I wonder whether we couldn't have a baby because of this. Because it's written, somewhere, that this was going to happen, and when it did, I'd fall apart, and no child should have to lose their father and watch their mother…this. I don't have the heart for this life on my own. I need you.

E xxx

MELISSA IS IN THE air somewhere above the Indian Ocean when Michael's funeral service takes place. She's been working on UK time since she got on the plane, so when 11:00 a.m. comes around, she puts her book away, takes her headphones out, and puts on her eye mask. She sits with her hands in her lap for what seems like the right amount of time for a funeral to take, remembering the man who her sister first described to her, eleven years ago, as "quite a sweetheart, for an English bloke." And so he had been. If Mel ignores the part where he persuaded her sister to move half a world away, she had no complaints about Michael, who made her sister happy, who came to Australia and sweated and swatted at insects and pretended that he loved the place for the sake of Elizabeth.

Later, when her solitary funeral tribute is over, Mel watches as the clouds below ignore her, and she thinks about how all of this global village stuff is crap when your sister's husband dies, and your sister is on the other side of the planet. She's talked to Elizabeth every day, and she's listened to all that she has managed to stutter out, about how she has to learn to live without Mike and she might as well start now, and how all she's doing is thinking and sleeping and trying to eat what Patricia tries to feed her, and how

Mel has her own life to live. Melissa had pretended to listen—or rather, she'd listened to what was happening between and behind Elizabeth's words, the scrabbling for some sort of purchase in reality, in sanity, in the place outside the nasty black bubble she was trapped in—and then she'd overruled.

"I've bought my ticket, I'm arriving on the eighteenth of January, I'm staying for as long as I need to, and you, Sister, are just going to have to suck it up."

"OK," Elizabeth had said, and it had pleased Melissa to hear relief in her voice, although she half knows that it was her imagination that put it there. She can't bear the thought of her sister in that funny little place she lives in, with a crone of a mother-in-law as the closest thing she has to a family. Mel doesn't try to sleep, or read, or do anything except watch the hours pass, and the miles decrease, on the screen in front of her.

When Andy picks her up he notices the wide-eyed, pale-faced shock of her, part long-haul flight, part landing in the real version of the abstract thing she's been thinking about ever since she got the call.

"How bad is it?" she asks as they walk to the car.

"Bad," he says.

"Is that a medical opinion?"

"It's everyone's opinion," he says. "You'll see."

❈

Andy stops at the gate and unloads the suitcase from the boot. "I'll see you later," he says. "I've hardly seen Luca and Toby. And Lucy. Since. And you'll want to—"

"Yes," Mel says, thinking, *I want nothing less than what's behind that door. I want nothing less than to see my sister in the way I'm going to see her.* She almost asks him to come in, then she sees the way he pulls at his tie, the places he's caught his chin when he shaved, the pinkness of eyes unused to crying.

"Sure," she says. "Tell them hello."

"I will," Andy says, and he nods, gets into the car, starts the engine, and drives away. Mel takes a breath and opens the gate. She's never been so sorry, and so glad, to arrive anywhere.

❋

It's Patricia who opens the door, more gaunt than Mel remembers her.

"I'm so sorry," Mel says, and Patricia says, "Yes," and there's a moment—just a moment—when the two of them could be friends. Mel almost forgives all of the barbed remarks about dyed hair and funny accents she's batted away with sarcasm over the years, and Patricia could forget how small and silly Mel makes Throckton seem—and, by extension, her whole life and all that's dear to her. But it's too much effort, especially now.

"Those boots will mark the floor, you know, they got rid of the carpets and Michael stripped the floorboards last summer," Patricia says, and Mel, momentarily cowed by this intimate domestic detail of the dead, bends to take her boots off on the threshold.

Magnanimous in victory, Patricia offers, "She's sleeping," then adds, "The pot's just warming."

"Oh, good," Melissa mutters at her back. "Tea."

There's time, before Elizabeth comes down, for Mel to hear about the funeral in the forensic detail of someone who must remember, as though the power of remembering is a measure of love. Patricia talks as though she cannot stop: who came, where they sat, what they said, when they cried. Elizabeth, scratching at the side of her neck until it bled; Blake, who was sitting on the other side of her, taking her hand and holding it, firmly, in his own, although the fingers kept fluttering and flinching. Andy's eulogy, touching and true, although it didn't mention Michael's father, which was a shame. Elizabeth slipping off her shoes and rubbing one foot against the other incessantly, and having to be reminded to put the shoes on again before they followed the coffin out. The Micklethwaite man, shame-faced, at the back. Patricia wouldn't have said he could be there when Blake came with the request, but Elizabeth had said of course he must come, how kind. (Patricia doesn't admit to Mel that, when Blake had left, she had objected to Rufus coming to the funeral, and Elizabeth had turned bemused blue eyes on her and said, as though it was the only possible option, "But, Patricia, you know what Mike would have said. He'd have said that this is no one's fault. He'd have said he was glad she was alive. We should let them come. If it was me, I would want to go," and she had felt ashamed of her own fury at that stupid, stupid Micklethwaite girl, who had not only killed her son, but also seemed to have done so in nothing more than a moment of fecklessness.)

Mel listens, and watches, and waits for a sound of Elizabeth. It's dark, and she's had two pots of tea and a sandwich selected from the funeral leftovers, and struggled to stay awake and listen to Patricia's memories of Michael—already well on the way to sainthood in his mother's heart—before they hear footsteps on the stairs. "I'll put the kettle on," says Patricia, and Mel's heart sinks for a moment before she recognizes that the tea is tact, and smiles her thanks.

Despite the warnings from Andy, the memory of her sister's sobs on the phone, and the litany of uneaten meals, unwashed hair and unopened curtains from Patricia, Mel is still unprepared for the way her sister looks. Elizabeth's skin has taken on a tint of gray, her eyes have dulled like glass tossed in a violent sea, and her body has defeat in every line and muscle. She looks half dead herself. The tears start in Mel before they erupt from Elizabeth. They hold on to each other, sobbing sadly and wearily, each remembering how they did this when their mother died, two frightened little monkeys clinging on to each other for dear life. In the kitchen, Patricia permits herself a tear before loading cups into the dishwasher, and is too tired to push away the thought that Elizabeth might—will, in all probability—find herself another husband, while she will never have another son, and yet they must all feel sorry for Elizabeth. Later, watching Mel spoon-feed soup to her sister, who opens and closes her mouth like a sad bird, she wishes she could take the thought back. *But,* she thinks as she lets herself into her own dark house, *if I could take things back, I'd start by taking back whatever happened that night, and then none of us would be where we are, and Michael wouldn't be gone.*

❀

The next evening, Andy comes for dinner—well, he brings dinner—and he, Elizabeth, and Mel sit around the table and have something that, given a casual glance from the outside, would look like a normal evening. Except that a normal evening takes no effort, and it's clear from the start that there is effort everywhere, from all of them.

Elizabeth has told herself over and over that she's allowed to do this, to sit at a table with her sister and her oldest Throckton friend and eat and drink and remember her husband. But when she walks into the kitchen where Mel and Andy are joking as they get out the takeaway cartons, something happens and she can't remember where the plates are, and Mel has to steer her to the table and sit her there, in pajama bottoms and the sweater that Mike used to wear in the evenings as he watched Pepper have a last-thing sniff around the garden. She's like a child coming to the table for the first time after a sickness.

Mel and Andy are genuinely glad to see each other. They work out that it's ten years since they met, on the eve of Michael and Elizabeth's wedding, and speculate about what Mel's then-boyfriend is doing now. (Andy reckons prison; Mel thinks she heard a rumor that he joined a cult. Elizabeth rouses herself long enough to point out that Mel seemed quite keen on him at the time. Andy and Mel look at each other as though they've won a prize.) There's no reason to wonder where Andy's then-girlfriend is: she's at home, with the boys, and so Mel looks through the photos on his phone and says, "You know I'm not a fan of the smaller members of the human race, but they are cute. They were just little tiny balls of wrinkles the last time I was here. Your eyes." "Yes, and Lucy's smile," Andy says.

But both of them are horribly aware of the ghost at the table, and the almost-ghost he has left behind, pushing rice around her plate and trying to smile, which is more pitiful than when she cries. The only other time Elizabeth has anything to offer—Mel and Andy have understood that as yet the conversation can do no more than nod toward Michael—is when Mel talks about the discomfort of the single bed in the spare room. Andy, who spent the first night after Michael's death in it, agrees.

"I didn't think it was too bad," Elizabeth says. For a second, Andy and Mel catch each other's eyes, then Mel asks, gently, when her sister has slept in that bed. "Oh, when I can't bear to go into our bedroom," she says matter-of-factly, and then something happens to her face—it's like watching a time-lapse film of one of those daisies that only come out in the sun—and she gets up from the table and goes upstairs.

Mike,

Everything's still black.

I keep telling myself that it doesn't matter what happened to you, but it does. I keep telling myself that you're—you know, gone—and that's the only thing that matters. But I can't bear that I don't really know. I feel like a failure. Mel won't let me listen to your voice in the night—she says it's unhealthy—so, instead, I lie in bed, or sit on the sofa on the nights when I can't be in our bed without you, and I imagine.

I imagine Pepper running off and you following him and finding Kate. Maybe she was waiting for a boyfriend. Even your mother can't dig up much dirt on her. The worst thing she's done seems to have been to have her nose pierced for a dare, though she took it out when her Oxford interviews came around—she's very clever, very hardworking, quite intense by the sounds of it. (I don't think you get 4 As at exams by being laid-back.) She was supposed to be doing some fantastic gap-year thing this year, but apparently she got cold feet and canceled at the last minute. God, how I wish she'd gone. Then she'd be shagging some floppy-haired traveler right now, and we'd all be happy.

Maybe the sound of you surprised her, and she got up and moved away and slipped and fell into the water.

I'm sure you didn't hesitate. I'm sure you were in there before you'd *thought it through properly. We promised we'd never mention the Burning Building Incident again, and I'm as good as my word, but you can't be surprised that I'm thinking of it. You stupid, stupid, brave, stupid, stupid man. It must have been so cold, so cold, and I bet she panicked and clung to you and made it really difficult for you. I think you got her as close to dry land as you could, and she pulled herself the rest of the way.*

But then I don't know what happened. I don't know why you didn't follow her onto the bank and get yourself safe. I can't believe you wouldn't have fought to get back to me. It just doesn't make any sense.

Sometimes when I'm thinking about this, in the night, I can't breathe and I feel as though I'm with you there, in the water, and I feel so cold and so frightened and my whole body is so impossibly heavy. Last night Mel came in and shook me—she thought I was having a nightmare, she heard me thrashing about and crying. I didn't tell her that I was awake all the time.

Come back to me, Mike. There must be a deal you can do. When I asked you, in the chapel, to send me a sign, I felt so sure you would. I haven't forgotten. I'm waiting.

E xxx

K ATE'S RECOVERY IS SLOW. Her body can't seem to remember what it was like before, when it was carefree, when it could trust itself to be strong and supple and had no idea that one day something might go wrong, and it might be overpowered. Her heart labors and burns under the weight of Michael Gray's death, and when interviewed she remembers nothing more of what happened that night at Butler's Pond, despite gentle questioning, vigorous questioning, and questioning under hypnosis, during which she kept her hands curled in on themselves so tightly that her fingernails bit her palms and kept her mind well under her own control.

✿

"She's barely coming downstairs, let alone going out, Rufus," Richenda says wearily as her husband picks up his car keys. He is dejected because Kate has declined another of his carefully casual offers of a run out in the car, maybe some lunch; he's sure that if they could only get her to behave as if she were recovered, she would recover.

"If only she'd gone to Thailand," he says for what must be the hundredth time in the last three days.

"Yes," says Richenda, "or if only she'd stayed in that night. Or not drunk so much. Or not slipped. Or left earlier and come straight home. If only there had been something on TV she wanted to watch"—self-control fails, and suddenly she is on-screen, scrabbling, incapable of controlling her rising voice, her speech getting quicker—"or she lived in a home where her parents weren't fighting all the time"—the tears start—"and her mother wasn't bitter and sour and her father wasn't planning his next"—Rufus rolling his eyes makes her pause, find a better word, something to make what she is saying find a place to grip and dig instead of sliding away—"dalliance..." She runs out of steam, turning away with a what-do-you-care set to her shoulders.

"I was working that night," he says. "I was upstairs and I was working. Planning regulations are—"

"Of course you were, Rufus. You're always working. All those nights you spend in hotels when you could drive home in an hour and a half. Just sitting there, on your own, in a hotel room, reading planning regulations. All night."

"I thought we were talking about Kate."

"We are talking about Kate."

"We need to bring her out of herself. Out of her room. We need something to...to coax her."

"She's not a sick puppy, Rufus. She's had a massive physical and emotional shock. A lunch in a country pub is not going to put her right."

"No, but it would be a start. What's your strategy, Richenda?" And he strides out, plans for a summerhouse rolled in a tube under his arm, car keys rattling. He leaves the door slightly ajar, a move he knows is worse than a slam, by virtue of being unexpected, and obliging Richenda to get up and push the door shut. He sighs as he starts the car, allowing himself to pull this door closed with just a shade of unnecessary violence. He really does try not to be petty, he thinks as he drives away, but every man has his limits. And anyway, there's absolutely nothing going on with Caroline.

❁

Richenda hates it when he has a point. She has assumed that love and time will heal her daughter. Rufus has made her wonder whether letting Kate sleep and cry, cry and sleep, is the best thing to do. The friends who have been Kate's world are mostly gone, digging wells to bring clean water to places that don't have it, handing out food in war zones, sleeping in hostels around Europe, working all hours in city bars to pay for the next chunk of their lives, some even at university already. While her peers are all agog at their new horizons, Kate's world is shrinking, shrinking. But Richenda has to admit that, actually, Kate wasn't quite right before this happened.

The gap-year adventure had been talked about more than anything else: more than exams, more than university, more than how dull Throckton was and how she couldn't wait to get away. Six weeks of working on a conservation project, with a break in the middle for some traveling and the option to change her ticket home so she could stay longer or travel more, was what Kate had her heart set on. When her friends had come around so that they could all revise together, more often than not Richenda would overhear them talking about how their adventures would intersect: meeting up and traveling around Australia, how once you are in Australia you may as well travel back via the States, it seems crazy not to. And Richenda, who likes her own bed and a world that she can reach out and touch the sides of, a steady, constant sky above, had been both terrified for Kate and in awe of the fearlessness that she saw in her.

And then Kate had decided, out of nowhere, to cancel her gap-year plans, and since then she'd done very little. A few weekend shifts at Benito's restaurant, some talk of going to join her friends in Turkey for a week, which came to nothing, sleeping in the afternoons. Rufus had taken the whole thing at face value and pointed out that their daughter seemed happy enough, which was certainly true, but Richenda had still wondered whether there had been more to it. She'd asked Kate and gotten nowhere. "I'm not doing anything wrong," Kate had said. "I'm just not doing anything, and when I'm ready to do something, I will." And so the Micklethwaites had soon settled into the line-of-least-resistance position of family life as they knew it.

As Richenda knocks on her daughter's bedroom door, she wishes she had listened to the instinct that told her there was more to Kate's change of heart than met the eye. She longs for the days when mothering was simple, when a Barbie bandage on a scraped elbow or an afternoon with a film about princesses was enough to cure all ills. She might have been tired and harried when Kate was a child, but she never had this sense of dread and sorrow as she looked to see how her daughter was doing.

"I brought you some tea," she says.

"Thanks," Kate replies, but her eyes don't move from the ceiling. The curtains are drawn. Richenda's eyes strain to adjust to the half dark.

"I thought we could watch a film this afternoon," she offers.

"No thanks, Mum. I think I'm going to take a nap."

"All right." Richenda bites back the question of whether Kate will sleep tonight. They had that conversation yesterday, and anyway, Kate seems to be able to sleep for eighteen hours a day at the moment. "I'll be downstairs if you need me."

❄

Richenda is half asleep herself when Rufus comes back. He is wearing what she recognizes as his guilty look, but she knows who his summerhouse client is—Bubbles McVitie, mad as a box of frogs and well over seventy if she's a day, so not really Rufus's type. And he's only been gone a couple of hours, which is not his style either: he likes to think of himself as a romantic, misunderstood and tortured, so his infidelities invariably involve lunch, or dinner. Also:

"Is that a new shirt?"

"This? No." He turns to face her and she recognizes the paisley and blue stripes. It's one of what Kate calls his "wallpaper shirts" although Richenda likes it. Even at this distance from the time when they loved each other, she can admit that her husband knows how to dress.

So, less than two hours and not a new shirt; it's definitely not a woman. But it's definitely a guilty face.

"What have you done, Rufus?"

"Why should I have done anything? I've been to a meeting. I've agreed to the next stage of the work. I've earned money so that you can sit here thinking the worst of me."

"All right," Richenda says mildly.

She's less mild when she discovers what he has done.

Rufus began by calling Kate downstairs with the promise of a present, trying to make her close her eyes. "I'm not a child, Dad," she said, "and I'm not really in the mood. Sorry." Then he disappeared out of the front door with the promise of being back in a minute.

"It's going to be balloons, isn't it," Kate says to Richenda resignedly, and her mother sincerely hopes so.

But it's not balloons. It's a puppy.

And for all that he's small, he knows what it is that he's here to do and goes immediately to Kate, snuffling at her bare feet, the wet nose making her toes curl, the big puppy eyes drawing her hand down to touch, to scratch, to marvel at the softness of his ears. Richenda's mouth opens but nothing comes out. No one notices, because Kate is stroking the puppy, and Rufus is watching the two of them, proudly, as though he's just discovered how to turn base metal into gold.

"He's a beagle," Rufus says. "Bubbles breeds them. He has a pedigree going back five generations and he's been wormed and had all of his vaccinations."

"Our house," Richenda says, her voice high and hot in her ears, "is carpeted in cream and most of the walls and furniture are shades of pale because you, in your architectural wisdom, want nothing but clean space and clean lines. We have never had a pet. We have never wanted a pet. Not so much as a goldfish."

"I thought he'd be company for Kate," Rufus says, still pleased with himself, but not enough to meet Richenda's gaze.

"And will Kate take it to university with her?" They both look at their daughter, who is laughing for the first time since the accident, as the puppy licks at her scrunched-up nose and eyes, and in this moment at least it seems that the answer is a resonating yes, barked from the rooftops. Rufus risks tilting an eyebrow at his livid wife, seeing how her face is softening. It's too soon. When she sees him looking at her, her features set back into fury.

"And will you take it with you when you go to work, or will I be looking after it?"

"He's housebroken," Rufus offers. "Almost, anyway. He knows about newspaper."

"Oh, good. Can he operate a door handle to put himself in

the garden?" Richenda curses herself for being bamboozled into moving from *it* to *he*. "Does he vacuum furniture and shampoo carpets? I'm sorry, Rufus, it's too much. He's just going to have to go back."

Kate, who hasn't been listening, looks up. "He can sleep in my room," she announces, "and we'll call him Beatle."

❊

Later that evening, Kate coaxes Beatle up the stairs and takes him into her room. She lifts him onto the bed, in direct contravention of one of the many doggy directives that her mother has spent the evening laying down, and strokes his silken ears. Crying feels easier in his company and more complete, validated by a witness but not complicated by comfort, questions, cajoling.

When she is calm again, she strokes the dozing puppy. Every now and then Beatle angles his ears to the sound of arguing from downstairs. Most of it is just rumble and squawk, but the odd word makes it up to them, *unilateral* and *thoughtless* and *uptight*. Kate tells him the story of the gold bracelet her father bought for her mother once, after what it pleased him to call one of his indiscretions had been discovered. "Indiscretion," Richenda had said very quietly, imagining Kate in the next room couldn't hear or wasn't listening, "is an understatement as far as you're concerned, Rufus. The new shirts. The whistling. The coming home at two a.m. and having a shower. I think I'd be slightly less furious if you made at least some attempt to pretend that you weren't screwing your way around your client list again." Beatle's eyes seem bright with understanding as Kate tells him the next bit: how she had leaned back in her chair and been able to see, unseen, through the doorway. Rufus's offered gift, Richenda's opening of the box, the way she had held up the bracelet, twisting it through the light, then gone to her bedside table and offered Rufus an identical box, containing an identical bracelet, with the words, "This is the one you bought me last time. Your taste, if nothing else, is fairly constant."

"He looked sorry," Kate tells Beatle. "Properly sorry." She hasn't told anyone about this before, afraid that in the retelling it would become comical, or trite, when it had twisted her up and made her feel so sure that, when she fell in love, she'd never fall out of it again. And before she knows it, she's crying, and she's telling Beatle other things that no one else knows.

Mike,

I'm wired all night, my mind won't stop, my heart just breaks over and over again and the noise and the pain of it are unbearable. I can no more sleep through this than I could sleep through being kicked in the ribs every two minutes. But every night I try. Stupid.

So this morning I was standing at the back door while Pepper had his morning scuttle—Blake takes him out when he walks his dog, which is just as well, because I don't think I'll step out of this house voluntarily ever again, despite your mother's incessant attempts to get me to go to one of her clubs or the library, and Mel's pleas for a change of scenery before she goes mad.

So, the back door is as far as I go. But this morning there was a patch of sunlight at the end of the patio. It was so pathetic and feeble that I sort of recognized it, and I went and stood in it, and then I saw the snowdrops.

My feet got wet as I walked through the last of the frost to pick them up: just half a dozen nodding white heads, tied with a piece of silver ribbon.

They were just in the corner of the garden, by the gate, the place that got the last of the sun in summer and where we'd sit with a glass of wine on warm evenings. I stood there with them in my hand and I remembered you, just back from work, just half an hour after I was back from work, walking *toward me as I sat there. You smiled and said, "I see you're already in our happy place." I thought of how, one winter, when I was so low, you bundled me up and walked me around to Butler's Pond because you said you had something to show me, and there was a tiny crop of snowdrops, huddling under a tree. "You see," you said, "there's always hope."*

So I knew that these were my sign. I knew, straight away, that these snowdrops are from you. They are what you'd leave. That's the place you'd leave them.

If you could. If I believed in that sort of thing.

I've put them on the windowsill in the kitchen, and I'm going to sit at the table all day and look at them.

Thank you.

E xxx

then

I S THIS YOUR FIRST time in Sydney?" Elizabeth had asked the
next guy in line. *Brit*, she said to herself. Something about the
pallor, and the haircut. Michael smiled.

"Don't tell anyone," he'd said, looking around the lobby full of
people who seemed to know how to do this traveling business a
lot better than he did, "but I've never been out of the UK before."
He'd handed over his passport, which was fresh and inflexible in
her hand. Valid from the month before. He wasn't kidding.

"Your secret's safe with me." She'd smiled, quietly upgrading
him to a room with a sea view. "And welcome to Australia. You
picked a great place for your first trip overseas."

"Well, it was my New Year's resolution to travel more, and if
you're going to do a thing, I think you should do it right," he'd
said, and he'd smiled a tired smile as he headed for the elevators.

Over the next few days she'd kept a lookout for him. She saw
him standing in the door way, studying a map. Buying postcards
and water from the hotel kiosk. He always seemed to be on his
own. On his fourth day, he approached her at the desk with a
leaflet about the city, and a question about public transport. The
skin on the bridge of his nose was peeling but his shoulders, broad
and thick, were turning a pleasing gold. She noticed that his eyes

were as brown as his hair, and that one of his front teeth was ever-so-slightly crooked.

"How are you finding Sydney?" she'd asked as he'd picked up the map and made ready to turn away.

"Honestly?" he'd replied. "Big and hot."

Elizabeth had nodded. "Fair comment."

Michael had rested an elbow on the desk and leaned in, a man with a terrible secret. "The place I come from has two bus routes through it and no more than six burglaries a year, unless someone comes in from another village for the hanging baskets and window boxes. I'm a little bit lost, if I'm honest." Seeing her eyes offering something like pity, he adds, "It's not as though I've never been anywhere, or anything. I've done London, and Edinburgh, and I've been on training courses all over the place. But everything here is just different. More different than I thought it would be."

"I grew up somewhere like that," she'd said, "but without the buses. It was cycle or die of boredom, where I come from."

Then Elizabeth did something that she hadn't done in four years of working in hotels, four years of at least once a day talking to a guest who was fit, flirtatious, and obviously ready for a fling with a pretty Australian girl. She offered to show Michael the city. He accepted.

At the end of the day, he kissed her on the cheek and thanked her. She was charmed. The next night, she showed him the night-life, and they walked on the beach in the darkness and he took her hand. "Are you being a gentleman?" she'd asked him as he walked her to her door, and he'd said, "No, I'm being a man who really doesn't want to blow it."

❀

Michael left after a week and a half for a two-week escorted tour of "Australia's Highlights," although he told Elizabeth that he'd already found his highlight. He'd be back in Sydney for two nights before his flight home. By the time he got on the coach, Elizabeth had shown him the city, the beaches, the harbor, and a few of the restaurants that the tourists didn't know about. She'd walked over the harbor bridge with him even though she didn't much like heights. She'd taken him to Luna Park where he'd laughed like a child on the rides, and she'd cooked for him and introduced him, casually, to her sister. She'd looked at photos of where he lived and tried to imitate his accent. She'd been charmed when he'd offered to come running with her—she was training for a marathon at the time—and liked how, although he was a head taller than her, they'd found a matching stride. She'd had sex with him, noisily all over his hotel room and quietly, gigglingly, in her little shared house. She was having, she told herself, a short-term romance.

Michael wasn't. He was smitten and he didn't care that she knew it. He felt ambushed by love and told her so. She laughed at him, telling him that he had sunstroke, infatuation, a bug. He curled her hair around his finger and shook his head. She told him she'd be forgotten as soon as he was back in the England he kept telling her about, rain clouds and gravy and all.

"No," he said. "No, Elizabeth, you've got me all wrong. You'll see."

She asked him how, if he'd never been out of his country before, he knew it was her and not Australia he was loving. He explained how he'd felt, this last year, that there was something missing from his life, but that at the same time he loved his job, and his home, and when he saw the TV ad for Australia he'd felt something speak to him, something telling him to come here.

"There you are then," Elizabeth had said, rolling herself closer to him. "The universe wants you to get a tan. That's all it is."

"No," he'd said. "It was you." But she'd refused to accept it. Refused the idea that she could tie her existence, her happy, easy days, to someone who would, by dint of his birthplace, make her life awkward, complicated, in need of compromise and planning and all of the things she had deliberately removed from it when she came to the city and started anew.

While he was away he texted her every day: good nights, good mornings. He called and left cheerful, thinking of you messages on her answering machine.

"He's behaving like my boyfriend," Elizabeth had said to Mel.

"He's behaving like your soul mate, Sis," Mel had said, scrolling through the messages, "and you need to decide whether you want that or not. He's not the casual sort."

"No," Elizabeth had said. "I suppose he's not."

"And neither are you," Mel had added.

"No. I know." She had been mostly happily mostly single since she came to Sydney, and could hardly believe that five years had gone by since her school sweetheart gave her an ultimatum about settling down and getting married, and she gave him the answer he didn't want. She'd known then that he wasn't really the man for her, although it had felt as though everyone except Mel had known better and had been lining up to tell her she had made a mistake. She had been sure that she hadn't. But now she came to think about it, she wasn't sure that the life she had made since was really the life for her either. It wasn't that she didn't like Sydney, and her friends, and running and swimming and working too many hours and saving for a deposit on her own place. She did. But perhaps it wasn't really right; perhaps that was why she was thinking about Michael the way she was.

But it was best to be sure. Elizabeth had spent the next week making a list to herself of all the reasons it wouldn't work. Not really knowing each other. Distance. Culture. Expense. Time apart. Away-from-home self, different from at-home self. The countless times she'd mopped the tears of brokenhearted colleagues when their One True Love had gotten on a plane home and never been heard from again.

Compared to the reasons for the relationship—getting on well, great sex, both like running, the feeling that, as she struggled to put it to Mel, she "just couldn't not"—the "against" list seemed overwhelming. So Elizabeth had ignored Michael's texts—or, at least, she'd not responded to them, which didn't stop her from reading and rereading them. She'd filled up her diary, booked some more shifts, started planning a trip of her own, and made a future with no Michael, and no space for Michael in it. She'd agreed to go on a blind date with a friend of a friend. She'd persuaded herself that the last ten days—only ten days, barely enough time to decide whether you like someone, let alone anything else—had been a madness that was over.

By the time Michael returned, Elizabeth had been so sure of her infallible heart that she had stood in the shadows by the hotel doorway and watched him get off the coach: a game of emotional dare. He had been more than she remembered him. More tanned, of course, but more imposing. More upright. More confident. Happier. She'd realized that he had no doubts about her, about them. She saw that he *knew*, and that was what made him aglow with something special. And in that moment she had recognized that she *knew* too. Unmoving, unspeaking, she had let herself love.

He had seemed to sense her change of heart. Just as she had thought about stepping toward him, about his mouth and his hair, he had looked straight at the place she was going to step into.

❋

He'd insisted on a plan. "Can't we see how it goes?" she'd asked.

Michael had said, "No. You can see how it goes on a picnic, you can see how it goes with a test drive, but this deserves a plan."

So they had made the rules. Some sort of contact—a text, an email—every day. A phone call at least once a week. No going to bed on an argument. No more than three months without seeing each other. An understanding that long-distance relationships were hard and they wouldn't lose heart too easily or too soon. Elizabeth was to come and take a look at Throckton before the year was out. And, if they were still together in eighteen months, a serious conversation about The Future.

"This feels like quite a serious conversation about the future to me," Elizabeth had said, and Michael had turned a solemn face to her and replied, "Elizabeth, there's nothing wrong with serious."

And for a moment, falling for some guy from the other side of the planet had felt not only good, but perfectly reasonable. She had groped for that feeling as she'd watched his flight leave, but there was no finding it again until the three months were up and she was stepping onto a plane herself.

now

Mike,

People are still coming, and I try to listen, and I try to talk, but I can't seem to. Especially since the snowdrops. Mel is so good. She's like a sort of filter; she sits next to me and touches my hand when she thinks there's something I might want to listen to, and the rest of the time I just look at the wall. Everyone says such lovely things about you.

Sometimes I wish everyone would go away and leave me alone, but then the thought of being alone is too much. Which is stupid, stupid, because I am alone, alone, alone all the time, because you're not here, and you should be. You should be. You know that, don't you?

Blake says Kate still doesn't remember anything after going into the water. Mel said, "Has anyone tried turning her upside down and shaking her until the memories come out? Because if they haven't, I will." Blake said, "Sometimes these things take time." I said, "Mel, accidents happen. We of all people should know that, after what happened to Mum. Tires blow out." "Yes," she said. "I've never understood how you were so accepting of that either."

I didn't say anything else to her, but I'm not accepting anything, here. Some days I can't bear not knowing. And then some days I couldn't care less, because it's not as though her remembering anything else is going to bring you back.

But I don't accept that you're not here, Mike. And I think—I know— you should come back. I can't believe you won't. This was never in the plan.

Come back. Come back to me. I don't care how. I'll wait. Because I can't, won't, don't want to be living my life—our life—without you. I absolutely refuse.

I've pressed the snowdrops in our wedding album. And I'm waiting.

E xxx

I T'S HARD TO KNOW what to do on Michael's birthday. Mel tells Elizabeth that next year she will be able to remember her husband and find happiness in those memories. Elizabeth agrees but doesn't really believe her, in the same way that she doesn't really believe that she's in the air when she's on a plane: it seems too impossible, too ridiculous, and looking down and seeing clouds only makes it all the more unlikely, somehow.

Patricia brings her photograph albums around.

Elizabeth hesitates before looking, but can see nothing in the chubby boy with the curly hair that she can relate to her husband. Until Patricia turns a page and there he is, only nine, eyes looking straight into the camera, mouth a solemn line. "I remember that year," Patricia says. "It rained and we had to have his party indoors, and so we couldn't have races. He wasn't very pleased." And everything the man will be sings out from the boy, and suddenly Elizabeth is gasping, gasping at how vivid he has become.

"I thought it might be too much," Mel says to Patricia as she holds Elizabeth's hand, Mel's other hand rubbing a rhythm up and down her sister's spine. Elizabeth's eyes are closed, her body shaking. Her head has dropped and it's impossible to see whether she is crying or not. There's no sound, but Patricia and Mel know that this means nothing.

"She's going to have to start making an effort, Mel," Patricia says in a half whisper that would carry through a stone wall. "Look at me. I've lost my son and I'm still going to the WI tomorrow. I don't much care about spring jams at the moment, but I have to keep going."

Like so much she tries to say to or about Elizabeth, it doesn't come out quite the way she means it to. If Patricia had more parts of her heart that weren't aching, if the constant battling back of the desire to give up and lie down would just stop for a minute or two, she thinks she could work it out. Somewhere in the air around her drifts the understanding that the generations grieve differently, in the same ways that they love differently, dress differently, raise their children differently. Close by is the feeling that if she could cry for help the way that Elizabeth does, by letting all of the desperate wordlessness out of her, then she would. But Patricia will do what she has always done: manage. She can tolerate enough sympathy to make her feel as though she isn't alone, but not so much that she can't take care of other people. When friends touch her arm, she smiles and nods. If she thinks anyone might try an embrace, she takes a step back. When people ask her how she is, she shakes her head but says she's bearing up.

Patricia would never tell you about her baby sister who died, because she never speaks about it. It's no secret: Patricia was five, little Sheila only two. She would never tell you, because she never thinks of the way that her mother gave herself over to her grief, becoming a shadow mother, ineffectual, incapable, insubstantial. She never thinks of it, but the memory is everywhere within her. And even though Elizabeth has no children—even though, in this house, there is no five-year-old being woken in the night by the strange, sad sound of muffled crying—she wants to save her from her mother's fate. She wants to do it with the kindness and the gentleness that, if she was the wishing sort, she would have wished for her five-year-old self.

But she can't do it. And when she tries, she says something that she shouldn't, and she could bite out her own tongue. In her heart she is saying, *Seeing my friends, having them touch my arm and say kind things will make me remember that I'm not as monstrously alone as I think I am. Taking home a recipe will mean that on one of these mornings when I wake up and I don't know quite how I'm going to make the day go by, I'll get out my jars and take the last of the elderberries from last autumn out of the freezer, and there'll be something to fill up the time, and there'll be a jar of warm jelly to take to a friend, and that's the only way I can do it.*

Elizabeth pauses for a moment and Mel looks at Patricia as if to say, *Well, here it comes,* but nothing happens. Or rather, nothing happens outside Elizabeth. Inside, she thinks about making an effort—about lifting her head and explaining her world to her mother-in-law, who she knows doesn't have a cruel bone in her body, not really, but that doesn't stop the things she says from sounding cruel, at a time when Elizabeth has nothing with which to protect herself from even unmeant cruelty. She thinks about how much of an effort every day is, that sometimes she feels as though she's going to have to reach into her own guts and move her own diaphragm up and down because her lungs can't find the strength to fill and empty, or her heart to pump and pull.

Instead, she says, "I think I'll have a lie down," and she goes upstairs and puts on her husband's sweater and waits for enough strength to get up again.

❈

Andy, Blake, and Mel have discussed the protocol for tonight and come up with a simple strategy for what should have been Michael's day: they will follow Elizabeth's lead. So when she comes downstairs, showered, hair brushed, and with the palest of smiles, Blake opens wine, Andy makes much of his allergy to dogs—Blake has brought Hope with him, and two dogs seem like one too many for the doctor as he sneezes and blows—and Mel begins some cautious reminiscing.

It's the closest thing to normal, or what any of them remember as normal, that there's been in the five weeks since Michael died. Elizabeth is unpredictable—sometimes present, sometimes worlds away, as quickly as if she is being switched on and off—but she is herself too, hand gestures and smiles breaking through the encrusted grief as if to remind her companions that she's in there, still, and might come out one day.

Every now and then she remembers that she will have to have her own birthday without Mike this year, and the next, and the next. Grief stacks itself up, waiting.

It's after eleven o'clock when the very-definitely-not-a-birthday-party breaks up. Mel walks home with Blake, taking Pepper, she says, "to give him some air."

The sound that comes from Elizabeth shocks them all with its strangeness. She's laughing. It's a rusty half laugh, but a laugh none the less.

"To give yourself the chance to smoke all the way home, you mean," she says. "I hear what you call Pepper when you think I'm asleep."

❈

As soon as Blake, Mel, and the dogs have gone, Elizabeth looks straight at Andy and asks the question she's sworn she doesn't want to know the answer to. Except that, after a drink and a loosening of the fear that binds her, it's all she can think about.

"What would it have been like," she asks, "for Mike?"

His expression tells her that he hasn't understood, and so she has the chance to back up and off this path, but she doesn't.

She just takes a deep breath—diaphragm up, diaphragm down—and says some words she doesn't want to have to use so close to one another. "Mike. That night. I keep wondering, Andy. What would it have been like? To drown?"

"Oh." Andy looks into his glass, and into Elizabeth's face—her eyes are alert, concentrating, sure—and takes a deep breath too. And he tells her, gently, calmly, simply, the way he knows he should.

Tears roll down her face and gather in his eyes but he keeps going. What he says is part medical opinion and part thirty years of friendship.

He says that, once the shock of the cold was over, Michael probably wouldn't have felt much.

He says that Michael would have been so focused on getting Kate out that he wouldn't have been thinking about his own body.

He says that physical strength and the instinct to save both himself and Kate would have taken over.

He says that the weight of Michael's own wet clothes and the weight of Kate and her wet clothes would have been a huge burden.

He says that Michael would have struggled but there would have come a point when he couldn't struggle anymore.

He pauses and looks at Elizabeth, touches her arm, a question: *Is this enough?* She nods. *Keep going. I'm OK.* Her eyes say, *Despite appearances, this is OK.* Her heart screams for him to stop talking, but something stronger in her needs to hear this.

He says, "Michael probably lost consciousness." He says—he falters as he says it—"He might not have known. About the dying. We can't know."

"No," says Elizabeth. "No. We can't know."

Later, in the dark, knowing how well Mel sleeps after a drink, she takes a blanket and sits on the stairs, listening to Mike's voice on the answering machine, over and over and over until it's a beloved white noise. She's consented to the machine being switched off, so that unwary callers don't have to hear her husband's voice, but she won't have the recording replaced. As she said to Mel the last time they talked about it, it's not as though she isn't here to answer the phone. Mel had made a face that said, *Well, I'll let this go for now, but this isn't the end of it.*

Andy's words have been partly reassuring: she likes knowing that Mike wouldn't have known, wouldn't have been thinking about dying, would instead have been focused on getting Kate out, getting himself out. But the conversation has also reminded Elizabeth of what she'll never know.

She wonders how he felt, what he thought about, whether he panicked or was calm, whether he thought about her. She goes upstairs and gets into bed and holds her breath, just to see if she can discover how it might have felt, but something more primal even than grief makes her pant and panic before she gets anywhere close.

Mike,

This morning, by the gate, it was a few crocuses—crocii?—tied with a silver ribbon again. I was out there early—it was barely light—but you'd beaten me to it. I felt as though, if I'd been fifteen seconds earlier, I'd have seen you disappearing around the side of the gate (or through the fence, or dematerializing, or however you do it). It seemed as though the air was still reassembling itself around the place where you'd been.

I put them in our bedroom, on my bedside table. I opened the curtains, a little bit, so that they would get some light, although I know it doesn't really matter once they're picked. Thank you for bringing them for me, today, of all days, when I've lain awake all night and thought about drowning.

I keep telling Mel she can go home, and she says yes, or she could stay here, because she can work anywhere she can plug her laptop in, and I'm a little bit glad, really, although I'm probably being selfish. Mel's the only person here who has a history with me that isn't also with you, so she isn't an automatic reminder. Not that I forget.

I'm making no sense. It's partly because I'm not sleeping, which makes the whole world slightly overexposed. But also because yesterday, you were supposed to get older, but you didn't, and now that's something else that's wrong.

I looked at your photo in the morning, and I wanted to wish you happy birthday, and then I didn't, and then I couldn't work out the tense—"It is, was, would be, could have been your birthday." In the end, I said, "Happy birthday, my darling, precious Mike, who brought me to this cold, damp, twisty-turny little place and made it my home." I said it because I'd found something to say that made perfect sense, whether you were alive or not. I said it to your picture, but if you'd been here, I would have said it to your sleepy, bristly, another-year-older face.

I miss you. I love you. I'm here. I'd rather be there, where you are. Wherever there is. But you know that, because it was always that way.

E xxx

ALTHOUGH BLAKE HAS BEEN very clear with the Micklethwaites, telling them that they can call him any time, for any reason, and that he'll help them in any way he can, Richenda has shied away from doing so. She blames her mother—she blames her mother for a lot, actually, one way or another—whose cry of "I'd rather die than take handouts from the state" had made for a long, cold, bleak childhood and a horror of taking any kind of help from any kind of institution.

As she dials Blake's number, she blames herself a little too, for her absurd idea that her family would be able to get through this time by relying on one another when, in reality, it's been years since they've had so much as a fully civil and convivial mealtime.

Blake arranges to come that afternoon, which gives Richenda enough time to calm down and feel a little foolish for making the call. She plans for coffee and questions about that poor policeman's widow.

But there's something about his face, as honest as the sky, demanding honesty in return. So when he asks her how she is, how things are, she tells him. She tells him in a headlong jumble. The dog, who at least has Kate leaving the house but knocks the bin over several times a day and trails rubbish everywhere, and no one seems to find it galling except her. Rufus slotting back into life as it was before this as though nothing much has happened, while she feels as though everything is tilting. The pictures in the local paper of that poor policeman's funeral, and his mother and his widow. Kate, hardly eating and vomiting and refusing to talk and how she'd looked up *bulimia* on the Internet and felt sick herself, all those girls destroying themselves as they tried to wrest control of something, and how she doesn't know where shock and trauma stop being a reasonable, understandable reaction and start being something else. How glad she feels that Kate is here, how terrible that Michael Gray is not. (She makes herself say his name, Blake notes, in the same way that Elizabeth carefully forms the words *Kate Micklethwaite*, although Patricia can only bring herself to spit "that girl," and rebukes her daughter-in-law for caring. Although only, Blake has noticed, when Mel is out of earshot.) The worry that having someone die in the process of saving you is a huge burden to bear, at any age, and because she is so young, relatively untouched by difficulty, Kate has no strategies for this.

"She has you," Blake says, his first opportunity to say anything at all since sitting down. "Don't underestimate that."

"Yes," Richenda replies, instantly underestimating it, "but she won't talk to me, or can't, and there's something different about her that I can't quite put my finger on. She's sleeping all the time and I don't know if that's good or bad. She still doesn't say much about what happened and I don't know what to think about that—should I be relieved, should I be worried? I wonder, if she did talk, would it be better, or worse..." She tails off, wiping her eyes.

"Right," Blake says. "I don't have any answers, but I can give you one piece of advice." Richenda looks straight at him, eyes darkened from blue to gray by the tears and the fading of the late afternoon light. "Don't worry about what you can't control. You can't make Kate talk and you don't know what will happen when, or if, she does. So put that out of your mind."

A retort is on the tip of Richenda's tongue—how easy those words are to say, how impossible to do—when she thinks about all of the times she's locked the front door at night, knowing that Rufus isn't coming in, knowing what he's doing and, sometimes, where he's doing it and who with, and choosing not to think about those things. She takes a deep breath, exhales, thinks about smiling and, although she can't quite manage it, Blake sees that the storm has passed.

❀

The trouble is, Richenda thinks later—apart from her marriage and Kate and the poor dead policeman—that she is working from home more, and being around for Kate more, she has more uninterrupted thinking time. Although her job, as a freelance bookkeeper, is easy to do from home, she's always preferred to sit in other people's offices, seeing how they work and getting a sense of lives other than her own. Since Kate's accident, she's been going out for a couple of hours to collect paperwork and spending the rest of the week in her beautiful, stifling house. Kate, whom she aches to care for, is mostly sleeping or going on long rambles with Beatle, who seems to be the only companion she will tolerate.

When Richenda hears Kate crying and goes to her room, she is sent away, not unkindly—"I just want to be on my own, Mum"—and so she sits in the office next door to Kate's bedroom and puts her head against the wall. She stares at the signed Beatles poster, one of Rufus's most treasured possessions, and waits for the sobbing to stop. And she wonders. She wonders where, when it could have been different.

Richenda unravels her life and looks for the knot that, had she seen it and undone it in time, would have changed the way things had turned out, and meant that Kate would have been safe at home that night. Or that she would have been confident enough to go to Thailand instead of being beset by last-minute nerves. Or that she had been anywhere, anywhere but here. She can't find it, or rather, she can find lots of knots, tied tight, not easy to undo, not clear what they are holding together.

Most of the knots attach to Rufus. But of course, without Rufus, there would be no Kate at all. Richenda knows that she's unkind to her husband, and sometimes unfair; she knows that there were times, earlier, when she was all too ready to let him sleep on the sofa bed under his precious poster while she sulked on their vast and expensively sprung mattress. She wishes she had made more effort and got the marriage really working, or made less effort and left him. She remembers their early days, and how the nervous young man, recently emerged from the double prison of obesity and merciless bullying, had been devoted to her, following her around the way Beatle follows Kate, dejected in her absence, ecstatic when she appears. He hadn't known then how handsome he was, those eyes as bright as cornflowers and those cheekbones and the way his hair wouldn't quite lie flat at the back of his neck. His shyness, his desire to please, was as true then as it is an act now. His interest in her studies was unfeigned, his enthusiasm for her body endless.

And she curses the fact that she didn't have the sense to realize that the way he reacted to a little bit of attention from her would be the way he would react to a little bit of attention from any woman.

Yes, that's the top and bottom of it, really, she thinks as she listens to Kate's sobs subside. *I can make it a lot more complicated, but it isn't. That's how he's always been, and that's how I've let it be. And now here we are. The mistake I made was to think that the state of our marriage wouldn't affect Kate.*

When Kate was born—and earlier, when Kate was unborn, swimming and growing inside her mother—Rufus and Richenda took their role as parents very seriously. Rufus set up a savings account on his way to work on the day that Richenda took the test. ("We don't want to have any worries about university fees," he'd said.) They'd read books about child development and attended prenatal classes with the fervor of newly signed up members of a cult. Richenda had felt thoroughly loved, from without and within, and put the unsteady early years of their marriage down to—well, it didn't matter, really, they were here now, and they were talking about what they'd be doing with their child in five, ten, twenty years, and they wouldn't be doing that if they weren't happy. Of course they wouldn't.

The birth had been uncomplicated. "I wish all of mine were like you," the midwife had said. "Seven hours and three tiny stitches, and baby as calm as can be." And Rufus had burst into tears. Richenda had hardly noticed, looking at the wonder of her baby's earlobes and the way her little feet flexed. Yes, Kate had been easy from the start: easy to feed, easy to get to sleep, easy to love.

Not so easy to give a baby brother or sister to. The miscarriages and the grieving and the sex fraught with purpose were like taking Rufus and Richenda's marriage and hurling it down a hill. When it came to rest, the part around Kate was still strong, but much else was broken. Simple intimacy had been one of the first things to smash; without it, honesty soon broke away.

As Kate grew and Rufus and Richenda grew apart, they did their best to parent together. However much they might whisper disappointments late at night, ignore the other whenever they could, they sat together at parents' evenings and school plays and made a point of being polite whenever they thought Kate was in earshot. Their heads touched as they put their diaries together and worked out who would take Kate to her riding lessons; they talked about her future without edge or rancor. Richenda allowed herself to cry only once Kate had gone to bed, and shouting was restricted to the times when she was out of the house.

They thought they did a good job. Of course, such a way of life was unsustainable. At fourteen—still quiet, still clever, sometimes sulky—Kate had said, quite matter-of-factly, that she really didn't think a family trip was a good idea this year because she could see how much strain it put on her parents to play happy families for a fortnight. They'd protested, but she'd said, "Don't insult me," and that had been that.

Of course, Rufus and Richenda had agreed that, even if they weren't all going away together, they could still be civil. Perhaps the lack of pretense would make things easier. Perhaps, conversely, admitting that they didn't get on might help them to get on.

It didn't.

Kate is quiet. Richenda, making her way softly down the stairs, is no closer to knowing whether she and Rufus should have done less, or more, to avert this disaster for their daughter. She remembers what Blake said, about not worrying about what you can't control. She starts to look for the knot again.

❉

Kate's bones gnaw with tiredness. She wants to be left alone, to sleep and cry and think, but that doesn't seem possible.

She sleeps all afternoon, sits downstairs with her parents for a couple of hours, goes to bed at eight, wakes early, and finds the only bit of the day that she likes: taking a walk with Beatle, before Throckton has rubbed the sleep from its eyes and so can't stare. She avoids Butler's Pond. Dog walkers, when she meets them, seem to be kind, but she already knew that.

When she gets home, she lets her mother make her breakfast and then she has a look to see what her friends are doing, in the posted pictures full of tans and new friends and sun reflecting from teeth.

She answers emails and texts and tells people that she's getting better, which she knows isn't true. Where before she wanted to talk, now she wants to be quiet. She toys with saying more to Bella, who is the one who knows the most and has understood things best over the last year. But Bella is in India, and when Kate looks at the latest pictures of her friend, she can't imagine how to talk to someone in such a bright and blazing world.

The relentless approach of the inquest dogs her dreams, along with Michael's face and the sound of him calling her name. *Grief, shock, trauma* seem like words too small to describe the way she feels, although her mother throws them around with a desperate fervor, as though they will heal her. Kate knows she will never be healed.

Mike,

I do know it can't be you, leaving flowers by the gate. (Winter pansies, silver ribbon, so pretty. And when I picked them up, I thought, it was you who taught me all the names of English flowers, and it was your mother who taught you, when you were so young that knowing about flowers was no different from playing with trains or poking ants with a stick. So you didn't think it was unusual for a man to go plunging through the undergrowth because he thought he'd seen the first of the bluebells. I love that in you. I'll tell your mother when she comes around.)

But I still think it is you.

I haven't told anyone about this. I know they'll think I've lost it. Patricia will shake her head and Mel will make a joke because she's uncomfortable and Andy will talk to me about grief and depression and how drugs aren't an admission of defeat. And then it will be spoiled.

Standing in the garden with the posy in my hand this morning, I wondered about all of the myths and stories there are in the world, about ghosts and visitations and that sort of thing. I thought about how many people have told me that when someone they love has gone, they've smelled their perfume, or heard them singing, or that their favorite book keeps falling out of a bookcase when there's no one there. And not the people you'd expect to say those sorts of things, not the fluffy people. Your mother's friend from the library, the one whose shortbread she complains about, who's as sensible as the day is long. The man in the paper shop. Susan-next-door's daughter. They've all got a story like that, that they've told me, when they've come here to tell me how sorry they are, and I've had to stop myself from asking them to tell me again, like a child with a favorite bedtime book.

So I think maybe this is just an extension of those stories. Maybe there is a way you can bring these things to me. Maybe you're telling me that everything is going to be all right.

I love you.

E xxx

E VERY NIGHT, PATRICIA TELLS herself that she won't get the photo albums out again. Every night, she does. She runs her fingers over the faces of her two men, and she smiles, and she cries, and she tells herself not to be so silly. She looks at the pictures of Michael on his birthdays—the plain sponge with jam and cream in the middle, his name iced in blue on the top; nothing like the cakes they have now, but Michael always liked them. She tries to remember what he got for birthdays. Every now and then there's a photo of him standing proudly next to a bike, slightly too big for him. She remembers *Star Wars*, but not when that started or stopped. There's no one to ask now.

She'd asked Elizabeth and Melissa what they did for birthdays when they were small. They had looked at each other, pulled faces, and said "joint parties," explaining that there was a year and two days between the two of them, so they could have either a joint party or no party at all. Patricia had said, "But you have each other, and you always will," and she'd meant it as a good thing, but it had come out sharply.

She knows that if John were here, he would tell her kindly that she just needs to get on with it, that the fact that it's terrible now doesn't take away from the good there was before. She knows that if Michael were here, he would tell her that he had loved his life and that she should be glad of that.

But they're not here. Unsure of whether she is angry with them for their sudden, terrible absences and their misplaced ideas of her strength, or with herself for this nightly indulgence, Patricia resolves to put the albums away.

Opening the bottom drawer of the dresser in the back bedroom, she finds the hand-knitted sweaters Michael wore as a toddler and a boy, lovingly made and kept, once Michael had outgrown them, in readiness for a grandson. Not that there will be one now. Patricia thinks of Elizabeth, childless, wearing Michael's sweater, refusing to let it be washed, claiming it holds a trace of him although it smells only of her own sweat and sleeplessness. She closes the drawer, gets to her feet, and shuts the bedroom door behind her. *I'm the last twig on the family tree*, she thinks.

And then, resolutely: *After the inquest, we will start to find a way. We must.* Although Patricia had had a hard time accepting the love of her son's life, she wasn't going to let her fade away.

Patricia had been unsure of what to think when Michael had come home from his great adventure full of talk and photographs of a pretty brunette who worked in a hotel and had, as far as she could see, taken advantage of her boy. "Who paid for all of this?" she asked halfway through the pictures of the pair of them at Luna Park, and Michael had said, "Oh, Mum," which Patricia took as confirmation of her suspicions. First, she waited for the whole thing to fizzle out. Then, she awaited Elizabeth's visit—Michael could talk of nothing else—sure that the girl was still taking him for a ride, and they would hear no more from her once she'd had her chance to visit England. Worried for her son, she'd cautiously aired this view to Michael, who'd laughed and said, "Mum, she's paid her own airfare and anyway, much as we love Throckton, I wouldn't have thought it was that much of a target for international gold diggers."

She'd said nothing else. There was no talking to him when he was in this mood—joyous, flippant, excited. Patricia hoped out loud that it wouldn't all end in tears, and hoped, to herself, that it would, and sooner rather than later, because it couldn't possibly work in the long term. Although Elizabeth had sounded nice enough. She looked pretty in the photographs, and the stories Michael told about her suggested that she was nicely brought up and good-mannered. If she worked as a hotel receptionist she must be polite, and well organized, qualities that Patricia valued very highly. What she really couldn't see was how such a girl could be so much more special than any of the ones Michael had grown up with. Girls whose history she knew, girls whose mothers she'd chatted with at school concerts and church services for almost thirty years.

But she had seen how he had been after that first trip to Australia and known that here was something new, something greater than her son having had his eyes opened to a different way of life. And she had understood that here was something she had no power over.

One night, she took a deep breath and asked the question that she didn't want to know the answer to. She asked Michael whether he thought he would move to Australia.

"Well," he said, "if it comes to it I was thinking I would ask Elizabeth to come here. To marry me. To settle."

"Oh," Patricia had said, then "Oh" again. And she'd thought, *Well, that will be something. Better than something else. Better than him being all the way over there.* She'd thought of one of her library regulars, always reading the same books as her daughter who lived in California as a way of keeping in touch with her. Frances is constantly counting down to Christmas or Easter or summer—with brittle excitement if her daughter is coming home, or stoic good humor if the flights are too expensive. "You get used to it," Frances had said when Patricia had asked her how she managed with her child so far away. Patricia hadn't believed her.

❋

Since the conversation with Andy, Elizabeth can think of nothing but drowning. Of the feel of water filling your body, the moment when you know, if you do, that you can't get out of the water. About how water muffles vision and stems sound and so there might be something dreamlike about the whole thing. About the remembered panic of being a child slightly out of your depth in a bright, clean swimming pool, and how darkness and dirt would multiply that feeling. About how it must feel to be truly unable to breathe, rather than trying to make it happen, the way she does sometimes in bed or in the bath as she tries to see how serious she is about wishing she was dead too.

But the medical details aren't enough. It's a taste of what Elizabeth needs to know. She thought talking to Andy would stop her from wondering, but it's made her want more details, more understanding. Now that she knows she can talk about it without falling apart, she looks for opportunities. So, when Blake comes around to talk about the inquest, she asks him to tell her what he knows about drowning.

She can see by his face that he's shocked.

"Are you sure you want to know?" he asks, and she nods. After looking into her face to make sure, he begins.

"I've been to six drownings in about twenty-five years," he says, "and every one of them has looked calm, although of course it depends if you get to them in reasonable time"—Elizabeth winces, and he reminds himself that he's not talking to a new recruit here, warns himself not to say *body* or *corpse* or *it*—"and people's faces are usually unmarked, so they just look like themselves, sleeping or dreaming."

"I didn't think Mike looked as though he was sleeping," Elizabeth says, "but he did look calm. Yes." Blake isn't sure whether she is talking to herself, or to him, or if she even knows that she is speaking out loud.

"The first death I ever attended was a drowning," he says, then stops, thinking through what he might say to make sure it's safe. He decides that it is.

"It was a little boy, a nine-year-old, who'd gone too far out to sea. It should have been terrible—it was terrible—but everyone who came to look at him—the police officers, the forensics people, the parents—just paused for a minute and drew in their breath because there was something about him. A serenity. It was—it was—" He can't find the words, but finds another way to explain it. "A month or so later, I went to my second fatality, which was a road accident, and I remember driving home thinking that if I had to go suddenly, violently, I'd take the water over the road, any day."

"Really?" Elizabeth hasn't considered the desirability of drowning before. She's thought about the unnaturalness, the choking and the dread, the coldness and the fear. She is drowning in another way, in love that has nowhere to go and memories that won't wait until she is ready for them. She considers the idea of drowning as the best option, shakes her head.

"Really. I still think that," Blake says. "I think it would be"— the first word he used is still the best—"calm."

Calm. Elizabeth rolls the word around her mouth like a marble. Calm. "I would like to think he felt calm," she says, and then she is anything but, howling again. Mel comes downstairs and settles herself next to her sister, resigned, routine, sad.

Mike,

I never should have given your mother a key. Every time she scratches it in the lock, there's a moment when I forget that it won't be you, and my heart bounces, and then it splatters back down again, like a watermelon on a hot pavement. Although I've forgotten what heat is, really. Mel says that being in England is like being trapped in a big, clammy, leaky cave, and that's why so many Brits are miserable and weird. I told her she's oversimplifying. I thought about how, if you were here, the two of you would have gotten into one of your endless England v. Australia arguments and I would have left you to it and gone to have a bath.

So. The inquest. Your mother offered to take me to the hairdresser, which I refused, but I did let her choose my clothes (dark green dress, black belt to gather it in as it hangs on me a bit these days but there's no way in the world I'm going shopping) and talk to her about whether the navy blouse went with her maroon suit, or whether she should stick with the ivory blouse she usually wore with it. We decided on the navy. I'm trying to be a good daughter-in-law. If that's what I am now.

I've agreed to the dress, and a lift from Blake, and Andy coming here for lunch afterward. I've had a grim conversation about "misadventure," which means that you knew that what you were doing was dangerous but you didn't mean for what happened to happen. Which is you, in a nutshell: so ready to help, to solve, to save that you wouldn't have seen another option.

Of course, they won't just say "misadventure"; they'll say "death by misadventure." I will think about how I used to think badly of your mother for still talking about your dad as though he'd just popped to the allotment when he'd been dead for twenty-five years, and how now I wonder how she's gotten through all of those years of it, when just these two months have been so bloody, bloody awful.

And Blake says the Micklethwaite family will be there, which means I might look up at a wrong moment and catch an eye, or see the girl you saved. And I don't know what I'll do. I'd like to think I'll be glad, and gracious. But I really don't know.

Mel says I have to remember that the inquest won't change anything. We know what the postmortem said and we know what the verdict will be. I say yes. Everyone thinks I'm worried about it but I'm not. What I'm worried about is what will happen afterward. Once the inquest is over, what will happen to us? You will be part of the past, dealt with and explained away, all tidy and neat. People will start telling me, out loud, that I have to move on, instead of just implying it and congratulating me whenever I do anything that isn't sobbing or staring at a wall. Soon it will be Easter and the hotel will be in touch to see if I want to work the summer again this year, and if I say yes, then I will have to put mascara on and smile at strangers all day, and your mother will smile at me in turn and say, "You see?" And I can't bear the thought of any of it.

E xxx

L UCY HAD BEEN AROUND a couple of times, with food and sympathy and the boys, but it hadn't been a success. The fact that the two women just don't get on all that well, so easily concealed or ignored at birthday parties and barbecues, became obvious as soon as they tried to talk about anything more meaningful than how sorry Lucy is or how helpful Andy has been.

They don't dislike each other, exactly. They have just never found a way to connect. It had been awkward during Elizabeth's first months and years in Throckton. Then one evening at the pub quiz, after a little too much to drink, Lucy had nudged Elizabeth, nodded toward Andy and Michael who were standing at the bar, and said, "If we can get those two to realize that just because they're best friends we don't have to be, I think everything will be a bit easier." And it had been. Until now, at least. Lucy fumbles for something to say. Elizabeth tries not to show how difficult she finds Lucas and Toby: not for themselves, but for the way that life and noise bursts out of them, barely controlled, when she cannot bear very much of either.

"Why don't we go for a walk?" Lucy had asked the last time she had dropped in.

Patricia was spending her afternoon off cleaning the kitchen.

"It's not dirty," Mel had said when Elizabeth told her.

"That's not the point," her sister had replied. "It's just what she does. I cry, she cleans. I get the cleaning more than I get the hairdresser and the social clubs."

Patricia looked up from where she was kneeling by the radiator—she's cleaned down the back; Mel would say later, "I didn't even know that was a place you could clean"—and said, approvingly, "It would be good for you to get some fresh air, Elizabeth."

And before she knew it she was thinking of Mike, lungs wrenching for good fresh air and finding only filthy, freezing water, and she was crying again, and Mel, who had been working in the spare room but was developing a sixth sense for when she was needed, was taking her by the arm and saying something about time, while Patricia shook her head.

Now, whenever someone mentions that she might want to go for a walk, Mel tells them that Elizabeth can make her own mind up about that, even though it's clear from the way that she has to be reminded to eat and drink and go to bed that that's probably not true.

So apart from the necessities—the funeral home, the funeral, the inquest—Elizabeth has yet to stray farther than her garden. Cold and dark and dead with the season, it's matched her, mood for mood. The sun, when it's come, has been watery and weak. She can stand on the patio and breathe the air with a hand still on the wall, for safety. Every now and then she puts on her wellies—unaccustomed to enclosure, her feet twitch when she walks in them—and works her way around the grass, cleaning up after Pepper, searching the earth for signs of spring and wondering if she will be able to bear them when they come, or whether the memory of Michael making her ring the bell of the first snowdrop will be too much.

And of course, the garden is the place where the posies appear.

Elizabeth likes it best in the morning, when Pepper is bouncing with energy, and watching him scurry gives her something other than the day ahead to think about. She stands in her pajamas and sometimes she is even able to make herself a small plan, the fulfillment of which will help to get her through the day: *I will change the sheets and duvet covers, I will reply to all of the emails that need a reply, I will defrost the freezer, I will sort out the photographs.* (Sorting out the photographs is one of the plans she often makes but has yet to begin. When it comes to it, she cannot bear to look at photos of them, smile upon smile upon smile.)

This morning, still wrung out after the inquest, she cannot face making even a small plan. She thinks she might try going back to bed. It's still early, not even morning really, light barely beginning.

She's just turned away from the garden, taken off her wellies and stepped into the kitchen, about to close the door behind her, when she hears the click of the garden gate, and turns back.

At first Elizabeth thinks she's seeing a ghost, or an angel. The figure is beautiful, and she stands just inside the gate, reflecting her own surprise, still as a deer in the dawn.

And then she recognizes Kate Micklethwaite from the inquest yesterday, from the photographs in the local paper, as the Girl Saved by the Brave Policeman Who Drowned. But up until now she has tried not to look at her too closely, instinctively afraid of what seeing her will do to her heart, in the way she'd once kept her eyes pointing away from her freshly broken arm, knowing that seeing the damage properly would make the pain worse.

But now she looks.

Kate has the lightly worn, unconscious loveliness of the young, with no idea yet that she will never be more beautiful than in these few years before age and sun and worry and sleepless nights and hangovers all find places to rest in her body. Elizabeth takes in a pale waterfall of hair, full-moon eyes of ice-blue gray. Kate is crying, grief and fright combining, and the tears magnify her eyes and make them shine, shine.

In her head she holds freesias tied with a piece of silver ribbon.

And everything makes horrible, awful sense to Elizabeth. Of course the flowers are a tribute. Of course the girl would bring them here. Of course she's grieving and confused and needs a way to express how she feels about Michael doing what he did.

Of course, of course, of course.

Time stops as they look at each other. Then Pepper barks. There's an answer from beyond the gate. Kate turns her head, says, "It's all right, Beatle." The second hand sweeps, and Elizabeth makes her move. She's in front of Kate, holding her shoulders, before either of them has fully realized what she's done.

"The snowdrops?" she asks.

Kate nods.

"The crocuses?"

Kate nods.

"The winter pansies?"

Kate nods. Elizabeth, just a shade shorter than Kate and barefoot on the earth, is looking up into her face, but Kate is looking away, down, to the left, to the flowers still clutched in her hand. Elizabeth shakes her, not hard, to make her look toward her. Kate refuses, eyes determinedly elsewhere. A burst of the sweet scent of the freesias rises in a clear cloud.

"I thought my husband was leaving them for me." Elizabeth's tears start. "Isn't that stupid? I thought he was"—her hands fall, and, freed, Kate's arms move to wrap her own body, cradling, protecting—"I thought he was coming back and leaving me flowers. I thought he was telling me, Elizabeth, it's all right."

Elizabeth is fighting, fighting for control of her breath, her tears, her words, her hands, which want to take Kate's face and force her to look at her, as though looking into her eyes will make her understand. "How stupid. How stupid."

Kate's tongue is a lump of dead meat. Her feet are buried in the earth. She can't move. She can't speak. The thought of her tributes so misunderstood makes her stomach shake. They were for him, in a place that was a little way into his life, not lost in a mass of flowers piled on his grave.

Elizabeth says, "He would be glad you are alive. Mike. He would be so glad that you are alive." What leaves her lips is different from what had left her heart, though, because the "you" comes out hard, an accusation, and she sees Kate flinch.

"It wasn't your fault," she says, aching with the effort to be the person Mike would want her to be. "That he died. It wasn't your fault."

For Kate, the truth of this widow, her neglected hair and sallow face, wrenches her heart this way and that, while her body stands, mute. She sees that Elizabeth is wrapped in a man's dressing gown that's too big for her, and suddenly her hand is alive and grasps at the sleeve, stroking. Now they are both watching Kate's hand on Elizabeth's sleeve, as though it's something on television, something neither of them has power over, and then Elizabeth takes hold of Kate's wrist and she says, "Tell me. Tell me what happened. Please. Tell me. I beg you. I beg you." She looks at Kate, cannot tell whether her mouth is sulking or planning to speak, and says, desperately, "Please. He was my husband. He was my husband and I was his wife and I need to know."

And the tears come, really come, a tempest, and Kate is suddenly free to move and she says, "No, no," the first words she has said to Elizabeth, and then she's out of the garden and gone.

❋

Two hours pass before Mel gets up and heads out to the garden for her first cigarette of the day. She had worked late the night before, translating a Spanish novel with so many characters that it made her head spin; although she keeps on telling Elizabeth that she can work anywhere, which is true, she is finding that she can only really concentrate when she's certain her sister is sleeping.

When she sees Elizabeth sitting by the fence, still in her pajamas and Mike's dressing gown and—well, just still, so still—for a second she thinks her sister has died too. Elizabeth's hands are freezing; she's wet from sitting in the grass; she doesn't respond to her name. Mel thinks about a conversation she had with Andy yesterday, about how if this was the 1800s he'd be confidently diagnosing Elizabeth with a broken heart, and he's not sure that the diagnosis would be too far off today.

But as Mel gets closer she sees a pulse in Elizabeth's throat, and takes her hand and rubs it, rubs her fright and fear into it, and Elizabeth looks at her and says, "Oh, Mel, I should have known," and she starts to cry, and she sobs the whole story out, her foolish-ness and hope, before she'll move a muscle.

Mel calls Andy at work, and until he arrives there's nothing she can do but sit in the grass too. It takes both of them to get Elizabeth—who seems to have only the slightest of connections to her body, and have no idea that she's cold, or wet—into the house, out of her wet clothes, and into bed, where she lies shivering, silent. Andy gives her some sleeping pills and a glass of water, and Mel says "no arguments," and so Elizabeth does as she's told and sleeps for six hours without moving a muscle, her color and warmth seeping back like morning through a northern sky.

❉

When Elizabeth comes downstairs, it's early evening, and Blake, Andy, and Mel are gathered around the kitchen table. Three pairs of cautious eyes turn toward her, assessing, appraising. "How are you doing?" Mel asks.

Elizabeth makes a gesture with shoulder, eyebrow, chin, which means, "I could say something in response to your question, but I have absolutely no idea how I am, so my answer would be meaningless." She says, "I should have told her off and sent her home, or called someone, or brought her inside and talked to her properly, instead of—instead of being stupid."

"Well," Blake says, "you need to remember that if she's upset it's not because of you. It's because of what happened to her. And she wasn't to know—"

"That I was thinking her flowers were gifts to me from beyond the grave? No, she wasn't."

"I've spoken to Richenda," Blake says, "and Kate's quiet, but she's all right."

"Good," Elizabeth says, then, "I begged her. I begged her." She shakes her head.

Blake picks up a look from Mel—before her sister came down, they'd been talking about Kate, and how she wasn't Elizabeth's responsibility—and offers, "Kate is having a hard time, but she'll come through it. She's young enough, and she has so much to go on to. This time next year she'll be at university. She'll be living a whole different life. And of course she'll always remember this, remember Michael; this won't be the end of her."

Elizabeth nods, understanding that Blake thinks he is telling her not to worry about Kate, but feeling that he's describing the opposite of her life now, that all of the reasons Kate will be OK are the reasons why she won't be.

Andy says, "It's time, Elizabeth. It's just time that we need."

She says, "Well, I have plenty of that," thinking of how every single conversation she has now, every single wretched conversation, ends up with someone saying something about time. Time heals. Time will make it easier. In time it will be better. Give it time. Elizabeth stands barefoot and exhausted in her kitchen, looking at the fridge with the photos on it and the cupboard that she knows still contains the half-eaten box of cereal that only Mike liked and that she can't ever imagine ever having the heart to throw away. And she's almost certain that time won't make anything better. It just keeps making it different, awful in lots of new ways.

❀

"The thing is," Blake says to Mel later, as he herds Pepper and Hope along the path and she lights a cigarette, "if I had to write what happened in an incident report, it would sound like nothing. A young woman is found trespassing in a garden. She isn't stealing, but bringing a tribute to the man who saved her life. The property owner found her there, talked to her, and then the trespasser left."

"Why the garden, though?" Mel asks. "The grave, I could see. Butler's Pond, I could see. But the garden? How does she even know where he lives? Lived. Oh, yes, it's Throckton."

Blake shakes his head. "Richenda said the same things. I'm not an expert, but I'd say that she might be worried about going to the grave: if she feels responsible for Michael's death, she might feel that she shouldn't be there. She'll be afraid of going back to Butler's Pond. Michael's home makes a strong, private connection with him."

"Or she's thoughtless."

"A lot of thought had gone into those flowers, Mel. And it must have been really early, so she didn't want, or expect, to be discovered. Richenda says Kate was home before six—she and Rufus didn't even know she had gone."

Mel stops to grind out her cigarette. "Well, we've been there before, haven't we? They didn't know she was out at Butler's Pond either." Blake puts an arm around her, hugs her to him. "You're like a bear," she says, "in a good way."

"Thank you." They walk on in silence for a minute or two. "It will be all right, Mel, somehow. We'll get her through this."

"I know," Mel says, "but it just—it feels like a bomb has hit. Another bomb."

Mike,

Writing to you seemed quite normal, before. Because when part of me thought that you were somehow leaving those flowers for me, it felt as though we were still doing this together, as though you'd gone away but you were reading what I was writing, and replying, in posies.

Now I sit here and I feel like a crazy woman writing into a void, when actually I was crazier before. How come I forgot that someone who has been pulled from a lake and isn't breathing and has been cut open and taken apart and examined and had all their organs put back in and sewn back up and nailed into a coffin and put into a big hole with a ton of earth on top, is not going to be in any kind of shape to leave flowers in his wife's garden?

Life is confusing, and crap, and just seems to go on endlessly. For me, anyway. Yours isn't going on anywhere. It seems I have no choice but to admit that I know that now. You, Michael Gray, my husband, my partner for all of these years, are dead. See? I can say that now. You are dead. You are dead. You, Michael Gray, are dead. You, my husband, are dead. You are dead. You died. You're gone. YOU'RE NOT COMING BACK. DEAD.

The stupid thing is, I am mad as hell with you. As though you made *her come here with her grief and her drama and her sulkiness and her double-take beauty, and mess with my head.*

God. I thought I couldn't do this before. I know it now.

E xxx

R UFUS COMES HOME IN good humor, and the greeting that
he gets from Beatle, tail swaggering aloft, only amplifies his
excellent mood, and makes him rash. "If I say so myself," he calls
to Richenda, who he notices from the empty plate on the table has
eaten without him again, "Beatle is a triumph."

"Yes, Rufus," his wife replies. "You're an absolute marvel, and
you deserve a prize." Her tone is slightly different from the one
she usually uses when she's about to go off into a dog-themed rant,
though, so he turns into the kitchen where she's unloading the
dishwasher, and he sees that she's been crying. Richenda rarely
cries—or lets him see that she's been crying, anyway.

"What's happened?"

"Kate," Richenda says, "has been walking Beatle to that
poor"—she stops herself, decides to do the hard thing—"to
Michael Gray's house when she goes out early, and she's been
leaving little bunches of flowers—floral tributes, I suppose—in the
garden. His widow found her there first thing this morning. Blake
rang to tell me."

"Oh, Christ," Rufus says, and he is so utterly crestfallen that
Richenda stops what she is doing, puts her hand on his arm, and
says only, "That's what I said."

"So, what do we do?"

"Blake says not to worry—"

"That's easy for Blake to say."

Richenda takes her hand away. "Blake says not to worry, because it's not unusual for people who've been through a trauma to find a way to deal with their feelings that doesn't seem completely rational to anyone outside. He says we should encourage her to visit his grave, or think about taking her down to the place where it happened."

"Well," Rufus says grudgingly, "that sounds sensible enough."

"Yes."

And then it's Rufus's turn to reach out to Richenda as he says, "I can't believe that I didn't realize. I was so pleased she was going out. I thought she would talk when she was ready. I thought time would put her right."

"Me too," Richenda says, and in the closest thing they ever get to closeness now, they clasp hands, briefly, look into each other's faces, more briefly still.

❀

Kate, upstairs, is scratching Beatle's ears—the look of bliss on his face makes it impossible for her to stop—and thinking about Elizabeth. Even before all this happened, she'd seen her around: months ago, she'd stood behind her in the line at the co-op once when she was picking up something her mother had run out of. Elizabeth's hair had been pulled back in a knot and she was wearing a black skirt, a white shirt, and heels, from which Kate assumed she was on her way home from work. There were potatoes and tampons in her basket and she wore tiny diamond earrings, and Kate could see from where she stood that her ears had been pierced for a second time and the holes left to close. She was wearing a scent that smelled summery and familiar but Kate couldn't quite decode: peaches, roses, maybe.

The Elizabeth of the inquest had seemed smaller in every sense, thinner, but also treated like a child, dressed up and then pushed and pointed into the right places, coaxed into the courtroom and out again, always a hand at her elbow, her waist, her shoulder. Kate, who could have been similarly supported if she had wanted—she had kept shrinking away from her mother's hand until Richenda had gotten the message and let her be—sat as straight as she could, hoping she looked dignified, imagining Michael watching her and seeing her strength and grace under pressure.

Kate had kept her head low and peeped up through her fringe to look at Elizabeth, until she caught a look from Melissa that had made her decide to concentrate on her fingernails until the hearing was over. She nodded and shook her head when she needed to, crossed and uncrossed her fingers, and spoke quietly, marveling at how easily these people were speaking of death, wondering if they would do it that way if they'd ever choked on water and felt sure that they were dying.

And then there was the Elizabeth of the garden, smelling of sleep, salt scabbing the edges of her eyes, skin pale, nails bitten, hair neglected. Smaller still than she had been at the inquest, but frightening in her grief and her insistence that Kate knew more than she was saying.

As Beatle dozes, Kate rewrites the history of Michael and Elizabeth that she has made. In the new version, she changes the neglectful, uninterested wife to someone clinging, needy, fawning. Michael remains the same: strong, loving, reliable, in need of true love. Although the meeting in the garden had thrown Kate, this new tale makes her happy and gives her courage.

The tiredness comes over her again, and she gives in to it, thinking as she drifts off that this might be her last night of thinking of herself as just tired. Because tomorrow morning is the morning when she'll do the thing that she knows she's been putting off for too long. She should have done it the moment she had that crashing, crushing realization. But she'll do it tomorrow. Tomorrow will be soon enough.

❀

Richenda cannot stop thinking about Elizabeth, and how she looked at the inquest. How she had seemed hollow, her clothes too big and her hands never still. How, when Blake had put his arm on her back to guide her to her place, Richenda wouldn't have been surprised if it went straight through her. How it was as though there was a wave behind her, swelling, and she wasn't moving away from it fast enough to stop it from engulfing her. She watches Rufus eating, as he reads the newspaper, and thinks, *If anything happened to you, if you died, I wouldn't care anything like the way that Elizabeth cares about Michael. I would care, of course, because we've shared such a lot, good and bad, and been together for so long, but the fact is I'm relieved when you leave, my heart drops when you come back, and I wish one of us had had the courage to call it a day before it felt too late to start over.*

Suddenly Richenda is tired, and although it's barely nine all she wants to do is sleep. "I'm going to check on Kate, and then I'm going to bed," she says.

Rufus nods. "I'll see you later."

"Yes." But Richenda pauses at the bottom of the stairs. "Actually, Rufus, would you mind sleeping in the spare room tonight?"

"If you like," he says. After a moment flicking through his

memories of the last few days, he adds, in the tone of a child given an undeserved detention, "But I haven't done anything."

"I know," Richenda says, and she gives him a sad smile that says, *Humor me, please, for the sake of all the times that you have done something that means you deserve to spend the night on the too-thin mattress under the* Sergeant Pepper *poster.*

Rufus nods. "It's been a tough day. I'll see you in the morning."

Mike,

I wasn't sure whether you would get any more letters, but it turns out that you do. I'm not sure how many more there will be, so make the most of it, wherever you are. I'm still angry. I know it's not your fault. I'm angry with Kate too. And with myself, for being stupid, stupid, stupid.

Being angry is exhausting, but if I stop I don't know what there'll be. A space big enough for me to drown in too.

Whenever there's something about a fatal accident on the news, a cyclist killed or someone getting shot or a car accident, you see so many people at the place where it happened. Parents, neighbors, school friends, whoever, laying teddy bears and tying flowers onto fences with twine. Messages to the person who's died, as though they are going to pop along and read them when everyone's gone.

But I've never wanted to go to Butler's Pond. Plenty of people have offered to take me. Blake, Andy, even your mother, who I think goes down there, quietly, every couple of days, and then goes to your grave. I haven't been able to see the point of looking at the place where you died. Maybe it's denial, or a desire to bypass that sort of mawkishness. To me, there's more dignity in staying here, in our home, and grieving for you. Your mother doesn't see any dignity in me sitting around the house in track pants, getting further and further away from the world, but it's felt right to me, so I've done it. The last couple of nights, I've gone to bed being able to remember what was on TV. I don't know why I resisted sleeping pills for so long. Anything that wipes out ten hours of my life at a swallow has got to be a good thing. In the fortnight since the Garden Incident I've taken them every night and the mechanics of life—sleep, food, night, day—are starting to make a semblance of sense.

Mel, your mother, Andy, and Blake are all acting as though I'm a marvel because I sleep at night and eat at the table. I've been out for three walks in the last two weeks, up to Beau's Heights with Blake and Hope. What everyone sees as going forward feels a bit like defeat to me. I'm not sure that I want to move forward, or on, or away, or whatever it is. These last three months have been dark as all hell, but dark is safe.

Anyway. Tomorrow, I'm going to go and take a look at the place where you died. I'm going to go quietly, on my own, except for Pepper, who'll be my excuse for leaving the house unescorted. (Andy keeps offering to take Mel to get some walking shoes. You can imagine how likely that is.)

I won't ever get over you, but I might learn to live with the fact that you're not here. One day. Not tomorrow, though.

I'll take daffodils from the garden and hope that it isn't too grim.

E xxx

then

ELIZABETH'S FIRST VISIT TO Throckton had been better than any of them could have hoped. For Michael, seeing the woman he loved in the place that he loved, after months of wondering and longing, was a simple, all-absorbing delight.

Elizabeth had been ecstatic to see Michael, bursting into sobs at the airport when she saw him waiting for her, his arms opening wide as soon as she stepped into his view. She had become awash with worries about what she was doing as soon as her flight took off from Sydney, and she spent a fair amount of the twenty-three hours of travel time checking the small print on her return flight and working out whether she could afford to change it and go home early. So the sight of Mike, not only looking top to toe exactly as she remembered, but also making her feel just as she'd hoped, a key sliding into a lock, had been a great relief. And a new worry.

"You do know," Mel had said into the quiet on the way to the airport, "that he's going to want you to stay, don't you?"

Elizabeth had protested, brandishing her return ticket.

"That's not what I mean," Mel had said. "I mean, he's never going to settle here, is he? You can see that, just looking at him. He's going to want you to live there, at some point. So you need to be thinking about whether you could learn to live there. He's going to want to know."

❉

Michael refused overtime and spent every moment he could with Elizabeth, showing her everything from the park where he played as a boy to the pub where he spent Saturday nights. They walked to the top of Beau's Heights, meandered around Butler's Pond, strolled by the river and ate plowman's lunches in quiet pubs.

"I've never wanted a dog before," Elizabeth had mused, "but it seems strange not to have one here."

Michael, looking for any sign that Elizabeth was giving serious thought to their future, had squeezed her hand a little more tightly as they walked home again.

They'd taken day trips to the Cotswolds and the seaside. "Now this is a beach," Michael had said proudly as they stood on a slab of pebbly damp sand, alone apart from a handful of seagulls and a dog walker, looking at the sullen, gray-purple water—and spent a long weekend in London.

Elizabeth, who would be running a marathon three weeks after she got back, went for long runs while Michael was at work. He only once had to rescue her. "I took a wrong turn and I'm in a phone box and all I can see is a bridge and a bunch of oak trees," she'd said, and instead of giving her directions he'd gone to pick her up and found her sitting on a five-bar gate looking at the sunset. "It's so lovely," she'd said, and Michael, watching his love for signs of something deeper than tourist appreciation, hoped. But it was hard to tell.

So Elizabeth had thought about it all. She'd looked at the pale sky and the pale people, casting off clothes at the first hint of sun, exclaiming at what seemed to her a laughable lack of heat. She'd listened to Michael as he explained the land, the reason the roads were the way they were, the importance of hedgerows. She'd been astonished by the history that everything seemed to have—not just capital *H* History, but how everything around Michael had significance. There was the wall he fell off where he broke his leg when he was nine, the place he first got really drunk, his father's grave. Everywhere Michael and Elizabeth went, there was someone to say hello to: an ex-girlfriend's mother, a colleague's son, an old teacher, someone who knew Michael's mother from the library.

"It's like a big web," Elizabeth had said, and Michael had said, "Yes, isn't it," smiling at her, delighted at her understanding, with no idea that she might not be offering a compliment.

❄

Michael had taken Elizabeth to meet his mother on her first night in Throckton. ("I've said we'll go around there," he'd said. "She's desperate to meet you. I'm sorry." And Elizabeth had smiled and said, "No, don't be silly. Of course she wants to check me out. It's what any mother would do. Mel did it to you. Just make my apologies if I go to sleep.')

They'd arrived, hand in hand and grinning like idiots at the simple thrill of simple touching after three months of the absence of each other's skin, and Patricia had recognized in an instant that this was no passing romance. Elizabeth, struggling through tiredness but charming nonetheless, had wanted to know everything there was to know about Michael, and when Patricia had offered to get the photographs out and Michael had groaned, she and Elizabeth had looked at each other and laughed, the smallest of bonds made and shared, and Patricia had thought, *Well, I still don't know why he had to choose a girl from Australia when there are so many lovely ones in Throckton, but if she's the one, he could have done a lot worse.*

"What do you think, Mum?" Michael had asked later, Elizabeth having fallen fast asleep on the sofa with no warning, and Patricia had told him that she was a lovely girl and, if she was really what he wanted, he'd be a fool to let her go. "I'm glad you like her, Mum," he'd said. She had been about to ask whether he was sure that they would be making their lives here rather than there, when she'd decided that she didn't want to know that, not yet. So she'd shooed them home and watched to see how Elizabeth got on in Throckton.

It was three weeks afterward when the two of them got to talk. Michael had gone to work. Elizabeth was helping Patricia with the dishes. She'd developed a simple strategy for being with Patricia—she asked a lot of questions, about Throckton, about Michael, and so the conversation never stopped.

But that night, Elizabeth had been quiet as she dried plates— methodically, thoroughly, front and back, Patricia noted—and so the older woman had seen a moment to understand more, and said, quietly, "A penny for your thoughts?"

"Oh," Elizabeth had said. "I don't think they're worth that, really."

Patricia had thought that that was going to be the end of it, but after the next plate was dried the younger woman had spoken again. The twang of her voice was still difficult for Patricia, who found herself paying closer attention, always, when Elizabeth said something. "I was just thinking about my mother. She died, you know?"

"Yes, Michael told me. I'm sorry."

"It was a long time ago," Elizabeth had said, "but we were young, my sister and I, and we went to live with our aunt and uncle, and we were happy enough, but—"

"You never quite get over it."

"No. And—" Elizabeth was feeling for just the right words now. "Because we never had a dad, not that we could remember—" Seeing Patricia's face, she hurried to be clear. "He's not dead or anything, was just a bit of a wild one, you know? And he left my mother, as soon as he found out that Mel was coming along."

Patricia tutted, although Elizabeth didn't think she knew that she'd done it, and she dried another plate (actually, it was the same plate again, though neither woman noticed) before continuing. "What I was thinking was that Michael and I, we've both lost a parent, and we understand what that's like. And it means we understand how important our close relationships are, and we know that we need to treasure them." And she'd put down the last plate, folded the tea towel the way Michael's mother liked them to be folded, long edge to long edge then on the oven door to dry, and smiled.

Patricia had said yes, and she'd put the kettle on. She wasn't good at conversations with the word "relationship" in them. So instead she touched Elizabeth's arm as she passed her, a touch that said, *I understand that you are telling me my son is safe with you, and I thank you.*

❀

Michael and Elizabeth's last night together wasn't easy. They went out for dinner and looked miserably at each other as they drank too much wine and ate almost nothing.

"Can we just go home," Elizabeth had asked when the dessert

menu came along, and Michael had paid the bill without a murmur, his idea of a romantic evening having died as soon as he'd seen the tears in her eyes when she picked up the menu.

"The food's not that bad," he'd said, and she'd said, "Mike, I don't know how I'm going to manage this next bit," and he'd said, "I know," because he had no idea either. Now that there was an imprint of Elizabeth everywhere in Throckton, there would be no way to stop missing her.

At home, he said, "We said we'd talk about things after eighteen months."

"Yes."

"Shall we talk about them now, instead?"

"Yes."

"Do you want me to come and live in Australia?" His face is solemn, true. Elizabeth takes a breath.

"No," she says, and his face is already crumpling, before she can get the rest out. "Mike, listen, I can't ask you to move to Australia because I can see how much this place means to you, and I've seen you in Australia, and I don't think it would work—"

"I'd get used to it," he says. "I would. It's just a question of acclimatizing."

She wants to kiss his stoical face. She does, because tomorrow there will be no face to kiss. "Maybe," Elizabeth says. In Michael's eyes, hope. "Or I could come here. Settle. I could settle here."

"Could you?" he asks.

"Yes," she says, "I could. I've thought about it. I could." She doesn't say, *This place is everything I don't quite remember, growing up, before my mother died, before we had to go and live on a farm, before I decided on the other extreme and headed for the big city that was just as lonely.* She didn't say, *There's something here, apart from you, that feels comfortable, for all of the oddness, for all the Wedgwood blue up above where the azure should be.* She knows how hard it will be to be parted from Mel, hopes, trusts that the agreement they made years ago, that they would always be there for each other but would never hold each other back, will be strong enough.

"Before you make up your mind," he says, and suddenly it's all gotten very, very serious again. "If you come here, there are some things you should know."

"OK," she says, and her voice is slow but her mind is fast, fast, flicking through everything they've said and emailed and talked about and not talked about, trying to find the shoe drop that she's missed before the second one falls.

"I don't want you to come here to live with me. I want you to come here and marry me and I want us to have hundreds of babies."

She laughs. "Hundreds?" Remembers their "Hopes and Dreams" emails, a mixture of the silly and sublime, marriage, children, happy old age mentioned by both, sandwiched between jokes about space travel and keeping pigs just in case they'd misjudged each other.

"Hundreds," he says, "and all of them with your eyes, please."

She says, "I could do that. But let's aim for three, first, and see how it goes." And he looks at her, as closely as he can look, to make sure that she is sure.

And she is.

She goes home, their parting a sort of triumph because it's the first step in their avowed life together. On the flight she stretches between sleep and not sleep, twisting the pretty silver ring that they bought on the way to the airport around and around on her ring finger. (Michael had taken a note of the size so that he could, he said, "organize the real thing" for when they were next together. The woman in the shop had as good as melted on the spot.)

They start the paperwork, Michael impatient and methodical,

Elizabeth by turns calm and frustrated, and after four months that felt like a long time apart but are forgotten as soon as the plane lands, they are reunited. Elizabeth has a fiancée's visa; the wedding is just less than a year away.

"You're here for good this time," Michael says.

"For good," Elizabeth agrees. She doesn't tell him that, for the sake of her sister's peace of mind, she's opened a joint credit card account with Mel. It's for emergencies only, the emergency being that if she's not happy, if she doesn't settle, if anything goes wrong, she'll get straight on a plane and come home. ("I'm only agreeing if it works both ways, and you'll use this to come to me if you need to," Elizabeth had said. "It's been you and me for a long time, and I don't want you to think for a moment that I don't know that this is a big deal for you too.") She does tell him that the sisters have agreed to spend a month together every year, here or there or in between, fortnights in European hotels or months as one another's houseguests.

Patricia manages to hide her horror at the idea of a beach wedding in Australia fairly well, comforting herself with the idea of Throckton grandchildren and the little bit of exoticism that Elizabeth is bringing to her family, remembering that conversation in the kitchen, sure as she can be that her new daughter-in-law-to-be is every bit as serious, as loving, as her son is. And Michael is nearly thirty, Elizabeth two years younger, so even if the wedding will be only eighteen months after they first met, they are old enough to know what they are doing.

Within a week of Elizabeth returning to Throckton they get a puppy, soon named Salty due to his habit of licking their legs when they come back from a run. Elizabeth has finished the first part of her unpacking, and they've found, or made, homes for everything in Michael's previously too-big house.

"So we're all set," Michael says.

"Happy ever after, here we come," Elizabeth replies.

Mike,

I've—we've—walked around Butler's Pond hundreds of times, so it wasn't as though there were going to be any surprises. The water was still, and Pepper frightened some ducks, but the noise they made frightened him right back. It's the sort of thing that used to make us laugh. This time I just felt jealous of Pepper, of his ability to be crushed, for a moment, and then bounce up again as though nothing bad had happened.

The ground was wet underfoot. I remembered those conversations we used to have, about little wellies. Still.

When I got to the place where you drowned I was all ready to cry, but I didn't. The swan's nest that we kept an eye on all last summer is abandoned now, and I sat down next to it. Pepper puttered about for a bit, and then he came and sat down next to me, and the two of us looked at the water. I thought about how cold it must have been, in the water and out, that night.

And then I sat and wondered at how I came to end up here, thousands of miles from the place where I grew up, with no husband, no child, no future to speak of. I kept waiting to feel something: some sense of you, some revelation. The full force of grief. I think I hoped that there was something I'd missed so far, that I would understand. Some secret of mortality, some understanding of what happened to you that night.

I waited, but nothing happened. Except maybe the knowledge that there's nothing worse to come. I am plumbing my own depths of grief. There's a strange sort of comfort in that.

Then Pepper ran off and I found him curled into the roots of a tree, looking very sorry for himself. I thought I could smell your aftershave.

On the walk home, I decided it's time to start making some little steps out of this awful place. I don't know how, or how well, I'll do it. I do know that I will never stop missing you, or loving you, even though you did the thing you promised that you never would, and left me.

E xxx

now

M EL IS SURPRISED BY how little resistance her haircut and new clothes suggestion meets. She'd agreed with Andy that if she kept it light, made it not too much of a big deal, Elizabeth was more likely to agree, and so she waited until she and her sister stood side by side making sandwiches in the kitchen.

"You know, Sis, if I'm ever going to find myself a decent English bloke you need to stop this trip down the crone road. I've made us hair appointments in Marsham, and then we'll get you a manicure, and then we'll buy some clothes that fit you and aren't jogging pants."

She'd stopped, watching Elizabeth carefully, kicking herself for making it sound like too much of a postmourning makeover, but her sister had just said that that was fine, so long as they came straight home if she said so.

"Do I look like a monster?" Mel had asked.

"No, you don't, but I probably do," Elizabeth said, then added, "I know I have to start somewhere, Mel," with such a wobble in her voice that Mel had been the one in tears, for a change.

When they'd pulled into the parking lot in Marsham, Mel had said, "You know, you're allowed to do these things. Shaving your legs is not a betrayal of Mike. Having your nails done doesn't mean you've forgotten him."

"I know," Elizabeth had said, but Mel hadn't believed her.

❋

Elizabeth flips through the hair magazines while she half listens to Mel putting the fear of God into the hairdresser about what she wants and what she doesn't. She's heard it all before—how many times she had to go back until they got the color exactly right, how in the end the managing director of the whole chain got in his helicopter and came to meet Mel to apologize in person—and while it used to make her laugh, now it's irritating, because a haircut feels so trivial. But then, suddenly, she's looking at a picture of exactly the haircut she would want, if she cared about how she looked.

Elizabeth shows the picture to Mel, who says, "It's very short," and passes it on to Chloé, the hairdresser, who has somehow come out of the other side of the hair expectations lecture as a trusted friend. Chloé looks at the picture, scrunches her nose, looks at Elizabeth, head on one side, and says, "It is quite drastic."

Elizabeth says, "In India, widows shave their heads. In comparison, this is nothing." Mel and Chloé look at each other. Mel nods, and before Elizabeth can get exasperated about not being allowed to decide on her own hairstyle, she is having her hair shampooed and her scalp massaged. She takes deep breaths and endures. She thinks she might have liked this sort of thing once, but now she's grown unused to such deliberate touching. This casual intimacy from a stranger feels wrong, when intimacy has become so absent from her days and nights.

As Chloé cuts and great swathes of dark brown hair fall, heavy, to the floor, Elizabeth watches her reflection and feels as though she is coming back from a long way away. Her eyes look bigger and her cheekbones are emerging from the shadows of her hair, casting shadows of their own. She has to admit that this suits her. And she thinks about how Mike wouldn't have liked it: how he used to hold her hair in his hands, how she used to joke about having it cut off so he could carry it around with him, how even joking about it made him uncomfortable.

She thinks about days at the beach in Australia, lying on her stomach reading while Mike stroked her hair, over and over, from the top of her head to the middle of her back, while he watched people go by. Every now and again she'd turn over and remind him that he was off duty, and he'd say, "Never." Which, as it turned out... Elizabeth watches her reflection and thinks about spilled milk, but it's not enough to stop the tears from coming.

Mel, trapped under a dryer at the other side of the salon, makes concerned faces and "honestly, it really suits you" eyes. Chloé says, "It'll grow back."

And Elizabeth, who is sick of crying, nods and dries her tears and doesn't bother to explain how everything she's done these last four months has been something Mike would have wanted, or would have approved of, or would have liked. This haircut, something he would have hated, is all for her. She can't tell whether she is proud of herself, or ashamed. She's definitely angry, but unsure of whether it's herself or her husband that she's angry with. But she feels strong. She is strong. She looks Chloé in the eye.

"Now dye it blond," she says. "Really, really blond. Icy."

❀

Mel is sitting in the garden in the late afternoon sun, feeling mildly optimistic about her sister, who not only had a haircut—a real, proper, wow haircut, not the swift removal of split ends that had been the most Mel had hoped for—but also bought jeans, and tops that suit her, and a new pair of shoes. They're not what Mel considers shoes—she admires her own new, red, patent leather boots, gleaming in the dull greens of the garden—but they are a start. And, as her experience of this funny little country is largely cobbles and mud, she can see why Elizabeth went the Mary Jane route. The important thing, she texts gleefully to Andy and Blake, is that she has done some things that are looking after her, and that she has done them willingly and without repercussions, apart from the tears in the hairdresser's, which, Mel thinks, any long-haired woman might shed when she made such a big change. Although Elizabeth had gone upstairs as soon as they got back, Mel isn't worried. This feels like a good road.

Mel hears footsteps stop outside the gate and braces herself for another chat with Patricia. The two of them tend to plow the same furrows, conversationwise: the wonderfulness of Michael, the delights of Throckton, how Elizabeth is doing. Patricia has gamely attempted to understand Mel's work as a translator, but none of those conversations has gone well. Mel understands that there's no malice in Patricia when she asks whether her job will be done by a computer one day ("There's no such thing as a literal translation," Mel had said, and Patricia had said, "Not yet"), but she tries to keep away from the subject. In what she thought was a moment of inspiration, she'd asked for book recommendations, thinking that this would mean that there was always something to talk about. Unfortunately for Mel, whose tastes are a little more varied, Patricia likes family sagas, and having supplied a dozen, interrogates her about them every time she sees her.

But it's not Patricia. It's Rufus Micklethwaite, carrying a bouquet. Mel recognizes him from an article in the *Throckton*

Warbler, when he'd been pictured at the opening of a school extension he'd designed. Patricia had pointed him out, wondering that he looked so pleased with himself after what his daughter was putting everyone through.

"Hello," he says. "I believe you're Elizabeth's sister." He holds out a hand, which Melissa shakes, although just hearing this man speak her sister's name has made her suddenly furious, her soul the color of her boots.

"That's right," she says. "I'm the sister in charge of picking up the pieces." She sits down again, without gesturing for him to do the same.

So he stands awkwardly and says, "I brought these for Elizabeth."

"You can't see her," Mel says. "She's sleeping." She lights a cigarette, blows smoke high, and ignores him to see what he'll do. He stands his ground.

"Well, I brought her these flowers—"

"I'd assumed they weren't for me." She nods, grudgingly, to a chair, and has a look at him.

She has to admit that he's handsome—at least, if you don't know what an idiot his daughter is. He has good skin, and he knows how to dress, with decent cuff links and trousers the right length so that when he sits down she doesn't get any leg.

The flowers too are well chosen. The bouquet has no ribbons or flounces, stating clearly that they are not for a celebration, and no lilies either, so nothing to make anyone think of a funeral. There's no fluff of fern or gypsophila, but there are sculpted leaves, framing roses, tulips, freesias, tiny orchids, all in shades of purple.

"They're nice," Mel says, but then, seeing Rufus plump himself up at the praise, thinking of her sister crying, sleeping, crying, pacing, crying months of her life away, adds, "The perfect way to say, 'I'm really sorry my daughter fucked up and your husband died and then, when it was all starting to get a bit better, my daughter fucked it up all over again.'"

"I just wanted," Rufus says, "to let your sister know that we haven't stopped thinking of her. That we won't stop being grateful to her husband. I'm sorry if you think that's inappropriate."

"What's inappropriate," Mel says quietly, so he has to lean a little toward her, "is a woman in her thirties being a widow. What's inappropriate is her knowing that her husband died in such a terrible way. What's inappropriate is you not knowing where your daughter is—which, frankly, points to how we are all in this mess in the first place—and so allowing her to upset my sister again. If Elizabeth was here she'd thank you for the flowers and say she was glad that Kate was alive, but she's much nicer than I am."

"I'm sure she is," Rufus says and gets up. "But I won't trouble her or you again. I was trying to do the right thing."

"I think that's best," Mel says, then adds, although she knows she shouldn't, "Would you like to take a photo of my boots before you go? You seem to really like them. You've hardly taken your eyes off them." And she stretches out her leg so the leather gleams. As she tells a horrified Elizabeth and horribly amused Andy and Blake later, it was like shooting fish in a barrel, but she couldn't help herself.

Mike,

Today I had a visit from Ian, who manages the hotel now. I think he was probably at your funeral though I don't remember. Mel let him in.

"Things are looking up, Sister," she said as she brought him through. He wants to know if I want to work the season again. He was very kind. He said he didn't know whether it would be inappropriate to ask, or inappropriate to assume that I wouldn't want to come back, so he was here to see what I wanted to do, and to give me the option of saying no.

I asked what he'd want and he said, "The same as usual, really. Three to five days a week, a bit of flexibility, from the end of May to the start of September." I said, "Well, I suppose so, I have to start somewhere."

Ian said, "Good."

Mel said, "I bet you've had more enthusiastic responses to a job offer than that one."

Ian didn't know what to say, but I told him to ignore her, and we arranged for me to go in and take a look at the updates to the computer system, and that was that.

So, in two weeks I'll be working, just like I was at the same time last year, and nothing like I was at the same time last year. I have no idea whether I'll be able to do it. We'll see.

When Ian had gone, Mel said, "I really didn't know what you were going to say."

I said, "Me neither, until I opened my mouth. But it's time, isn't it?"

She said, "Yes, it's time."

I think maybe it's time for her to go home too, but when I mentioned it, she said her career's been going brilliantly since she's been here because there isn't a decent daiquiri to be had within thirty miles so she's in no hurry to leave. I think that's Mel-speak for "I'm not quite sure that you're ready to do without me just yet," which is probably fair enough. For all that I probably look a bit more together on the outside, I think it's more of a scab that I've formed than anything else.

I mean, look at me. Look inside. Underneath.

I'm still writing to you, for a start.

I loved you. I love you. I will love you.

E xxx

then

ELIZABETH HAD GOTTEN THROUGH her first British winter with relative ease. The fact that she was newly, glowingly, excitedly married had helped. So had the winter itself, a snowy, bright one rather than the dull, wet months she'd been warned about. The days matched her mood. She watched in wonder at the snow coming down, laughed as it made a clean squeak in her hands.

Michael in his turn had watched her and hoped, with all his heart, that she would settle to life here and keep on being as happy as she seemed to be. Back in Australia for their wedding, she had asked him whether he really would have been prepared to move for her. He'd said yes, and he'd meant it, because he would have done anything for her and for the sake of being with her. But he doesn't think he would have liked it the way Elizabeth seems to like it here.

They had decided to run the Marsham March Marathon together, and so even on the darkest days they were out training, putting in the miles as Michael says, clocking up the miles according to Elizabeth. A training run is the setting for their first serious argument: Michael trips, and his wife laughs and tells him not to make such a fuss, then keeps running. Somehow—and neither of them can ever work out how—that night Mike insists on sleeping on the sofa after Elizabeth has told him that if he wants to be mollycoddled then he's picked the wrong woman, and he's said that yes, maybe he did, he had no idea she could be so selfish. Sometime around 4:00 a.m., he'd climbed into bed beside her, and she'd said, "I have no idea how that all happened," and he'd said, "No, me neither," and that was the end of it, although their training runs seemed to lose their rhythm for a while. But they both ran a personal best in the marathon.

"We're so good for each other," Mike had said as they crossed the line.

That spring, Elizabeth found a job in the new hotel on the outskirts of Throckton. So, on their first wedding anniversary, spent in a country house hotel just the other side of Marsham, because Michael could only get one night off, Mr. and Mrs. Gray seemed to be settling down well enough.

❈

"Are you really happy here?" he'd asked her.

"Yes, Mike, I'm as happy as can be. I really am." Elizabeth had noticed how much reassurance he needed. Even now they were married, settled, and she was the one on the wrong side of the world if it all went badly, he still needed her to tell him that everything was all right. Which it was. So that was fine. She kissed him, hoping to distract him.

"I'm so glad. When I look at you I still can't quite believe my luck."

It was the next anniversary when the baby question became the baby answer. Elizabeth and Michael were in Edinburgh, walking down the Royal Mile, dodging strollers and laughing about the increasingly unsubtle hints coming their way from Patricia, when Elizabeth had said, in the casual way that only comes out when things mean a very great deal, "Well, I'm game if you are, Mike."

"Really?"

"Really." She'd only glanced toward him, not so much as broken her stride as they walked together down the hill, but he'd still known that this was no spur-of-the-moment offer. His beloved wife wanted their first baby now. His beloved wife would have one. Michael must, somehow, prepare for a better life than he had now, a job he loved, a place to live that had always looked after him, this woman beside him. It seemed impossible to him.

But not to Elizabeth, who had been ambushed by her desire for a baby. Motherless since the age of nine, she thought of mothers as something that happened to other people. When she watched friends with their children, she more often than not found herself overpowered by anxiety on behalf of the baby, imagining itself safe in the unchanging world of its mother's arms when in fact anything could go wrong, at any time. She had to stop herself from interrogating her friends about what provision they had made for their children should disaster strike. When she and Michael had talked about their own plans for a family, she'd known, in the abstract, that that was what she wanted, but had no idea of how the hot, visceral need would hit her.

One ordinary day, a couple had checked into the hotel, bleary from a long drive, bickery from tiredness as they gave their details. By the woman's feet was a baby car seat and the child in it, dressed all in pink and still peachy with newness, stretched in her sleep, and it was as though that wave of a tiny arm flicked a switch in Elizabeth. In that instant, she loved the child, she longed for her own child, and when the woman sensed her baby waking and picked her up, all tension draining out of her as the little one found its place against her shoulder, Elizabeth felt such jealousy attack her that she wondered if she was ill.

❀

The next anniversary, they were still in good spirits. Marriage had failed to settle down into something mundane, every day, uninteresting. Michael and Elizabeth were still walking hand in hand, seeking each other out, planning time together, mainly delighting in the life they were making.

But there was the nonappearance of a baby, or any sign of a baby. To Michael, Elizabeth looked more beautiful than he'd ever seen her: six months into Operation Puppy, as they'd called it—a joke that was becoming less funny with every despondent month that passed—she'd started drinking less, running more (but not too much more), taking multivitamins, and as a result she was fitter, healthier, lovelier. "You look..." He'd struggled to find a way to express it, every word that came to him—*glowing, radiant*—too pregnant a word. "You're just lovely. Lovely."

"Well, you'd better make the most of it, because I intend to let myself go completely to hell when the baby comes." She'd laughed, but her eyes had dulled a little bit at the apparently limitless size of that "when."

Michael couldn't see that there was anything to worry about. A book about fertility had appeared at Elizabeth's side of the bed, but when he'd read the first chapter while waiting for his wife to come to bed from her bath he'd discovered that, until they had been trying for two years, there wasn't any reason to suppose there was a problem.

"I know," Elizabeth had said when he'd ventured this view, gently, later. "But I thought it would just happen."

"I know," Michael had said, and he had admitted that he had expected the same.

"It's just going to have to be three times a week for the foreseeable future then," she'd said, and rolled herself in close to him, and he'd laughed and agreed. But checking a date in her diary the next week, he'd realized that she was keeping a record: *P* for *period*, *O* for *ovulation*, *S* for *sex*. He felt as though he'd been handed a school report with "must try harder" written across the bottom of it.

Folded into the back of the diary was the list of baby names they'd made one evening, early on, when there was nothing in the world to worry about. Elizabeth's girl suggestions were Amelie, Kayleigh, Seraphina, against Michael's of Rose, Daisy, Lily. Elizabeth's boys were Arthur, Archie, Tom, playing Michael's John, Jack, Sam. "We're going to need nine months to thrash this out," she'd said. He'd said, "Why don't you name the first and I'll do the second."

The book about fertility became a pile. "They're new," Michael had said.

"I went into Marsham to get them," Elizabeth had replied, sidestepping the real discussion. "Living in Throckton really gets on my nerves sometimes."

"Do you want to move then?" he'd asked mildly, sensing the onset of premenstrual syndrome and knowing (finally) not to ask whether that was the problem.

"No. I don't want to move. I want to be able to walk into the bookshop here and buy a bunch of books about babies."

❊

Eighteen months after they started trying to conceive, Elizabeth began taking her temperature every morning, and the bathroom cabinet always contained an ovulation predictor kit. They tried having more sex. They tried having less sex, at the times when it was more likely to work. Elizabeth trawled the Internet for clues about what might add the magic ingredient that they were missing. She drew up lists of things that could be wrong with either of them. Mealtimes became combinations of foods high in one thing and low in another, in the hope that they would add the missing something. Wine was for weekends. Sex was not for fun. Once, Michael had come in from work on a night shift to his wife saying, "We need to do it now, but we need to be quick, because I have to be at work in fifteen minutes, and if I drive instead of walk I can be there in five."

Michael was the one who suggested going to see a doctor. He wasn't sure they needed to, couldn't believe that their good health and their bodies and their love wouldn't do the job sooner or later, but he was afraid for Elizabeth, for the way she seemed to need a baby more than she needed him. One night, she had said, "Maybe that's the one that's done it," as she turned over to go to sleep, and her husband was fairly certain that she hadn't known she'd said it out loud. Their world, once everything they needed, was becoming a place where they could only see what was missing. Elizabeth longed for her baby, Michael for his wife. A baby seemed the best way of getting his wife back.

So they went to see their GP about it, properly, at the office, although the topic had come up between Andy and Michael not long before. They'd been at the pub quiz and Andy and Lucy had announced that they were expecting. Elizabeth had said the right things and gone quiet; the men had gone to the bar. "You've had better luck than us," Michael had said. "We've been trying for a year and a half." "Give it a bit longer," Andy had replied. "A year and a half doesn't mean anything. Honestly. Medical opinion. But come and see someone about it, if it will put your mind at rest."

Back at the table, Lucy had caught something of Elizabeth's mood and said, "It will be you next."

In the waiting room, Elizabeth whispered, "I haven't felt like this since I went to get the pill when I was seventeen." Michael smiled and squeezed her knee. Elizabeth added *contraceptive pill too early/too long?* to her list of possible reasons for her empty arms.

Their doctor told them that there was probably nothing amiss, but referred them on to a specialist. The appointment was another six-week wait. "Makes a change from a four-week wait," Elizabeth had said, and she'd suggested that they go for a run. It helped her to clear her mind, and tire her body. It was the first time she'd proposed that they do anything except have sex in a long time. Which, Michael reflected as he pulled on his sneakers, sounded a lot more fun in theory than in practice.

The fertility unit was bright and full of couples holding hands. As they waited Elizabeth read leaflets and Michael looked at the notice board thick with thank-you cards and pictures of babies and hoped. Only Mel and Andy knew they were here; only Mel and Andy knew that they were trying for a baby.

If Michael and Elizabeth had thought they were trying before, then that first appointment at the clinic showed them that there could be a whole new level of endeavor. They had tests for everything. They had medical histories taken, as far back in their families as either could remember. They had hormone tests, blood tests, swabs to be taken and sent on. Elizabeth's menstrual cycle was recorded. The doctors needed to check that Elizabeth was ovulating, that Michael both made and delivered good, healthy sperm. Because of the cystic fibrosis that ran in Michael's family, because Elizabeth knew nothing about her father and knew of no one living on her mother's side, there would be genetic testing too.

"It's like forensic evidence," Michael had said, on the way home in the car.

"Isn't forensic evidence exactly what it is?" Elizabeth had asked with something that was shaped like a smile but wasn't really. "And I can't believe that you didn't tell me about the cystic fibrosis, seeing as it usually means infertility in men." She was driving, glaring at the road. He was afraid to touch her. It seemed like a long time since the one of them who wasn't driving would rest a hand in the other's lap.

"I didn't tell you," he had said, "because I never really think about it, to be honest." He'd tried for the positive angle. "I know I don't have it."

"That's not the point," she'd said.

"No," he'd replied, "I don't suppose it is."

❋

"So," the specialist had said to them, when they sat in front of her, holding hands, another sad month later. "There's nothing really wrong with either of you. Michael's sperm count is a little below average, but the sperm are healthy, so that shouldn't present a problem. Michael, you do carry the cystic fibrosis gene, although you don't have cystic fibrosis"—Elizabeth's fingers had stiffened in her husband's hand—"but, Elizabeth, you don't, so we would have no worries about any child that you had on that score." The stiffness became a squeeze. Michael was forgiven.

"But it's been two and a half years. If there's nothing wrong with either of us…" Elizabeth had said. Her voice had slid to a halt. She had looked at Michael. His face had said, *I don't know.* He had realized that they were both hoping for a problem, something that could be fixed with pills or an injection. Michael had felt Elizabeth's body soften; not relaxation but defeat.

"What else could we do?" he had asked.

"First of all, don't despair. We can't find anything wrong with thirty percent of couples who don't conceive naturally. That doesn't mean we can't help them. In your case, I suggest we try IVF using your own eggs and sperm."

Mike,

It's only now I've started dreaming about you. Andy said that dreaming about you is a good thing. He says it's part of the process. I said, "Don't call this a process. Making a cake is a process. Taking out an appendix is a process." He said, "OK, dreaming about Michael is a good thing, and we'll leave it at that."

Except in the dreams, I can't see you. I know you're there, but I can't reach you. Sometimes you're just around the corner, and I'm waiting because I know you're coming, but you don't. Sometimes I can hear you, taking off your boots without undoing the laces, pushing one off with the toe of the other, the bounce on the kitchen tiles and Pepper welcoming you home. Sometimes you're lying in bed with me, curled into my back, but I'm trapped in the sheets and I can't turn over to you.

Andy says it's still a sort of healing. Mel says, "Like leeches, you mean, Andy," and he said, "I know, but it's hard." I agreed, with the hard part.

I haven't told them the other part. The other dreams. There's you—you're still not there, you're always just out of shot, parking the car or putting the kettle on, something ordinary—and there's me, and there's our baby too. And it's just normal. You're going to work, or we're watching

TV, or the baby is playing with something, a ball, a train, on the floor. His age changes in the dreams, sometimes I think we're just back from the hospital with him and sometimes it seems that he's ready to go out on his little bike, but he's always a boy. Always a boy, a little you. I don't think I'd have been good with a girl, but in these dreams I am very good with our boy, and he is plump and smiling and towheaded, like you were when you were small. If I'd told Andy about these other dreams I know what he'd have said. He'd have said, "You're mourning for what you didn't have, as well as what you did." He'd have told me that although we always said we'd come to terms with not having a baby, there was probably still a part of me that hoped, and that your death means no more hope. And he would be right. All those books I read about infertility when we were trying, and the ones about coming to terms with childlessness when we stopped, made me good at this stuff.

But I didn't tell him, partly because I don't need to hear people saying things like "no more hope" to me, and I don't like how Andy looks when we have those kinds of conversation, so full of grief and worry.

But the main reason I keep quiet is that I quite like those dreams, and I quite like the way I feel the next day: after the kick in the guts of understanding that you're not here, and that the baby never was here, I feel as though I have a secret, a hidden little bit of something special, a shiny pebble in my pocket that I can touch and rub my thumb across and hold on to when the day darkens.

Dreams are better than nothing. Dreams are better than flowers in the garden that aren't from you. Dreams are mine, and I'll keep them close for as long as I want to.

Oh, my love.

E xxx

now

EVER SINCE THE MORNING when she took the pregnancy test six weeks ago, Kate has walked around unable to understand why no one can see what is going on inside her. It seems to her that she has the words "mother-to-be" picked out in flashing neon above her head. Every time she walks into a room with her parents in it, she waits for one of them to see what's happening in front of them, but they never do, although they look at her with love and concern and, she thinks, more than a suspicion that they don't know the whole story. She hears her name spoken softly at night, sometimes, as she goes downstairs for bananas and milk.

Although Kate has been sad, so very sad, since the night at Butler's Pond, still she feels a deep, uncomplicated joy at the thought of this baby nestling itself into life inside her. She cannot tear her thoughts away from it. She'd thought, for three months, that the sickness and the tiredness she felt were the understandable aftermath of the horrible night when she nearly drowned; everyone around her seemed to think the same thing. But then she'd added coming off the Pill at the beginning of December into the equation—it had seemed like a good time for a break—and a baby became a much more likely explanation.

The first time she felt it move, her whole self lurched with love in response. She reads, secretly, voraciously, about this miracle her body is making, fascinated by how it grows: grape, plum, lemon, avocado, grapefruit. She wishes she wasn't doing this alone.

She knows what her parents will say; she knows she doesn't care. She knows the worst they can do to her is make her leave, and that they won't do that, because then there would be just the two of them, and they all know how well that would work.

She knows, she tells Beatle, who keeps on wagging his tail in spite of the weight of all the secrets he is carrying, that there will be a bit of temporary unpleasantness. There will be a conversation in which the words *disappointed* and *education* and *future* will feature, heavily. Her mother will look tragic and her father will sulk and tut and sigh. They will all three of them—all four of them, if you count the baby, all five of them, if you count Beatle—be upset for a couple of days. But then, they will all find a way to get on with it. She's sure they will. It will be all right, she promises the pup, and promises herself.

Kate has known since that morning when the word *pregnant* materialized like magic in front of her that the longer she can keep her secret from beaming, blurting itself out, the better. The further on the baby is, the more of a fait accompli she will be able to offer the world. So she's done her best to sleep unobtrusively, vomit discreetly, crave privately. She hears her parents talk about her, about shock and trauma, and she slides her hand to her belly, rounding now. The plan is to wait, until six months if she can, and then tell them. She thinks it's a good plan.

But then, one morning, there's blood.

✤

Richenda looks up from her laptop as Kate flies down the stairs, Beatle at her heels. There's an urgency in their approach that alerts her. Since "that night at Butler's Pond," as the family has come to refer to it, Richenda has grown used to Kate being lethargic at best. She is anything but now. Her eyes are wide and her hands are reaching for her mother. "I'm bleeding," she says. "Mum, I'm bleeding."

"Where?" Richenda is thrown. There's been no crash, no clatter. There's no sign of injury, no blood on her hands.

"No," Kate says, and she takes her mother's hands, and a deep breath, and forces herself to look straight into her mother's face, although this is not how she planned this, not at all. "Mum. I'm five months pregnant. And I'm bleeding."

❁

In the car on the way to the hospital, there's one of the most uncomfortable question-and-answer sessions that either has ever taken part in. It reminds Kate of the conversation she'd had with her English teacher after failing her mock exams because she'd misunderstood the instructions on the paper. Richenda recalls talking to Rufus about one of his "work weekends away."

"Do you have any pain?"

"No, no pain."

"What color is the blood?"

"Mum—"

"It's important. Bright red, brownish red?"

"Bright red."

"How much?"

"Mum—"

"If you're pregnant, Kate, you need to be able to answer questions like this like a woman, not a girl. How much?"

"Not much. Spots."

"OK."

Kate hugs her baby to her, as though her arms could hold it in its right place, as though the force of her love will make this all right. She hopes her mother has stopped with the questions. She hasn't.

"How long have you known?"

"About six weeks."

"Why didn't you tell us? Me?" Richenda's voice is breaking. *Concentrate*, she tells herself, *drive carefully. Don't cry. Don't look at her, look at the road. This family doesn't need another near miss.*

"I thought you'd try to make me get rid of it."

The baldness of this makes Richenda pause. She stops thinking about a place at Oxford thrown away and a life narrowed and limited in ways that Kate cannot imagine. Instead, she remembers how she might have been a mother of three instead of having one perfect, beautiful baby girl and two wretched, painful miscarriages, how easy it is to be objective about someone else's pregnancy, how your own is your own cosmos.

She decides that she will leave the education/potential/future-abandoned-for-the-sake-of-one-mistake stuff to Rufus.

"Who's the father?"

"No."

Richenda, negotiating a series of mini roundabouts, thinks she's misheard. "You don't know? Oh, Kate—"

"That's not what I said, Mum," Kate says. "I said no. I'm not telling you who the father is. There's just me and the baby. If the baby is all right." Her voice starts to fray with tears. They pull into the hospital parking lot. Richenda stares ahead for a moment, then takes her daughter's hand.

"The baby's survived a pretty rough time already," she says. "Let's hope for the best, shall we."

❋

They are through Accident and Emergency and into the Early Pregnancy Unit before there's been time to say much more. Kate has been pale and still, but she's answered questions in a clear, unapologetic voice, and while she hasn't invited her mother to come into the consulting room with her, she hasn't stopped her either. Richenda, calm on the outside but a scramble of worry and disbelief inside, is within arm's reach, should Kate choose to reach. So far, she hasn't, but her mother is sure that the time will come.

Until then, Richenda does the math, and wonders about Christmas parties, and that boy whose mother manages the restaurant where Kate sometimes works, and the possibility of violence. And she wonders, yet again, how she could know so little about her daughter.

She thinks of how Kate had been tested for pregnancy when she was admitted to the hospital after the accident. She remembers because Rufus had had to be placated when he found out.

"It's completely routine in admissions of women of childbearing age," the consultant had said. "We have to know, just in case."

"You'll find it's negative," Rufus had said. "She doesn't even have a boyfriend."

Richenda wonders, not for the first time, whether Kate had been at Butler's Pond to meet someone. But surely, if she had, he would have come forward by now, come to see her, come to make sure she was all right?

❋

When they go for the scan, Kate does hold Richenda's hand. Richenda looks at the small, taut mound of baby when Kate pulls up her top, and cannot believe she didn't notice. She shakes her head. "Please, Mum," Kate says, misunderstanding, and Richenda smiles and touches her daughter's hair, which is the same cream-blond it was when she was born, although everyone said it would darken.

"It will be all right," she says.

"Let's see if we can find a heartbeat first," the radiographer says, and Kate's whole world shudders to a halt, holding its breath. And then there is noise, filling the room, strong and fast, like feet running along a wet pavement. She looks at her mother, sees a mirror of her own delight and relief, and starts to cry.

"You see, it will be all right," Richenda says, looking at the mixture of child and adult in front of her. She thinks of how, whatever the circumstances, you can't really regret a baby. She remembers her own mother, saying, "A baby brings its own love." And she thinks about how this almost-young woman is her daughter still, and if ever there was a time for a mother to stand with her daughter, it's now.

And then there's a picture on the screen, and for a moment the radiographer, who has been all business so far, softens and says, "You never get tired of this bit."

She starts to measure and check, while Kate and Richenda watch the heart blipping away and the arms and legs moving and point to the outline of a nose and chin.

Kate has to be asked twice whether she wants to know the sex of the baby, not because she hesitates over the yes, but because she is so absorbed in the graphite image, greedy for the sight of her child, that she doesn't hear the question. Her last few months of worry and fear and living in a strange, secret universe vanish as she watches her baby's tiny feet flex. The grief, the loss, remain, but they move back to make room for this new, greater reality.

✳

"You can say what you like to her," Richenda says to her poleaxed husband later, "but I'm telling you, Rufus, there's no point."

"She has options," Rufus spits, "other than her preferred option of throwing her life away."

"You can see that, and I can see that," Richenda says, "but I saw her face when she looked at the scan and they told her it was a girl. I've never seen her so—"

"Don't be ridiculous, Richenda, of course she was going to look like that. It's hormones. It's instinct. The biological imperative to reproduce, nothing more. We're outside the hormone cloud. We can see clearly. We're her parents. She can't keep it. We can't let her."

"We can't make her do anything else. She's nineteen. She's an adult."

Rufus pauses, absorbing this. His wife watches as his brain flicks through the possibilities: threaten to throw her out, throw her out, buy a little house to throw her into. He looks at Richenda. His eyes say, *All right, all right, you're right. There can be no throwing.* He sighs.

"She's supposed to be going to Oxford, for crying out loud. Four As at exams. For this?"

"We know that she's a bright girl. Which means she won't throw her life away. She'll have the baby then she'll find her path."

"That's a matter of opinion. She wasn't very bright when she got herself—" Unable to say the word, Rufus gets up, sits down, gets up, walks to the window, glares into the garden.

Watching him, Richenda is thankful for the bargain she struck with Kate on the way home from the hospital: she would break the news to Rufus, if Kate would consent to a sensible conversation with him when he'd calmed down.

Kate had agreed, with the caveat that the baby's father was not, and would never be, up for discussion. "He's not going to be part of our lives," she'd said.

"Well," Richenda had replied, "that's fine, except that your father and I will both want to know that you haven't been…" She had rejected "forced," deciding instead on "hurt."

"Hurt?" Kate had looked puzzled for a moment, then understood. "No, Mum. Not the way you think, anyway."

Rufus turns his back on the garden, annoyed by its rampant fecundity.

"You don't think she'll have an abortion?"

"No. I'm certain she won't. And anyway, at five months, it's—it's not an easy thing. Not pleasant."

Rufus makes a half-shrug gesture, dismissing these mechanics as irrelevant to the much more pressing subject of his daughter's future, having no idea that he's just added another reason for his wife, already primed, to loathe him a little bit more. "Adoption, then?"

"No."

"Are you sure?"

"I'm completely sure, Rufus. Don't think I didn't think about everything that you're thinking about. But she's not going to be talked out of this. She's having a baby. She's made a choice, and the only choice we are left with is whether we support her or not."

"And where will the father be in all this? Do we know who he is?"

"No."

"Does Kate know?"

"I think so. She's not telling, though. Not yet, anyway. I think the less we ask, the better, at this stage."

"Well, that's obvious. Christ, Christ, Christ." Rufus is still glaring. "What do we actually know? Do we know anything at all?"

Richenda chooses to answer the letter of his question, and ignore the spirit. "We know that she's twenty weeks pregnant. We know that the baby is a girl. We know that both of them are well, and the bleeding was nothing significant. We know that we only know about the pregnancy because of the bleeding, and Kate would have kept this a secret for longer if she could have, because she has no intention of giving this baby up. We know that we don't know who the father is and Kate is unwilling and unlikely to tell us, until and unless something changes. We know that, if things go as they should"—she ignores her husband's furious snort—"Kate will have a baby sometime around the middle of September."

She judges that the storm has passed, and she sits down next to Rufus, speaks quietly. "We know that we've always supported our daughter."

❀

When Patricia arrives, bearing one of her pies, she looks as though she's going to burst. Elizabeth braces herself for another tale that she won't be able to follow. It starts unpromisingly, about how someone who had come into the library today had been talking to someone else who had had a hospital appointment the day before, for a lung complaint that won't be cured, which is a terrible shame.

She was just launching into an explanation of who, exactly, the person with the breathing problem was, when Mel looked up from her laptop and said, "Christ, Patricia, I can do Spanish into English, but not with Throckton rattling away in the background, so do you think you could please get to the point? I'm on a deadline here."

Patricia pauses, waits until both Elizabeth and Mel are looking at her, and says, "Well, the Micklethwaite girl—"

"Kate," Elizabeth corrects, automatically, one of the many small ways she's found to show her mother-in-law that, despite everything, she's not prepared to vilify the girl. She knows that making a target out of Kate won't bring Michael back.

"Well, Kate Micklethwaite was seen at the hospital, leaving the Early Pregnancy Unit, with her mother, and they both looked a bit teary, and the girl—Kate—was holding what looked like a scan." She looks at Elizabeth and Mel, who don't seem to be getting it. "A scan. Of a baby. A baby picture that you get when you're pregnant, these days."

"OK," Elizabeth says. "Well, I suppose she might be. We don't know a lot about her, really." She looks to her sister for rescue; babies plus Kate Micklethwaite in any combination aren't going to make her evening bearable.

Mel adds, "There's no law against it. Girls will be girls."

"It seems that she's no better than she should be, that's for sure, for all of her picture-in-the-paper-with-her-place-at-Oxford." Patricia sniffs. "And where was the boyfriend when she needed pulling out of a lake. That's what I want to know."

This is just the sort of malicious triumph that Elizabeth can't stomach. She gets up, walks to the kitchen, switches the oven on, breathes. Deep, deep breaths. She remembers the girl in the garden, beautiful and frail, just as broken as she is, in a different way. Slow, slow breaths.

In the other room, Mel is pointing out that they know nothing, really, and even if she is pregnant, that's her business.

Patricia is arguing for a baby as further proof that Mike Died For Nothing. When Elizabeth hears Mel asking if Kate had fallen into the water because she was reaching for her library card, whether that would be an acceptable reason for Mike to go in after her, she interrupts to see if Patricia wants tea. She doesn't: she's on her way to a meeting of the church council.

"You know," Elizabeth says to her gently, on the doorstep, "she might be ill. Maybe the Early Pregnancy Unit is in the same direction as the MRI scanner, or the place they take your blood for testing. Maybe it's Richenda that's ill. Maybe Kate is pregnant, because since Mike died she's been reckless and upset. Maybe she is pregnant, but there's something wrong. We just don't know, Patricia."

Patricia, who has listened quietly to all of this half turned away, turns back, touches Elizabeth on the shoulder, looks straight into her face. "Michael always said you always see the good," she says, but the way she says it makes Elizabeth feel that her mother-in-law is telling her off, and her husband is joining in from beyond the grave.

❊

Every now and again Mel thinks about going home, about her sociable Sydney life and the way her friends are changing, new jobs, new relationships appearing on Facebook and making her home-sick. But there's something in her that won't let her leave her sister. Not just yet. Even though Elizabeth seems to be ready to go back to work and is sleeping better and spending less time looking like a woman trapped at the bottom of a well, it feels too soon.

But they are establishing a new sort of normality.

Elizabeth is back to full-time dog walking again, although she strides out looking at her feet and the six feet of pavement in front of her. Sometimes she arranges to meet Blake, but any discussion of shift patterns makes her sad, and she quite likes the chance to concentrate on her body and think about the things it can do that aren't crying and aching—stride, climb, breathe deeply, hurl a stick. She has ordered a new pair of her favorite running shoes. She wants her lungs to burn with something other than tears. The thing she likes least about going out is the coming back: the whole weight of Michael not being at home when she gets there, never being at home when she gets there, crashes down on her again. Not quite again, because every time it happens it happens in a slightly different way, so it's always surprisingly, shockingly painful.

Blake is filling the absence created by the death of his friend with more overtime, more sports coaching, more time at the gym. He's not good at dropping by to see how Elizabeth is, but he often finds a purpose for a visit. He mows the lawn; he's battled back the leylandii that Michael and Elizabeth somehow never got around to dealing with.

Lucy had put her foot down when Andy suggested that they might not take an Easter trip in case Elizabeth needed him.

"What Elizabeth needs," she'd said, "is to start to learn to live without him. And so do you."

"He would want me to look after her," he'd replied.

"Yes, but he wouldn't want you to move in with her, and there are times when I think that you might as well." It was almost six years since Elizabeth, looking closed off and uncomfortable, had come to see them after the boys were born and refused to hold either of them. "I'm not going to make you take one away with you," Lucy had joked, and Elizabeth had shot her a look full of fury. Lucy would like to think that she didn't hold this against Elizabeth, after all this time, all this tragedy, but she suspected that she did.

"I'm trying to do the right thing," Andy had said. But he'd known that his wife was right.

Then she'd said, "The right thing is to put your own family first now and treat her like your friend, and let her work out how to cope on her own"—and she'd taken his hands—"and you can start working out how to manage without him as well. Don't use helping Elizabeth to stop you from missing your friend. You can't fix this, Andy. Don't break other things trying."

So they'd agreed that he would go around for an evening every couple of weeks, invite Elizabeth to their home now and then— "Not yet," she'd said last time, "but I think I will, soon, thank you"—and drop in for a coffee sometimes in between. It seemed to be working.

Meanwhile, Patricia is doing what she always does: being busy, being helpful (in the ways she judges to be helpful). She can't talk to Elizabeth about Michael, much—can't even bear to hear her call him Mike, a version of his name that he'd rejected with everyone else—but she can feed her, and encourage her, and try to keep her interested. So that's what she does.

The evening before Elizabeth goes back to work sees her, Mel, Andy, and Blake gathered in the garden. Mel is cooking chicken and salmon on the barbecue; Elizabeth has assembled a salad and bought a pavlova; Andy and Blake have brought the beer. Elizabeth had suggested this, wanting to mark the occasion. "Although it's not an occasion, and it's definitely not a celebration," she'd said to them all. "It's just a—" But she couldn't find a word. "It's a gathering," said Blake, and Elizabeth had agreed that that would do. Patricia, who is at the WI this evening, has brought some bread and said not to worry about her not being there, she doesn't really like food cooked outdoors anyway.

It's not an uncheerful evening. Elizabeth is more present than she has been, and Michael is an occasional, gentle topic of conversation. Tonight it feels as though it's Mel's turn to be quiet. "My head's in Spanish. I'm having to translate you all," she explains, when Elizabeth puts her hand over hers and asks if she's OK, as the others talk of nothing much.

When Blake gets up to go, Mel goes with him, picking up her cigarettes and clipping Pepper's lead on. "You're a hell of a good excuse, and that's all," she mutters as she takes him to the door. "Don't go thinking I like you."

"I assume," Blake says, "you're talking to the dog."

She waits until they turn into the corner of Blake's road before she tells him the short version of Patricia's story. "Well," he says, "that's Throckton for you. They were probably visiting someone, and before you know it, Kate will be having triplets."

"Yes," Mel says, "but, Blake, if we didn't know Michael, if all we knew was that she went into the water, he was there, close by, he went in after her, he died, and now it turns out that she's pregnant, what would we think?"

"Mel, you can't be saying…" Blake is standing very still. He's looking over her shoulder. She can't read him.

"I'm not saying anything. I'm just saying, if we hadn't known Michael, what would we be thinking?"

❀

Walking away from what he still thinks of as Elizabeth and Michael's house, Andy remembers a time—the only time—when he and his friend were both at the scene of an accident. A cyclist had got caught in the wheels of a truck, just along the road from the office, and a horrified witness had come to find a doctor after calling an ambulance. Andy had been standing in reception at the time. He'd picked up the emergency kit and run.

In the event, there wasn't a lot for him to do. The cyclist had possible spinal injuries and a crushed pelvis at the very least, but it didn't look good. The guy would be lucky to walk again, let alone get on a bike. Andy cleared his airway, got a line in ready for the paramedics, and told Michael, who was standing on the pavement making sure that no one whose curiosity got the better of them would be able to have a look, that he'd never complain about doing a diabetic clinic again.

And then the man's phone, on the road by the doctor's knee, started to ring. "Gran" came up on the display, shaking Andy more than the blood and shattered bone and the sound of the truck driver sobbing.

He'd held the phone up to Michael, mute, horrified, thinking that the next time this Gran was likely to hear her grandson's name would be attached to some very bad news. The cyclist was no longer a jigsaw of bone and blood, a game played against poor medical odds.

Michael had taken the phone from him and switched it off, then put it back in the cyclist's bag.

"What you have to remember on days like this," Michael had said, "is that everything works out, somehow, in the end." Seeing the look Andy gave him, he'd added, "I'm not saying it happens for a purpose or a plan. I'm saying, even with the terrible things, it works out somehow, in the end. The river always gets to the sea."

Mike,

Well, I did it. I put on my black skirt and my white shirt and mascara and tights and heels, and I went to work. I said, "Welcome to Throckton," and I smiled and I chatted a little bit, and I was all right. Ian hovered for the morning, and Emily took me to lunch, which I'm sure wasn't as casual an arrangement as it seemed, but I'm getting to be graceful when people try to help me, because God knows I'm not good at life without you, and I need all the help I can get.

It's funny to see people arriving and exclaiming over how pretty this place is, something I'd forgotten. I just see the bits I don't like: the sky too close, the streets too narrow, the people knowing exactly who I am and where I fit into the Great Scheme of Throckton. But today, walking home, I remembered how I felt during my first spring here, and I was happy. I remembered my amazement at how green everything is, all the time, not just during spring and autumn, like it is back home.

When I left, walking back through town, I think I saw Kate Micklethwaite.

I shouldn't be jealous of that girl. I shouldn't. She nearly died, she's traumatized, and she's fucked up her superbright amazing future. I should feel sorry for her.

Or I should be like Patricia, who is angry. She's muttering about how, when she was a girl, if you got into trouble then you at least had the grace to keep a low profile, rather than "flaunting your shame." (There seem to be as many ways not to say pregnant as there are not to say dead.) Mel asked her what Kate had been doing. Surely it was a bit chilly to be wandering around Throckton in a bikini? But apparently she'd been to the library to borrow a book about pregnancy. Mel said, "I wouldn't call that flaunting; I'd call it making the best of a bad job." I don't know whether to laugh or cry at the two of them. Mostly I ignore them, or intervene if it's getting out of hand.

But now I'm jealous of Kate Micklethwaite, who seems to have gotten, accidentally, I presume, what we wanted so badly. She got the baby. And she got the last touch of your life.

In a funny way I'm glad we tried, and failed, to have a baby, because those four years of trying made me understand that life isn't fair. And I'm glad I knew that before you died, because if I hadn't, I can't imagine how much worse these days would be.

I love you. I do.

E xxx

then

ELIZABETH ONLY ONCE THOUGHT she was pregnant. It was not long before they went to the fertility clinic. Her body was fraught with hope. She was fit and healthy, making of herself the best possible nest, and at the same time anxious and aching for a baby. She'd given up on trying to note things in her diary and now kept a spreadsheet to track everything she thought might be important: sex, menstrual cycle, exercise, alcohol, working hours, unusual events.

She had always had regular periods, with less than forty-eight hours' variation month to month. Later, she would describe her cycle to the nurse who took their details at the clinic, and when it was all written down, the nurse would look at Elizabeth and say "perfect" with a big smile and no irony. And Elizabeth had laughed, because surely a perfect menstrual cycle would have made a baby. A perfect baby. "That's the spirit," the nurse had said.

But there was one Wednesday morning, the second summer that they were trying, when Elizabeth got up and ready for work and was putting tampons in her handbag and feeling a bit sad at the sight of them, when she realized that there had been no pain, and there was no blood, and there should have been by now. Mike was at work; they had an agreement that he would be in the house when she did pregnancy tests. ("You don't need to be in the room," she'd said. "I'll have enough of accompanied trips to the bathroom when I'm home with a toddler.") She had gone to work and every spare second she had was checking herself over for anything, any sign at all.

At first, Elizabeth was scanning for cramp, the feeling of heaviness, of bleeding, but then, by lunchtime, she was looking for nausea, tiredness, or a feeling of knowing, so that later, she could say to Mike, "I just knew." She calculated dates, worked out that she would have an early April baby, and thought what a perfect time of year it would be to be born, to be new parents.

She saw the three of them in the garden under the apple blossom, and they were as clear as if she were looking at a photograph. Elizabeth herself would be rounded and smiling, the baby on her lap as pretty as a picture—she had seemed to be a daughter—with her father's eyes and her mother's hair, and Mike, proud and protective, standing over them. Their family, happy and complete at last.

She was bursting to get home and do a test, but it was a day when she was staying until six, so she had thought, well, she would just practice waiting, because she would have until April to wait. Mike would come off shift at four, and so he would have walked Pepper, thought about dinner, and be in the perfect mood for finding out that he was going to be a father.

Then, as Elizabeth was walking home, heart twittering and soul contented, thinking about how she would tell Mike the news, but being fairly certain that she wouldn't need to say a word, because she could feel herself glowing, she felt the cramp tear at her.

When she got home, on the edge of tears, it was to find a message from Mike to say that he'd gone for a run. They tended not to run together so often, these days. (There had been an argument when Mike had suggested that they should both enter the London Marathon next year. "Is that because you've given up on the idea of us ever having a baby?" she'd asked, and he'd said, "No, it's my way of trying to enjoy the life that we have. Do you remember it, Elizabeth? It used to be enough for you.")

Elizabeth had lain in the bathwater until it was lukewarm. When Mike came in, he was whistling, but he stopped when he closed the door behind him, and she had thought, *Have you stopped because this home has become a house that you can't relax in?*

So when she came downstairs, and she saw the look on her husband's face, half hoping, half ready with the sympathy, she had just said, not this time, sweetheart, and left it at that. Life went on. The cycle had kept on cycling their hopes away.

When she lay awake at night, Elizabeth would think about that day and remind herself that nothing had been lost. She hadn't been pregnant. Her period had been late, that was all. But she had felt bereft.

She could have woken Mike and told him. She knew she didn't have to lie there, feeling the way that she did. But she knew that if she told him, he would be upset for her, and it would be more pressure for next time.

Instead, she thought about what they were doing to themselves, about how in not being completely honest she was keeping a secret, for the first time, from this man she loved more than anyone. It didn't feel right. But then, all the books said that having difficulty conceiving wasn't good for a relationship.

Mike,

Your mother looks terrible. Drained and tired and obsessed with Kate Micklethwaite and her baby. Yesterday, she came in—it was raining—and before she'd even taken her coat off, she'd started talking about what she'd have done with Kate. How at the first sign of trouble she'd have kept her busy, put her in charge of the ironing, including the sheets. "People iron sheets?" Mel mouthed at me before she made her apologies and bolted.

It would have been volunteer work or helping with a church group, a part-time job in the library. Kate wouldn't have been allowed to "moon about" after she decided she wasn't going abroad, if Patricia had had anything to do with it. (I started to feel sorry for the poor girl at this point.) How she'd have taken her shopping on the weekends, and invited her friends around, and made sure every second of her time was accounted for.

Under your mother's hand, Kate would have spent a lot of time with people who loved her, and when she went to bed at night she would have been tired out, and have had no time or thought for mischief.

And then, she said, and then, within a month, I'd have turned her around, and she'd be a normal, well-behaved girl with a bright future ahead of her, and I might be proud that Michael had saved her, and understand it a bit more.

It was just as well that Mel had ducked out as soon as this all started, because your mother was in tears and I know she hates to cry in front of—well, of anyone at all. I sat her down and I said, "Patricia, we might not like what's going on here. It's hard. But I think of it as Mike saving two people. I didn't want him to die, but there are going to be two people walking around Throckton, Kate and her baby, for a very long time, for longer than you and me, probably, because of what Mike did that night. It's cold comfort, but it's something."

She was quiet for a minute while she dried her tears. So I told her that I'd baked a cake, and she looked so proud. God knows what she would have been like if we'd had our baby. She declared it "a bit dry but not a bad effort" and then said she'd write down the recipe for her fruit cake that you liked.

I said I'd like that and we'll call it "Michael's fruit cake," even though you're not here to eat it.

She told me how she's always thought of her steak and kidney pie as John's pie because he liked it so much.

And then we were both crying. I was having a better day until then, feeling a little bit like me.

Mel came down and put the kettle on. This is a long road.

E xxx

now

K ATE FEELS LIKE A lion cub in one of the nature documentaries that she and her father used to watch. There are times when she seems to have gotten cornered by something with big horns, and she can't see her way out of it, and then the mother lion appears, all claws and teeth, and the predator is gone, running for the hills.

Her mother seems to have developed a sixth sense for trouble, so that every time Rufus appears, his eyes cold, and starts talking about Oxford and the future and hard decisions now being the best in the long run, Richenda will come in and say something like, "Rufus. We had a long talk about this and we agreed that Kate has made her decision and we'd say no more about it."

At the library, when Mike's mother had been at the desk, horrible staring and pursed-up face, Richenda had appeared at her shoulder and said kindly, "Mrs. Gray, I hope that you're well. I know things must be very difficult," and ushered Kate away before there was time for a response.

When they had gone to see the midwife, and she had asked about the baby's father, and Kate could barely trust herself to speak, Richenda had said firmly, "The father isn't involved," and that had been the end of that conversation.

Afterward, Richenda had said, quietly, "When you are ready to talk about the father, Kate, I'm ready to listen. Until then, I'm not going to badger you about it. I trust that you have your reasons."

Kate had nodded, and just for a moment she'd been ready to tell her mother the whole of it. But then, she'd remembered her promise.

❀

Blake finds himself at the Micklethwaites' house. He hasn't called in advance; he was just walking past and thought he'd drop in on the off chance. That's what he tells himself, anyway, the conversation he'd had with Mel the other night refusing to leave him. He pushes the gate open, winces at the squeak as he does every time.

"Infuriating, isn't it," Richenda calls from where she's kneeling by a flower bed. "I've asked Rufus to deal with it a thousand times, and so I can't do it myself now. It's a sort of garden argument. Neither of us will give in."

She gets to her feet, pushes her hair out of her face. Blake notices that she's barefoot, her toenails painted pale purple. "I didn't know you were coming today. Have I forgotten?" She makes a gesture—a twist of her palm, a drop of her shoulder—that says, *The way things are at the moment, I could forget anything, so please forgive me if I have.*

"No, no," Blake says. "I was just passing, and, well, I thought I'd see how you are doing."

"You've heard then?"

"I've heard."

She smiles, and moves toward the house, speaking over her shoulder to him.

"I can't believe how calm I am. I had no idea, of course, although looking back, it's obvious…" They are in the kitchen now, Blake leaning close to hear her over the sound of the water filling the kettle. "But there you are. I think it's because I was there for the scan. It makes it real. My mother used to say, a baby brings its own love, and, well…"

It's as though now Richenda has started talking, she can't stop. She blurts it all out: due date, Rufus's fury, Kate's calmness, the planned decorating, how much easier it is when you know what sex the baby is, the university place released, the way that four months isn't anywhere near as long as you think it is. And, as she does so, a waterfall of words, she recognizes that she hasn't had a true conversation with anyone. Kate she protects, with her words as well as her actions, her watching. Rufus she bickers with, over the father and the future and the fact that he can't accept what's happening to them.

She's had the briefest of conversations with everyone she needs to in the wider family, who have sympathized and said things like "Well, I suppose you'll make the best of it," with an undertone of "My child would never/has never done such a thing." Richenda hadn't noticed how much she is holding on to, how many words, how many worries and doubts. But now here is Blake.

And Blake is telling her things that resonate with her own, unexpressed thoughts. That an unplanned child is not the same as an unwanted child. That these things can be the making of a family. That babies are born into circumstances thousands of times worse than this one will be, and that there's no reason why Kate shouldn't be OK, with the right support.

Richenda's face makes a shrug, because her hands are holding mugs. "She's not getting a lot of support from her father. Or from the baby's father, come to that."

"Do you know who he is?" Blake's voice, well trained, is behaving exactly as it does when asking any other question.

"No. She won't say. I'm not going to try to make her. She's as stubborn as me and her father are over that wretched gate—she gets it from both sides—so it wouldn't do any good, anyway. Not that Rufus isn't trying. But, well…" Richenda pauses, hands coffee to Blake, takes a sip of her own as Blake waits. "All that she'll say is that he's not around, and that could mean anything. It must have been after Christmastime when she got pregnant, because it was too early for the pregnancy to show in the hospital tests, and she didn't leave the house for three weeks afterward. So he could have been someone here, visiting, over Christmas. He could be away on a trip, or already at college. She might not even know who he is."

She looks to Blake, who, understanding what's required, nods a nod that says sad but true. He's turning over "he's not around," examining it. Looking for clues, not wanting to find them.

"I've got a shortlist of her friends who came back from their gap-year things for Christmas, but, well, I just don't know." She pauses, going through the lineup in her mind. She remembers them, part of the group of almost-adults sprawled over her sofas, waiting for Kate before going out on New Year's Eve. While the girls downstairs had been flirty, giggly, already a little drunk, upstairs Kate had been sullen, dragging her heels. Maybe—

"There's no point in speculating," Blake says gently.

"No," she agrees. She remembers that Rufus had a junior working with him, from September to January; he'd come to the house a few times, seemed to get on well enough with Kate, although she'd rather assumed he was gay. Still, there's no telling. She wonders how she can ask Rufus about him without appearing to ask; she'd gotten furious with him last night for doing exactly what she is doing now.

"And how are you, Richenda?" Blake asks.

"I have absolutely no idea," she says.

❀

Upstairs, Kate teases Beatle with a ball, waiting for the grumble and throb of the voices downstairs to fade, so that she can take a walk. She knows she will soon be tired again, her body too heavy to be easy with, but for now she feels strong and her breath moves happily in and out of her. She doesn't have to hide her baby anymore, and she knows how to hide her eyes, looking constantly away from people, above or below or toward the ever-helpful Beatle, so that she can't be stopped, chatted to, engaged in conversation.

Her favorite walk is to Butler's Pond, the place where the mix of emotions is so sharp and strong that she doesn't know whether she'll be elated or distraught. But both feel true, and in most of Kate's world at the moment truth is not an easy thing, but rather, something to be protected, hidden, cosseted away, as her pregnancy has been.

She won't tell her mother where she's going. She's been letting her assume she's going to the graveyard with her posies, sure that no one will find the flowers where she really lays them, between the roots of an ancient tree, hidden from the water's edge and the people passing by with dogs and children on bikes, trikes, and scooters. She wished she'd put them here all along, but she'd been so afraid of coming back to this place, for all the power and the pull it might have.

As she waits, she thinks through her list of names. And suddenly, she has it, and she doesn't care who's downstairs or what they're talking about.

She heads down to the living room, and sees her mother and

Blake look up at her, startled, caught out. Yes, definitely talking about her. Well, let them. Blake takes his hand from her mother's arm. Kate almost changes her mind about what she's going to say. She hesitates, and in that moment Blake gets up, faces her, and says, "Congratulations, Kate. You must be very excited about the baby." He looks straight at her as he says it. And he smiles.

Kate is thrown, completely thrown, because it's the first time someone has congratulated her about her little girl. She stands very still, absorbing the feeling of it, thinking of all the other people who have babies, who are washed in congratulations for months, who would think nothing of this heartfelt reaching out, these simple words. She looks at Blake again, just to make sure there's no ill will, and he's still looking at her, still smiling. She remembers that Mike had said he was a good man, but then, Mike had only good things to say about everyone. And she smiles back.

"Kayla," she says. "I've decided to call her Kayla."

Mike,

Everything is dull. People say I'm doing well, and I suppose I am. They say it as though I've been crippled and am learning to walk again, which I suppose is also true. I'm doing well in the sense that I don't spend every minute of every day beating my breast and wailing. But everything is dull. Flat.

You know that argument we used to have, when you used to say I didn't like the weather in England, and I used to say that it wasn't that I didn't like the weather, it was those days when there was no weather I couldn't bear. When the air is still and the sky is gray and it's not sunny and it's not raining and there's no wind and it's certainly not warm but it's not exactly cold either. Those days. My life is one of those days. The sun doesn't shine and the wind doesn't blow and everything is just going along. And it's fine, bearable anyway. So long as I don't look up from this dull, gray path and see my dull, gray life stretching on and on and on.

You were a third of my life, which feels like so little. One day you'll be a quarter of it, then a fifth, maybe only a sixth if I live to be 72. Awful thoughts, when I look up from this gray path on this gray day.

We had made a little nest of our life, you and me. Our favorite places, our long weekends away, our barbecues and our crosswords and our walks and our wine.

You, saying, "We're just like an old married couple."

Together, it was lovely. On my own, it's too sad. But I'm just getting on with it.

I've told Mel she should go home. She still says no. I think I'm glad. I miss you, so much.

E xxx

M EL'S ONLY REAL SOURCE of Throckton gossip—if she cared, which she doesn't—is Patricia, with her blending-into-one-after-a-while tales of babies born and conservatories built and cruises embarked upon.

Elizabeth had done a good job of stopping her mother-in-law from talking about Kate Micklethwaite and her baby, and so Mel hears very little about her. Until the day when a flurry of texts between her, Andy, and Blake means that she is sitting at the kitchen table while Elizabeth is at work, having a conversation that she really doesn't want to be having.

"I know I complain about Throckton being boring, but I take it all back. I didn't know how much I liked boring, until now," she says as they settle with coffee that she has insisted on making, although none of them wants it.

"It's never boring," Blake says.

"Too damn right," Andy adds.

Mel remembers that the brother-in-law she was very fond of had been a decades-long fixture in the lives of these two. So she takes charge.

"Come on then," she says, "from the top."

Andy nods. "When I got to the office this morning, Peggy,

who's our receptionist, brought me a coffee along to my office. She doesn't usually. She shut the door behind her. I assumed that she wanted to talk about something medical—you know, the staff are supposed to make proper appointments like everyone else but they never do—but she said she knew that I was good friends with Michael Gray, so she thought I ought to know there was a rumor going around that he was the father of Kate Micklethwaite's baby."

"Which we don't think he would be," Mel clarifies, "although we can see how people might put two and two together, after the accident."

"Which we don't think he would be," Andy says.

Blake says, "Richenda says she won't say anything about the father, except that he's not around. Rufus Micklethwaite is playing holy hell with her every chance he gets, but she won't say a word."

"Just like she won't say anything about when Michael died," Mel adds, "and she's lying about that as well."

They all look at one another.

Mel says carefully, "We're assuming this is no more than a rumor, right? Blake, I know what I said to you, about what we'd think if we didn't know Mike, but we did know him. I can't imagine…" Her words falter, fail.

Blake says, just as carefully, "Elizabeth and I were talking, at the Christmas party, and she was saying that between work and his marathon training and Pepper having taken to running off on walks, she'd hardly seen him."

Andy adds, "She went into the water. He was there. He was near enough to get her out. It was cold. She wouldn't have had long."

"What are the chances of that?" Mel asks.

"Not high," Blake offers.

They look at each other, seeing in each other's faces the chasm that they've opened. Andy shakes his head, a furious clearing motion. "No. No. He wouldn't. He adored Elizabeth."

Mel says, "Unless he'd met her nearby, and she was upset. He'd have walked her home, wouldn't he? He'd have been near enough then."

"Yes," Blake says, "but—"

"Oh God." Mel puts her head in her hands. "I'm always telling Patricia that there's no bloody point in speculating, and here I am, chairing a speculation meeting."

"We might never know," Andy says, and the chasm closes again, thanks to all of their good efforts. Mel reaches for her cigarettes and is about to head for the door, when Blake speaks, and brings her back to her chair with a bump and a groan.

"Surely the point is not whether or not Michael fathered that baby," he says. "Surely the point is that people are speculating about it, and sooner or later someone is going to say something to Patricia, and then Patricia will say something to Elizabeth, if someone from the hotel doesn't first."

"You're right," Andy says. "We need to do something."

between

K ATE HAD ARGUED, PASSIONATELY, against helping her mother with the tombola at the Throckton Fair.

"I know, Kate," Richenda had said. "I don't especially want to do it either."

"So why are we doing it?"

"Because we do almost nothing in the community, and so when one of your father's clients, who is one of the organizers, asked if I would help, I said that I would because it seemed like the least I could do."

"But that's your decision. I didn't agree to it."

"No, I know you didn't." Richenda has had a sleepless night and a long day of snippy exchanges with Rufus and she is too tired not to let it show. "But, Kate, your exams are finished, you have nothing else to do, and I presume you'll be expecting me to drive you around while we—or rather I—buy the rest of what you need for your trip. So I was hoping you could see your way to giving up an afternoon. I think, quite frankly, that you owe it to me to help."

So Kate, knowing that "quite frankly" was a phrase her mother used only when she was very near the end of her tether, had agreed with as little grace as she could get away with. She had been roped in for this kind of thing before, and she never knew how to talk to people, or liked the way older people treated her as though she was a child still.

It had started every bit as unpromisingly as she feared. The early June sky glowered but didn't rain, so every other conversation that she had was about the weather. The wind whipped raffle tickets out of the basket if she didn't watch them. Her father had slept in the spare room the night before, which meant that her mother was taciturn and complaining by turns, wondering out loud what on earth she would do when Kate went. "Why don't you just leave him, Mum," Kate had eventually said in exasperation, and Richenda had looked at her daughter and laughed and said, "Well, you know what, I just might, one of these days," and she'd disappeared and come back with a bag of hot doughnuts, which they'd eaten while taking the mickey out of Rufus.

Kate had enjoyed that part, because she was almost never allowed to be rude about her father, his separate trimmers for nose hair and ear hair, the way he claimed to be able to tell fresh pasta from dried after it was cooked, his near-obsessive polishing of his car.

Then, just as Kate was about to suggest that she might go and her mother could probably cope now, Richenda had gotten up. "I'd better do the rounds," she'd said glumly. "Stock up on tea towels with cats on and lemon drizzle cake."

Kate had told her off for being a snob and resigned herself to the loss of the whole day, envying the friends who had come to say hello earlier before heading off to Marsham in a cloud of good feeling that only the end of exams could bring. She'd texted them to say she wouldn't be able to join them. And then she'd been left alone with the last few tickets, a bottle of port, a jar of pumpkin jam, a ginger cake, and the *Throckton Warbler* for company.

And then it happened. The oddest thing. On the front page

of the newspaper was the story of a policeman who had saved a mother and child from a house fire. The rescued mother was a friend of the chef at the restaurant where Kate did the occasional weekend shift, so she had already heard all the details: the iron left on when the baby started to cry; the assumption that it had fallen into the basket of clothes waiting to be ironed or maybe the cat had caught the cord; the mother settling down on the sofa to feed the baby, the broken nights before; the next thing she knew, the smoke, the panic, and then the man appearing in front of them, like a dirty, coughing angel, holding out a hand. Kate looked at the photograph, the grateful mother, the police officer holding the child, looking handsome and ever so slightly embarrassed.

And then she had looked up when she heard a cough, and there he was, in front of her, the man from the photograph, looking handsome and ever so slightly embarrassed.

"I can't wait for next week's newspaper to come out," he had said to Kate, then, leaning forward conspiratorially, added, "I am in so much trouble."

"Why?" she had asked.

"I wasn't really supposed to go in. It wasn't safe. There are rules. You have to wait for the fire department. And my mother and my wife are giving me a lot of grief about it."

He had glanced over his shoulder to a couple of women standing a little distance away. It was obvious which was his mother; the other woman was in jeans and a navy jacket, thick brown hair being whisked around her face, pushed back, whisked around her face, pushed back. She was holding a dog under her arm; it looked as bored as Kate had felt until this lifesaver had showed up.

"Well," Kate had said, made bold by his bright eyes, the scent of limes that splashed toward her every time he moved. "I think you were very brave."

"Thank you," he had said, and he'd grinned, and inside her head Kate had said, *I wouldn't give you a hard time if you were mine.*

Michael picked up the ginger cake. "We brought them," Kate explained. "We bring them back from France because they taste wonderful there, and we always forget that they're not as good here. Somehow they don't have the same flavor back in England."

"Don't let my mother hear you say that," Mike had said. "She thinks Throckton is the best place in the world."

"I'm going to Thailand, in September, to work on a turtle conservation program," Kate blurted, then wished she hadn't. Her attempt to sound interesting had come out like a schoolgirl showing off.

But Michael had only looked at her, grinned again, and said, "Turtles, eh?" in a way that made them both laugh, and then he had given her a five-pound note and said, "Well, we don't have any pumpkin jam at home, so here's hoping."

And he had won the pumpkin jam, and the ginger cake, and she'd said, "Congratulations," and he'd said, "Thank you. There'll be a feast in our house tonight," and she had watched him walk back to his family, touch the dog on its head and his wife in the small of her back, give the ginger cake to his mother and the jam to his wife, who pulled a face and said something that made them all laugh.

And Kate had felt different. Queasy. As though the world was a different color now.

now

A M I IN TROUBLE?" Elizabeth asks when she comes in from her shift to find three solemn faces awaiting her. One day, she thinks, she will take a photograph of the three of them when they are like this, and show them exactly how obvious it is when they're thinking that poor Elizabeth thinks she's coping, but she'd barely be alive if it wasn't for us. She pauses, takes a breath. *No,* she tells herself, *no. Grief can make me sad and lonely. It does make me sad and lonely. That's OK. But it will not make me bitter, or ugly, or unkind.*

Andy looks away. Mel studies her nails. Blake looks steadily at her and says, "Sit down, Elizabeth."

She slides into the fourth seat. "What's happened?" she asks. "Just tell me, will you? I've had a long day."

A long day of relaxed couples and heedlessly happy families checking in, and a wedding party coming by to make sure everything is ready for the weekend. Elizabeth's face hurts from smiling and her feet ache from standing. In her mind, she runs over the possibilities for disaster.

The three of them are here. Mike is already gone. Pepper came to greet her with his usual yapping joie de vivre before flopping back into his basket. So, she should be able to manage it, whatever it is.

Andy sees the pulse beating in the top of her jaw as she sits and looks around at them all. There's no point in dragging this out. He takes a deep breath and begins.

"There's a rumor you should know about," he says. "Just a rumor. About Michael."

Elizabeth almost laughs. She can't imagine any rumor that could hurt her. And he is safe from everything now. "Is that all?" she says. "You should see the three of you. You look as though you've murdered somebody."

"It could come to that," Mel mutters.

Blake says, "There's a rumor that Michael is—was—the father of Kate Micklethwaite's baby." And then they all look at her, watching.

All Elizabeth can think is that no one is telling her it's not true. She sits very still, her hands clasped in front of her, her head dropped, as though she is pleading, or praying.

She waits.

Still nothing.

So she says it herself. "It's not true."

The trouble is, she can't seem to say it just once. Now she's started saying it, she can't stop. "It's not true. It's not true." Without looking up, she can feel the uneasiness around her grow. There is a small part of Elizabeth that is very clear that for as long as she keeps saying it's not true, it cannot be true. The words are blurring, losing meaning, taking hold of her tongue.

Mel says, too late, "Of course it's not true," but Elizabeth is caught up in her own rhythm now, three words the only fragile wall between her and a tidal wave.

"It's not true."

Andy is the one who gets her to stop. He takes both of Elizabeth's hands in both of his.

"Elizabeth." He says it very quietly.

"It's not true."

"Elizabeth." He says it more quietly still.

"It's not."

"Elizabeth." The third time is barely a whisper, and it's the smallness of it that lets it slip through.

She stops talking. She looks up, at each of them in turn, and she says, "What do you think?"

Mel says, "I just don't know. I don't know."

Blake says, "I'd be very surprised, Elizabeth."

Andy says, "Michael loved you so much."

And suddenly, Elizabeth is furious at the stupidity of these people, who are supposed to love her, to have loved Mike, but cannot see what's in front of them. She stands up, leans forward, the tips of her fingers and thumbs making mirrored churches on the table top. And she lets them have it.

She tells them that Mike wouldn't look twice at some doe-eyed teenager.

"I knew him better than anyone," she spits. "I knew where he was, what he did, what he liked, and I can tell you for sure that it wasn't screwing teenage girls."

And then she tells them that if anyone is even thinking about saying anything about smoke and fires, then they can go now and not come back, that she doesn't want to hear another word about it until they can tell her who the father really is and how sorry they are for thinking ill of the dead. Then she turns, and she goes upstairs, and she waits for her breath to come evenly, and she waits for her tears to stop.

between

MICHAEL FORGOT THE GIRL from the fete as soon as he turned his back on her. Or he thought he did. But every time pumpkin jam was mentioned—and it was mentioned often, quickly becoming the joke of the moment—he'd see a pair of pale eyes, hear a laugh, listen to an echo of himself saying, "Turtles?" When his mother complained about the cake, he smiled to himself.

And then he started to bump into her. He knew it was too often to be coincidence, really, but he couldn't see any harm in it. She'd wander out of the end of her road as he passed, and say, *Oh, hello, I was just going to get some fresh air.* He'd be almost at Butler's Pond and he'd hear running behind him, and there she'd be, hair swinging out from side to side, pink cheeked with effort.

I thought I recognized Pepper, she'd say. *I wish I had a dog, but with going away soon, there's no point.*

You'll have a turtle, Michael would say, and they'd laugh, even though it wasn't that funny.

Yes, Michael knew it happened too often to be coincidence. When she took his arm at the water's edge where the ground was slippery underfoot and then he moved away, just a fraction, and she dropped it, he knew that he wasn't being very clever. But he thought he was safe.

now

PATRICIA'S HEART SINKS WHEN she answers the door to Andy. He's a nice enough lad, and she makes a point of telling his mother so whenever she comes into the library, but she sees an awful lot of him at Elizabeth's, and she can't imagine what he has to say that won't wait until tomorrow. She stands at the door for a moment, hoping that he's dropping off a pie dish as she isn't far out of his way, but no. He stands his ground, says he's sorry to disturb her, but he needs to talk to her about something.

"Is everything all right, Andy?" she asks. She'd planned a quiet half hour with her photo albums before bed. If he'd arrived ten minutes later, she would have answered the door in her dressing gown. She likes to think that she won't answer the door after nine at night, but actually, if there's a knock after nine it's more likely to matter.

"Yes, it's nothing like that," he says. "Just something I've heard that I think it's best you know about."

"You'd better come in then," she says, thinking that there's not a lot that happens in Throckton that he would know about before she did.

"Yes," he says. "This won't take long."

Patricia offers him coffee. She thinks she can smell whiskey, which will be down to Mel again. "I'll sleep when I'm dead,

Patricia," she'd said the other night, which was all very well, but Michael and Elizabeth were never big drinkers, and Patricia would hate to see Elizabeth being led astray. Especially with those pills Andy has her on.

"I saw that Elizabeth and Mel were drinking whiskey again the other night," she says as they wait for the kettle to boil, "and I wondered about those pills you've given her. If it could be dangerous."

"Oh, it's all right, Patricia," Andy says, though he seems a bit distracted. "It's either the sleeping pills or the whiskey. One or the other, I've told her."

"Well, good," Patricia says uncertainly as she carries their drinks through, coffee for him, chamomile tea for her. But she soon understands why she hasn't had his full attention.

Sitting in the room full of photographs of two dead men, Andy tells Patricia that he's heard a rumor that Kate Micklethwaite's baby had been fathered by Michael. He tries to be as matter-of-fact as he can. He tells her that Kate has said nothing about the father, and that he couldn't see that there was any truth in it, just people putting two and two together to make five because he was near enough to save her when she went into the water. He says he really didn't think it was worth worrying about, and he's only here because he doesn't want her to hear it from elsewhere.

And then Andy braces himself for the rant about That Girl, and the goodness of Michael. Part of the reason he is here now, on the brink of when she will think it acceptable of him to call, is because Blake had said that she would need time to think about it, and Mel had wanted to put the maximum possible distance between her hearing the news and her being able to talk to anyone—especially Elizabeth. So he'd gone home for bath- and bedtime, told Lucy the tale, and come to do the deed.

But Patricia doesn't rant about Kate and she doesn't reminisce about Michael. Her mind is tumbling and turning like ferrets in a sack. She knows, of course, that Michael would be very, very unlikely to do anything as sordid as get involved with a girl when he was so happily married himself. But she also knows, with the wisdom of a long life, that these things will and do happen, no matter how contrary appearances are.

She starts to think about Elizabeth: such a lovely girl, but always working, no babies. Michael wasn't brought up that way, and she should know.

Well. Stranger things have happened, that's for certain.

She puts down her cup and saucer, carefully, by her feet, and she puts her hands on her knees and takes a deep breath, bracing, and then she looks straight at Andy and says, "You're telling me that I may have a grandchild?"

Mike,

When you died there were a lot of things I had to do that I didn't like. Go to your funeral. Look into your poor mother's devastated face every day and understand that it was a reflection of what my own face looked like. Read letters with the words "late" and "deceased" in them. Go to sleep on my own, every night—or try to—and wake up on my own, every morning. Not be able to talk to you, or at least not have you talk back to me when I did. Look at your weird beer in the fridge and your horrible sweet cereal in the cupboard and know you wouldn't be back for them.

And I know that there are decisions I will have to make that I won't like either. Mel wants me to think about going home with her, she says for a change of scene, but I know what she's thinking. I'm refusing, for now, but the day might come when I have to really think about where I want to spend the rest of my days, and whether to move back to Australia or not. One day I might have to make decisions about Pepper without you—he's started limping, sometimes, when he's been running too hard, and it makes me think that one day he'll have something really wrong with him. It was hard enough to make the decision about Salty together, and then to take him to the vet and leave without him. I remember how you wouldn't let me go into the consulting room with you. I said good-bye to him in the waiting room and then you did the hard thing. I can't imagine losing Pepper, let alone having to be the brave one when the time comes.

I can't even bear the thought of the mundane things, replacing the double glazing, renewing the insurance, buying a new car before our beloved banger rusts itself to death during another crappy, damp English autumn/winter/ spring. But I've come to accept that I can manage to do these things without you, when I have to, because I tried lying down and dying and that didn't work, and so now I don't have a lot of other options.

One thing I never thought I'd have to do—something that wouldn't have crossed my mind until I got ambushed into that vile conversation— was to stand up for your good name. I didn't think I'd need to tell people who loved you too that you didn't screw a teenage girl, that you're not the father of her child. Because it's so blindingly obvious. Why would anyone even think that you would do such a thing? Everyone knows we were happy. Everyone knows that we loved each other and that we didn't need anyone else. For crying out loud, it's Throckton. Your mother once asked me why you'd been buying white bread when we normally had brown. Someone would have known if you'd so much as looked at Kate Micklethwaite. And even if they hadn't, I would have known. I was your wife. I loved you. You loved me. I would have known.

I know that you probably don't care about this stuff anymore, because you're all made of grace and starlight now, or whatever, and human suffering is something that you've forgotten, or are seeing from a long way away, like watching a rainstorm through a window.

But, wherever you are, whatever you're doing, I need you to know that I care, and I don't believe it, really don't believe it. I won't believe it. It's not true. I know that.

I'm standing up for you.

I love you.

E xxx

then

THE TRIP WAS MEANT to be blissful. "Remember," Michael had said when they booked it, a break before IVF began and therefore, very possibly, their last time away as a couple rather than a family. "My darling Elizabeth, we are going to relax because you've worked hard all summer and we need to top up your sunshine before winter comes. We are not going on a baby-making expedition." She'd laughed, and said no, of course not, but she did rather hope there would be some sex, and she'd kissed him, but she'd wondered if he had been reading her mind. Because just at that moment she'd been thinking about the advice she'd been giving Mel—that the best way to find a man was to stop looking for one, and just go and enjoy having her own life—and she'd thought, *Yes, perhaps the best way to get a baby is to forget that that's what we're trying to do. All those teenagers with baby carriages who thought it could never happen to them: maybe that's what we need, to be forgetful of the consequences.*

And Michael and Elizabeth had tried. Elizabeth hadn't taken her temperature; Michael had tried not to watch her for signs of excitement, disappointment, premenstrual syndrome, tried not to step carefully around her, calculate dates and times—although at this point it wasn't really possible for him to unlearn everything he knew about cycles and timings. They had lazed in bed in the mornings, gone to markets, gone snorkeling, lain in hammocks, reading, during the hottest part of the day, settled on the balcony at night. All in all, they did an excellent impression of people who didn't have the baby they had yet to make on their minds all the time.

Elizabeth had tried to remember how much she loved, simply loved, her husband; he had tried to appreciate her, turning golden in the sun, beautiful and fit and strong, although her shoulders drooped when she thought he wasn't watching, and her eyes took on a fairy-tale hunger as she watched toddlers splashing in the shallows on the beach.

They had drunk too much on the last night. Elizabeth had been bright and brittle during dinner, but afterward, walking along the shoreline, warm evening water lapping at their ankles, she'd confessed how much easier it was for her to be happy here, at night, when all of the children were safely tucked up in bed. How she dreaded the flight tomorrow, the babies who could only be comforted by their mothers, the fathers proudly pretend-apologizing as their big-eyed offspring tried to play with everyone around them. Elizabeth tried to explain how it's the assumption children have that they will be loved that broke her heart: because she would love—oh, how she would love—a child of her own. Of their own.

Michael had held her and they had stood in the warm tide until the water lapped at the backs of Elizabeth's knees, tickling her into the now again. They'd walked up to the hotel hand in hand, and Michael had told her that he thought they were getting some help with this, just in time, before they both got broken, and she had nodded and smiled and said, "Yes, Mike, it's time. I know I'm breaking. I know you're holding me together, and that's not fair on you." That night they had both slept better than they had in a while, and in the morning they'd smiled straight into each other's eyes.

During the flight home, Elizabeth had played peek-a-boo with the toddler on the seat in front of her for what seemed like hours, and Michael had watched her: the patience on her face, the smile in her eyes. The child's mother had thanked her as they got ready to get off the plane; Elizabeth, still smiling at the child, had said that she was getting some practice in. "Oh! Congratulations," the mother had said. "You'll make a lovely mother." And somehow, in that moment, it had been easier for Elizabeth and Michael to smile at each other and squeeze each other's hands and say thank you than it had been to embark on an awkward correction.

"It's a sign," Elizabeth had said in the car on the way home, and although Michael didn't believe in signs, he'd just smiled and said, "Well, you will be a lovely mother." And then they were back in Throckton and it felt as though everyone was lining up to tell them how well they looked, how relaxed, how happy, and the baby seemed no longer a distant, fading possibility, but a little plump gurgle of newness waiting just around the corner.

❀

Two months later, the first cycle of IVF had a certain novelty value to it: the daily injections, the appointments, the schedule, all meant that Elizabeth and Michael had a sense of purpose. Things were happening at last.

Elizabeth was shining with excitement. The baby-naming conversations started again.

"Does it have to be a flower, for a girl?" she'd asked.

He'd said, "What's more beautiful than a flower?"

Elizabeth had shrugged and said, "OK, but I'm crossing Rose off. Too thorny."

Michael had known he should have said something, just a cautionary word or two, but he couldn't quite bring himself to remind her of everything that the consultant had told them—that it might take a while, that it might not work, that Elizabeth's body would strain and that their relationship would be tautened and tested, that it would be hard, and unpleasant in places, and that the success rate was a lot better than it used to be, but it was not guaranteed.

Elizabeth had smiled and said, "We think we've waited long enough," and, well, that had been it. They were off. Blood tests, pills, injections, dates in their diary. In the coldest November Elizabeth had experienced since she came to Throckton, she glowed with warmth and excitement. Patricia had kept commenting on how well she looked, even risked the word "blooming" a couple of times, but Elizabeth had stuck with their resolve to tell no one anything until they had something to tell. As she injected her thigh every morning, she reminded herself that there didn't seem to be anything wrong with either of them, so what they were doing was a boost. Michael kissed the little circles of bruises on her thighs better and brought her flowers. And so she bloated, and she ached, and she waited, and she was absolutely certain that she'd taken the stern advice of the nurse to heart: that on no account was she to think that she might be pregnant during the two-week wait to see if an embryo had implanted. That there was no way to know. That she must put the whole question out of her mind.

But when the bleeding started, and the scan confirmed the gaping black emptiness of her womb, tight and cramped inside her like a clenched fist, something in her broke a little bit more.

Still, that first time, it was almost easy to talk about bad luck. They had known it might take more than one go. Elizabeth could find a brave face, although she started to go to bed earlier and earlier and sometimes didn't wake when Michael got in beside her after a long shift or a late dog walk.

Salty died two days before they went back for the embryos to be implanted the second time—he'd gone from being a little bit off his food to being put down in the space of two weeks—so it always seemed unlikely that a baby would come from those sad days. When the bleeding had started, Elizabeth had felt sad but not surprised.

It was during the third try that Elizabeth and Michael started to struggle. With their new pup Pepper a force of scuttering, chewing enthusiasm for life, and bluebells everywhere on their walks, and a feeling of warmth returning to the world, they couldn't quite believe it when a baby still didn't materialize. To not be pregnant seemed perverse. To sit, weeping, over blood once more, while everywhere Elizabeth looked there seemed to be growth and newness, was wrong. But it was what happened.

Sitting in front of the consultant like two bright high school students who hadn't done as well as they should have done in their exams, Michael and Elizabeth had talked about options again. Their NHS-funded treatment was at an end. Michael remembered being a boy at a fairground, looking at his empty hands where three hard rubber balls had been a minute ago, the coconut still obstinate on its stand. His father, clapping him on the shoulder, saying some things are harder than they look, son.

The consultant had advised a break and suggested that they could come back in six months and fund their own treatment, if they wanted to. Elizabeth had cried. The consultant had offered tissues, with the gesture of a man who mopped tears with great regularity. And Michael had said thank you, and taken his wife by the hand, and walked her to the parking lot, and put her in the car, and tucked the belt around her. And in many ways he had felt not a lot different from the way he felt when he spent a day at work dealing with the aftermath of a car accident, a house fire, a sudden death. He was sorry; he was helpless; he was hurt; he was strong with the strength that comes of having a role to play. These things were all the same, whether he was taking his distraught wife home or doing his job on a difficult day. But there was a difference that made all the difference. At work, he was not responsible for whatever had gone wrong to begin with. At work, he could hand over to someone else, and go home, to a life that had once been so perfect he could barely believe it would last. Well.

"Maybe we should have a weekend away," Elizabeth had said, in an attempt at making an effort, a couple of days later. Michael had agreed, although he used to like it when such weekends were fun, rather than attempts to recover from the last failure of trying to make a baby or prepare for the next. But neither of them had the heart to organize anything, and if they were going to pay for IVF they'd have to watch their money. So Michael bought a set of all the James Bond films on DVD—he couldn't remember so much as a single baby in a Bond film—and they watched them, one a night, and when they had worked their way through them all, they went back to the fertility unit and started IVF again.

Mike,

I've started driving to work. I don't talk to anyone any more than I have to. I drive home and I come upstairs, to our room, and I wait for all this to pass.

Because it will. It will. All I have to do is wait. I can wait.

But when I close my eyes, and I want to see you, instead I see her.

Standing in our garden with that look on her face.

Leaving the flowers.

Help me.

E xxx

between

I T WAS ONE OF Michael and Elizabeth's trips that brought everything to a head. Michael and Kate had just bumped into each
other, in a way that could have looked casual, Kate coming out of
the café at the entrance to Butler's Pond just in time to see Michael
arriving with Pepper, Michael setting off slowly on his walk so that
anyone walking quickly would have been able to catch him up just
out of sight of the parking lot.

Kate had had a lot to say about waiting for exam results, and
how far away university seemed, and how boring her parents'
arguments were, how repetitive, and how every time they whined
or shouted each other's names she was glad that they had, at least,
given her a sensible, easy name. "Although my middle name is
Eris," she'd said, "so I didn't get off completely when it came to
weird names."

"I'm Michael John," Michael had offered. "You can't get much
more functional than that."

"Like bread and butter," Kate had said, and she'd smiled.

Up until then, that smile, Michael had been pleased with how
things were going. It had all been as he'd been determined it
would be, what he had in mind when these walks started. These
conversations made what he was doing a sort of public service. He

was striving to mentor a teenager who was under pressure, to show her that there was life beyond exams and parents arguing. He knew what it was to be an only child; he knew what it was to feel the borders of Throckton as restraints and frustrations.

But then there was that smile. It gave him a glimpse of what she was feeling. That smile, that in another man—a man less devoted to his wife, his beautiful, generous, sweet-natured, unreproaching wife—might feel an answering glint for.

By mutual consent, they had seated themselves on a fallen tree a little way away from the main path. On warm days like today, Michael would pour some water into Kate's cupped hands, and she would stretch down her arms so that Pepper could drink before he settled at their feet. No one would be passing close enough to see who they were.

Michael had unlaced his boot to take out a stone, and as he'd done so, he'd said, "I won't have this problem next week. Next week it will be flip-flops all the way."

Kate had looked at him, an animal alert for danger, and he'd said, as casually as he could, "Oh, Elizabeth and I are going to the Canary Islands for a fortnight. Just to get her some sun before the hotel gets really busy in July. Even after all this time, she can't completely get used to the climate."

Kate hadn't been able, in that moment, to fathom what was worse: the thought of two weeks without seeing him, or the way he had talked about his wife, so casually, the way you'd talk about your arm, so much a part of you that you barely think of it. She had watched Michael's foot being swallowed up by his boot again, and watched his hands, lacing, pulling, back and forward, back and forward, snap, snap, snap.

She'd thought about how, if he'd cared for her even the smallest bit, he would have explained it better, added some preamble, tried to let her down gently. He wouldn't have told her that he was going away in a blurt like that. He wouldn't have flung it in her face.

Kate had wanted to get up and go but she felt weak all over, and the tears came without announcing themselves in advance so she had no chance to dig her nails into her palms and stop them.

Michael had fastened his boot again, stood up, and turned to Kate to suggest that they head back, before he noticed that she was crying. He sat down again, cursing his stupidity, knowing that he knew better than this, and he said her name. It was meant to be a coax, a teacher to a student, but it came out as a plea, a man to a woman.

But Kate wouldn't look. She kept crying, every now and then the heel of her hand swiping up her face to knock the tears aside. When Michael put an arm around her, she sat solid, not showing that she noticed.

So he put out his free hand, and he turned her face toward him.

It was the way his thumb fitted so exactly along her cheekbone that did it.

And once he had kissed her, he was done for, and he knew it.

When they had walked back to the parking lot, he said, "This can't happen, Kate. You know that, don't you?"

And she had said, "I know, Mike." It was the first time she'd ever dared to shorten his name.

❄

When Michael had walked away from Kate that afternoon, he was sure he'd never put himself in that position again. He'd planned to rearrange his shifts, persuade Elizabeth to do more dog walking with him, get organized to go out with Blake and Hope more often. He'd stick to busy places. He'd explain to Kate that it was inappropriate for the two of them to spend so much time together and apologize if he had hurt her feelings or misled her in any way. By the time his hand was on the gate at home, half an hour later, that kiss had felt like a thing of the past, or an ill-judged moment in someone else's life.

But it hadn't stayed that way.

The Canary Islands had been fine. Good, even. Elizabeth had read books and slept and been charmed by local bits of tourist nonsense, and she had worshipped the sun. Michael had read a bit, and gone to the gym once or twice, and stroked Elizabeth's hair while she lazed and dozed. They went to couples-only resorts these days, so everything had felt quiet, and calm, and civilized. They had swum in the mornings and chatted over cocktails and meals and promised each other that they would cook fish more often when they got home. It had been every bit what they had planned, the kind of trip they always had these days.

It was two weeks designed not to remind them of the fact that they didn't have a child, or two children, or three. Designed to remind them of how lucky they were, to have each other, to have love, to have a happy home, to have the money to do this sort of thing.

Except…maybe it wasn't the thumb/cheekbone. Maybe it was the eyes, or the soft, waiting unsureness of two mouths new to each other. All Michael knew was that, all the time they were away, Kate Micklethwaite filled his mind. He didn't think that she was anywhere near his heart, but he didn't trust himself. Because he had already done something he had been certain he would never do.

He was a loyal man, a true man, a faithful man. He loved his wife, and since the moment he'd set eyes on her, standing behind the hotel reception desk with her uncomplicated eye contact and her unforgettable smile, he'd thought of no one else. No one. It had felt like madness. It had felt like walking toward those flames, the heat building, the cries behind him, powerless to stop.

❀

When he and Elizabeth had gotten home, Michael hadn't been able to wait to take Pepper out and see whether Kate would appear. He knew how much could happen in a fortnight, and he half hoped that she had found herself a boyfriend—there was someone she mentioned sometimes, a lad who worked at the restaurant where she waited on tables on the weekend—and the other half he ignored.

But Kate was nowhere to be found, although he walked Pepper in all the familiar places, and dawdled past the end of her road. It's for the best, he told himself, imagining her hand in hand with someone nearer her own age, single, full of things to give her. It's for the best, he said to himself, as he came home from work late and curled in bed, wrapping himself around his beautiful wife in the way they knew worked best for their bodies, Elizabeth waking only to mumble something with the words "love" and "night" in it.

And after five days without so much as a whisper of Kate anywhere, he had given in, and he had texted her. He had remembered as he'd done so how he'd protested, politely, as she'd put her number into his phone. He hadn't wanted to say, "But why would I ever need to call you?" So he'd just said, "Well, we often bump into each other, so I shouldn't think I'd need it." And Kate had smiled and said, "You never know," and then rung her own number from his phone so she had his number too.

And Michael had paused before sending the three little words that he knew would change his world. But he had sent them.

❉

Kate had been waiting. After two weeks without seeing him, and another week since he'd gotten home—she'd checked the flights and worked out exactly when he would be back in Throckton—she was starting to wonder whether her strategy had failed. Her decision to let him find his way back to her if he wanted her had been much easier when he'd been out of the country. Since he'd been back in Throckton, tanned and smiling, she'd found it much harder not to put herself in his path. Much harder to press Delete rather than Send after writing another text message.

And then Kate's phone beeped, and she was looking at three magic words: "Dog walking tonight?" She didn't reply. But she went. And they sat on the tree trunk, and they kissed, and Kate smelled limes and fresh sweat, and Michael tasted lip gloss and breath mints, and they were both of them lost.

Mike,

I remember, once, we were talking about a trip, and I said, "How about a boat?" "Like a cruise," you said, and I knew you were thinking about your mum's unending list of people she knew who were either planning a cruise, going on a cruise, away on a cruise, or coming back from a cruise. And I said, "No, not a cruise—a gulet. A little Turkish boat, maybe five or six other couples, just kind of doodling around the coast. Swimming, reading, sleeping, sex, watching the sun go down."

And you shuddered, and you said, "No," as though I'd suggested going clubbing in Ibiza or trekking through a rain forest or any of the other things we'd agreed that we never needed to do.

You said it was the idea of being surrounded by water that you didn't like, a tiny little boat and nothing but sea.

I asked you whether you'd looked at a map, if you knew where you lived, on a tiny little island full of people obsessed with going to the edges of it and looking at the water while they were lashed by the wind?

"I know," you said, "but—I can't stand the thought of it."

And you shuddered again, and I stopped laughing at you, because I could tell that you weren't fooling around, that you felt the way I felt when I walked past a pet shop and saw anything in a cage.

And I thought, How funny, I never knew that about you. We must have been married for eight years by then. I think it must have been about two years ago.

Still. I never told you about the day I thought I was pregnant. You never knew that. You never, ever knew.

So. My not-baby. Your surrounded by water thing. I think that makes us even. One secret each. No more. I know that.

I refuse to talk about the rumors or have anyone talk about them in our house. I've hardly seen your mother; she obviously can't trust herself to keep off the subject. But in our bedroom, it doesn't matter. In our bedroom, there's just me, and the memories of us.

I wish, wish, wish you were here.

E xxx

now

B LAKE FEELS AS THOUGH he has a foot in both camps, and is fully welcome in neither. Elizabeth's eyes are hostile when he asks how she is feeling, and she snaps back that she's feeling every bit the way he might imagine, and does he ask the Micklethwaites the same question?

She'd gotten up and left the room, and he and Mel had caught each other's eyes, and Elizabeth had called, from the bottom of the stairs, that there was no need to look at each other like that—she wasn't mad, she just knew her husband.

With Richenda, Blake can't manage to have a constructive conversation either. When he tells her tentatively that there are rumors about Kate that she probably ought to know about, she holds up a hand and says, "Blake, I'm not at home to rumors. I don't need them."

"But," he says, and she says, "No buts, Blake, thank you." And he stands in her kitchen while she grinds beans for coffee and then tamps them with what seems like unnecessary force, and he sees what it would be like to have this woman as a teacher, a mother, a lover, the sort you could only push so far and if you overstepped the mark you'd know about it.

"Rufus just wants to argue, because if he's making a big noise he doesn't have to think," she says. "And Kate is so busy thinking about what color to paint the spare room that there's no getting any sense out of her, but I can see it's going to hit, sooner or later, and when it does, well, heaven only knows, and here I am, trying to keep us all together, which is a joke because we weren't even together to begin with—"

"These things—" Blake begins.

"Please don't tell me that these things can bring a family together, because I'm sure it's true, but I don't need to hear it now, while my husband is behaving like a spoiled little boy who can't believe that everything isn't going according to his plan, and my daughter is having to be way older than she should be, but I still hear her crying in her bedroom at night."

"I won't," Blake says. Richenda takes coffee mugs from the shelf, puts them on the countertop, then looks at them as though she has never seen them before, and has no idea what they are doing there.

"Coffee," he says gently and is rewarded with a smile, quickly erased by a shake of the head.

"You can see," she says, "why I don't need to hear any more bad news."

❀

Mel's desperation for a change of scene has brought her, Andy, and Blake to the pub. "I'm having an early night," Elizabeth had said, and as if to prove her point had gone upstairs and started running a bath.

So they'd gone. Blake had asked, halfway down the drive, whether they ought to leave her, but Andy had said they could, and Mel had grinned and said, see, a medical opinion, then added, sadly, all she does is work and sleep and cry.

Mel manages to get what she declares to be a half-decent martini—"If I can't smoke, I need a real drink, not a pint of something cloudy"—and sits back in the corner of the corner table, a place they've chosen in the hope that they can talk. "Right. Where do we start?"

"No new rumors," Andy says. "I checked with Peggy when I left work. I know where you can get a kitten if you want one, though."

"Well, that's something," Blake says. He has been over and over it. He keeps thinking about Michael: his dedication to the job, his burning need to help, to put right, to resolve. He had been a dream to work with from the beginning—punctual, willing, meticulous, able to talk to anyone. With time, a good judge of which situations needed a gentle hand and which needed to be shut down fast. Apart from the time when he walked into the burning building, the man had been everything he should have been.

"So it might just die out of its own accord, if no one else says anything," Andy says.

"Or if the father shows up," Blake adds.

"Or if it's not true," Mel adds, although it's more of a moan. "Please let it not be true."

"Of course it's not true," Blake says.

"It's hard," Andy says.

"I tried to get her to agree to come back to Australia with me again, but she just said she can't leave Michael behind. Not even for a couple of weeks." They all shake their heads, helpless. Mel doesn't tell them the other part of the conversation, when she'd pointed out that Elizabeth never visited the grave, and her sister had said, with chill dejection, that that didn't mean she didn't know how close to it she was.

And they have another drink, and they try to talk about something else, they really do, but it's like pushing water uphill: it won't work, and it's exhausting.

"OK," Mel says, returning from a smoke break with two pints and a fresh martini on a tray, "I'm just going to name the baby elephant in the bar, and if neither of you know what I'm talking about, or neither of you think we should be talking about it, then we'll all pretend I was pissed and I made it up. OK?"

Andy and Blake tip eyebrows at each other, nod.

"Right," Mel says. "I know that Mike and my sister tried for years to have a baby and it never happened."

"I didn't know that," Blake says, "though I was a bit surprised they didn't have one. After the wedding, Mike told me I'd be his first choice for godfather when the time came."

Andy says, "I knew they were trying. Michael said that there didn't seem to be anything wrong with them. They went for IVF. Still nothing." He remembers how wan Elizabeth became, how sad. Lucy saying that she thought Elizabeth had ignored her and the twins in the street, and it wasn't as though they were easy to miss, the noise they were making. How he'd told Elizabeth that she could come to see him if she wanted any help; how she hadn't. He adds, "They were very private about it."

Mel nods. "I think I only knew because I was over here once when they were getting ready for IVF, and Elizabeth realized that she wasn't going to be able to keep it hidden. I think it started because they didn't want Patricia to know they were trying, and the only way to make sure Patricia doesn't know something is to make sure nobody knows." They all pause, drink, pause again at the wisdom of this. Blake opens a packet of chips, tears down the side of the packet, lays it flat on the table.

"But what I was wondering was," Mel says, "Elizabeth always

said that there was nothing wrong with either of them; it just wasn't happening. When they had IVF, I couldn't get any details out of her. She always just said it hadn't worked and it was too horrible to talk about. So I was thinking how neat it would be if she was lying to me to defend Mike's honor, as it were. That if he was the one who had a problem…"

"She could certainly be sure that Kate's baby wasn't his," Blake agrees.

"Exactly!" Mel takes a chip, beams at it, balances the end of it on the tip of her tongue, brings it back into her mouth, crunches, beams again. Both of them look at Andy, hopeful.

Andy remembers an afternoon he and Michael had driven into Marsham together to collect some secondhand furniture that Lucy had bought for the twins' room. Not taking his eyes from the road, Michael had said, "So, a below-average sperm count isn't disastrous, right? Because that's the worst they can come up with." Andy had told him that no, it wasn't disastrous at all, that it was the nature of averages that some people would fall below them.

"His sperm count was a bit low, but a lot of men's are. Half the fathers in Throckton will be the same. The tests didn't find anything else. Elizabeth was telling the truth."

"Of course she was"—Mel puts her head in her hands—"so there was nothing wrong with either of them, and they wanted to have a baby, and they tried to have a baby, but no baby? That has got to fuck you up."

But Blake is on another path. "So there was no reason why he couldn't have gotten someone else pregnant? In theory?"

"Nope," says Andy, wondering how it is that they are talking about something they were sure could not have happened. "But he probably thought he was infertile, whatever the tests said. People do. They'd rather believe an answer that they don't like, that fits the evidence in front of them, than live with uncertainty, or the idea that there might not be an answer at all."

"Oh, wise one," Mel says, muffled by her own palms.

"It's true, though," Blake adds. "Sad, but true." He thinks of a family he knows where the mother, decades after her teenage son left home and never came back, still refuses to spend a night away from home, just in case she's not there on the day he returns.

"So if—hypothetically—a man who thought he was infertile, despite all medical evidence except the evidence that after years of relentless sex his wife still isn't pregnant"—Mel raises her head, pauses, gathers her jumbling thoughts—"if that hypothetical man was, hypothetically, shagging someone else, someone nonslutty and young and fertile, he might well not bother with a condom?"

Mike,

There's an alternative universe in which none of these things are happening.

In my alternative universe I got pregnant, and the fact that we'd had to wait a couple of years for our baby made us all the more excited about him. You watch the baby grow, and you talk to him and sing to him and we take sedate walks around Butler's Pond and just let Pepper take a run around the garden last thing, so we can go to bed together and you can have a little chat with the baby before we go to sleep.

We can't decide what to do for the baby's room and your mother knits horrible, scratchy matinee jackets in terrible pastel colors, even though we've showed her the scan picture, because she doesn't trust the technology.

In my alternative universe, on the night you died here, we were sitting on our sofa, reading TV credits in search of the perfect name. In that universe, at the moment you died here, we were drinking tea and bickering about shortlists.

But I can't get my alternative universe any further than that.

Where are you?

I miss you. Everything is going wrong without you here.

E xxxx

P ATRICIA HAS KNOWN, SINCE the night Andy came to see her, what it is that she needs to do. She's waited, though, to make sure that she can't think of a better way.

She's almost talked to Mel but thought better of it, knowing how, at times of crisis, the sisters' need to protect each other is stronger than any reason, or any consideration of others. Her visits to Elizabeth this last week have been difficult: mostly, they've been visits with Mel, who has stood at the kitchen door, smoking, while Elizabeth has stayed in her room.

Once, Patricia had been there when Elizabeth had gotten home, and she'd been shocked by her daughter-in-law's paleness, thinness, the curious look to her hair where the natural color is growing back in. Elizabeth had seen Patricia, and dropped her bag, come over and embraced her.

Even though Patricia is not a fan of hugging and caressing and hand-holding and all of the intimacies that seem to take place so casually now, she had submitted, waiting until Elizabeth stepped away, looked straight into her eyes and said, "Patricia, this must be so awful for you too. I'm so sorry. I just can't talk about it yet."

And then she'd gone upstairs, and Mel had said, "Well, you just got more out of her than anyone else has since somebody put two and two together and all of Throckton made five."

And Patricia had left, and gone home to her photo albums, back beyond Michael to her baby sister who didn't make it beyond two, her uncle who never got to be more than a handsome teenager, and she felt the weight of what she was going to do.

But Patricia has never been a shirker. So, this fine Saturday afternoon, she finds herself standing on the Micklethwaites' doorstep, and she takes a deep breath, and she rings the bell.

Richenda answers the door, in jeans and a paint-splashed shirt. She's expecting to see Kate, who often forgets her keys when she takes Beatle out, and makes cautious jokes about pregnancy brain. Richenda jokes back, while Rufus looks daggers at them both. But Richenda is coming around to the view that this baby is a good thing, especially now that she is no longer a secret. When she compares the Kate now with the Kate who was hiding her pregnancy, she can only see health where there was illness, anticipation where there was brooding misery. Kate is relaxed, easy, more like herself than she has been for—well, for a good year, now Richenda comes to think of it. Her sulky teenager has gone for good. Her daughter is a woman with whom she is building a more equal relationship.

It takes Richenda a moment to recognize Patricia out of her library context, although she looks just the same as she always does, neat and smart and sharp, Margaret Thatcher without the hat.

Patricia says, "I'd like to come in and have a word with you and your daughter, if I may," and Richenda replies that Kate is out but shouldn't be long and invites her unexpected visitor in to wait.

Patricia sits, very still and erect, in the living room while Richenda makes tea. Much as she wants to dislike Richenda, she has to admire her manners, the way she was obviously in the middle of something when Patricia arrived but hadn't made a big thing of it, and she has to admire her taste. She thinks that everything here must be the best, that you can somehow tell, even if it's just a little table for a lamp or a plain white china vase holding a trio of peonies. She's surprised they can't afford a bigger television, and is looking curiously at photographs—she's not quite close enough to see them, not prepared to get up and look—when Richenda comes in with a tray.

"That's Kate when she used to horse ride," Richenda says, seeing where Patricia is looking. "Funny to think that it was only four years ago. And that the most difficult part of parenting was getting up at five on a Saturday morning to take her to some show-jumping event on the other side of the country. Still."

Seeing Patricia's rigid face, Richenda decides against following that "still" to the place where it might lead. Instead she pours tea, and when Patricia says, "You can always tell when someone's warmed the pot," she feels more pleased than she ought to.

"I'm not sure whether I should mention Michael or not," she says, these days of new conversations and unexpected turns in life making her bold. "But we are so grateful to him for what he did for Kate."

"You may not be," Patricia says sharply and ignores Richenda's look of incomprehension. She wants to say it all only once. So she starts to admire the rug, and as Richenda launches into the story of them buying it in Egypt, she thanks one set of stars that Rufus is off looking over something at the summerhouse this morning, and begs another to bring Kate home soon, so that they can get this over with, whatever it is.

The stars are on her side. Kate blows in the back door with Beatle, starts talking before she's looked through into the living room. "This baby is kicking me in the back like you wouldn't

believe," she says. "Either that or it's a fantastic elbowing tech-
nique. But I think it's feet. Isn't it funny, how you can tell?"

Richenda's voice is pretend-bright and heavy with warning as
she calls back, "Michael Gray's mother has come to see us, Kate."

Kate can smile at the sound of his name now and thinks how
funny it is to hear her mother call him Michael Gray, as though if
she only said "Michael" Kate wouldn't know who she meant. She
wonders whether the grief that held her paralyzed for so long is
really starting to ebb, or whether it's just masked by her hormones,
her baby, her sense that all of her love is not lost. Only the nights
are really bad.

She takes a deep breath and walks into the living room, and sits
down next to her mother, which means she is directly opposite
Patricia, who is looking her up and down as though she is trying
to decide something. Kate thinks of standing with her father at
the county show, watching as the horses were judged. Patricia is
prodding at her with her eyes. She drinks the tea her mother passes
her, even though it's too strong and not quite hot enough, and she
waits. Beatle settles by her feet.

Patricia chooses her words carefully. Or rather, she recites, with
care, the words that she has been choosing for the last ten days.

"I've come here to talk to you today about a rumor that's going
around." She senses that Richenda is going to try to interrupt her,
but she keeps on, looking at her knees. "I hear most things, sooner
or later, and I've heard a rumor that my son Michael might be
the father of your child." She moves her eyes, briefly, to Kate's
impassive face, then Richenda's, not yet stricken, rather the face
of someone who is working out a difficult equation in her head,
not quite sure that the answer she has come to can be the correct
answer. "The father of Kate's child."

Patricia sees that Richenda is holding Kate's arm, above the elbow, and she recognizes the gesture: like a mother with a baby about to have an injection, big hand wrapping the little chubby hand, knowing that it won't stop the pain that's coming but saying, gently, *I'm here, I'm here; you have me.*

"Well," Richenda says, sliding a look at her daughter, who is giving nothing away.

"That wasn't what I'd come to say," Patricia says, not unkindly. "I'd come to say that any child Michael did father would have to be watched very carefully, because there's cystic fibrosis in our family. In our history. I had a sister who died when she was no more than a toddler—I barely remember her—and my uncle, my mother's brother, only made it to his teens."

"No," Kate says. "No." And the tears and the look in her eyes tell Patricia what she's come here to discover. Richenda is saying something, but the mother and the grandmother ignore her, facing each other, absorbing, adjusting. There's a blind panic in Kate that jolts the rest of what she planned to say from Patricia, with more compassion than she thought she had for this flighty, feckless girl.

"I don't think cystic fibrosis is the end of the world anymore, even if your baby does have it—and the chances of that are slim, I think. I don't think it can be cured but I think people can be helped, more than they used to be. And the more you know about it, about what to look for, the better. When Michael was a baby he didn't grow quickly enough for a while, and we were afraid that that was what it was, but it turned out he was just a slow baby."

Kate is crying, nodding, crying, nodding, her eyes fixed on Patricia, her hands rubbing round and round on her belly, something she doesn't seem to know she is doing. And Patricia feels her own tears coming, but she's damned if she's going to cry in front of these people, so she stands up, and she says, "No matter what the circumstances, I would like to be able to get to know any grandchild I might have. Even if it is born on the wrong side of the sheets."

She gets as far as the garden before the tears come, so she stands for a moment and lets herself cry and lets herself wish things were different, before drying her eyes and walking home again. When she gets there, she looks out her jam recipes.

❁

Kate's sobs are violent and the tears go on and on. The only thing that will stop her is when Richenda looks into her daughter's frightened eyes as her breathing slows and she says firmly, "Kate, this will not be doing the baby any good." And Kate nods, and Richenda can see her fighting, fighting, to regain some control.

"I would know," Kate says, "if there was something wrong with her. Wouldn't I?"

Richenda remembers an afternoon, long ago, when she was lost in a daydream of blue onesies dancing on a washing line when the cramps started, another when a colleague took her aside and said to her, quietly, that maybe she'd sat in something or maybe she was bleeding. She takes her daughter's hands and tells her not to worry. Tells her that, these days, if anything was wrong, the doctors and midwives would be able to tell, and help, that it isn't the way it would have been for Patricia's mother anymore, these days. And Kate half smiles and puts her hand to the place where her baby is kicking her and says, "She's perfect. Whatever she is, she's perfect."

She saves the tears that she has for Mike, and for the secret she promised to keep, for later. Richenda lists her questions and puts them to one side, and sits back on the sofa, strokes Kate's back, and wills calmness through her fingers into Kate, although she doesn't feel very calm herself.

Rufus gets home to find his wife and daughter on the sofa, asleep, Kate's head on Richenda's lap, Richenda's hand on Kate's shoulder, Beatle curled in the triangle behind his daughter's pulled-up knees. He leans in the doorway and looks, and watching them he has the first moment of true peace that there's been for him since Kate went into the water. He makes himself look at his daughter's changing body the way he might look at a gouge on his own leg, forcing himself to examine every detail until he's not looking at a horror but a fact, something that needs fixing.

It's the fact that Kate seems still half girl that breaks his heart. Her hair is in a ponytail, her fingernails are painted pink, her cheek is as smooth as it was when she was born, and Rufus had held her while Richenda slept and promised her that he would look after her, and protect her, and be the best dad that there had ever been.

He remembers all of the parent-teacher evenings where he and Richenda were told how bright their daughter's future was, and how she could do anything she wanted to do. And he could not believe that this was what she wanted: this domestic shackling, this deliberate shrinking of her world.

Unless she had gotten scared. Unless all of that promise, all of those possibilities, had been too much, too soon.

After a quick check on the summerhouse project, Rufus has been to Marsham to have lunch with Caroline, a woman he has lunch with whenever he can contrive it, and will do more than have lunch with if things continue as they are. Caroline has interesting theories about human behavior, something that attracts Rufus almost as much as her walk, the shape of her forearms, the high warm glug of her laughter. The fact that she laughs a lot.

Caroline thinks that everything people do they do as a way of getting something that they want, so, according to her, if Kate isn't ready to go away, if Kate feels insecure, then getting pregnant is a clever way of making sure she doesn't have to do the things that she's afraid of. The baby makes her safe from too much change, safe from being alone in the world.

But she's not alone, Rufus had said, and Caroline had said, no, but she probably feels that she will be, would be, if she went away. She has no idea that after two days on a beach or three evenings in a university bar, she'll have made friends who she feels as though she has known forever. Those of us who live in these small places, these fixed places, can forget how much the world can flex.

Then she'd reached across the table, rested her hand on his, and said, apologetically, "Of course, Rufus. I don't know Kate at all; you must ignore me, or stop me, or tell me that I'm wrong. I'm just going from what you've told me; you are her father and you know much better than I do," and he'd said, "Honestly, Caroline, I feel as though I know nothing about my daughter. Nothing. Not anymore."

And so, as Kate sleeps, he walks over and touches her, lightly, on her head, and then he takes a breath and touches her stomach, and leaves his hand there, waiting to feel, if not love, then some sort of affinity. The baby moves and Rufus remembers how miraculous, really, it all is and he thinks, *Well, new baby girl, none of this is your fault, and you and I are going to get along just fine.* It's the best he can do for now.

Richenda has woken, and she puts her hand on his arm. He looks at her, smiles, stops smiling when he sees the look on her face. "What now?" he asks, and that tiny peace inside him wilts away, vanishes, takes with it the memory of it ever being there at all.

Richenda sighs, moves herself gently out from under Kate, who is sleeping in the way that only the emotionally exhausted can, and says, "Let's talk in the garden. You're not going to like it."

Hey, Mike.

There are other alternative universes that are much worse.

There's the one where Pepper dies so you don't need to walk him, and you're safe at home that night. We're doing the crossword, or watching a film. We might even be talking about getting a new puppy. Mustard, I imagine we'd have called him. Or Ketchup. When I look at Pepper now, I feel bad about this universe. I give him too many treats to make up for it, and he's getting fat.

The next alternative is worse. I only think of it when things are very dark. In this universe Kate dies and you live, because you don't see her go into the water, or you realize in time that you can't get both of you out and you get out yourself, or you call for help. I'm really ashamed of that one, in spite of the lies that girl is telling about you.

And then there are those alternative universes where you would have died anyway, because in some book somewhere in the beyond, your name and that date are written, unchanging. So there's the heart attack universe, the car crash universe, the meningitis universe, the undetected cancer universe, the eating a sandwich with a bee in it universe.

But if you were always going to die, I have a bunch of other universes that are much better than those, because I die too. In the same car, killed on impact universe. *The plane crash universe. The house fire universe, where the smoke suffocates us in our sleep.*

But none of those are this universe. This is the slowly dying of a broken heart universe, and I wish it would hurry up and be over.

There is no universe in which that is your baby.

E xxxx

between

T HAT SUMMER—HIS LAST summer—Michael was like a man possessed. With Elizabeth at the hotel, and Kate with nothing to do until she went off on her gap-year trip in September, it was as though it was meant to be, as though he had been given this small gift, these few months of uncomplicated sex and simple adoration. A little bit of time off from good behavior. A little bit of time off from wondering whether he and Elizabeth should have tried a little bit harder for their baby for a little bit longer, whether the sad way she looked sometimes, when she thought he wasn't watching her, was her thinking about the family they didn't have.

Everything was all right between them, of course: good, even. They had enough money, a happy home, a way of living and working that suited them both. When they argued, it was angry and fast, and soon forgotten. The three-trips-a-year agreement they'd made when they stopped trying to have a baby still stood and their evenings of planning and wondering, researching and deciding, were some of the happiest he ever knew. His wife laughed at him and accused him of liking the anticipation more than the time away. He denied it, but she might have been right. When she was absorbed in brochures, bookings, dates, flicking between web pages and asking herself where she'd seen something that she'd meant to show him, she was all his own Elizabeth, the one he remembered from the first, serious and sweet and excited, not disappointed yet.

She still avoided babies, and that made Michael wonder. He had noticed that she would make any excuse not to see Lucas and Toby, left the room as soon as his mother started talking about one of her friends' new grandchildren. It didn't worry him, exactly, because he knew that they loved each other, even if the loving was quieter. But sometimes Elizabeth looked wistful, and he was afraid of what she might be thinking. Did she ever wonder whether, if she had picked a better man, she would have a life that didn't include a pair of pristine white baby shoes still tucked in the corner of her underwear drawer? Michael couldn't find a way to ask.

One day, as Michael had been coming home from work, he'd looked in through the living room window to see her sitting on the floor with her head in her hands. He'd rushed to the back door, immediately and thoroughly worried, his years of being a good husband leading him to think only that someone else has hurt his wife, not that he could be part of whatever the matter was.

What happened when he got to the back door shocked him. He went in to find Elizabeth as she always was, happy and smiling, delighted to see him, with a shortlist of next year's marathons and a new travel book.

Every time she tucks her hair behind her ears, the diamond earrings he gave her for their tenth anniversary last year wink at him and remind him that he walked into the jeweler's with an eternity ring in mind.

Kate had asked to talk to her parents on the Saturday after her exam results came in. She had thought it would be the best time: they were so proud of her, of her success and, by extension, their own success as parents, that the three of them had managed to spend a genuinely enjoyable evening together, with no snipes or sulks. When the mood had still been cheerful two days later, Kate had decided that there wouldn't be a better time.

"I just want you to hear me out, please," she'd said, and her parents had looked at her and waited, her mother with half a smile, her father with half a frown.

"I've decided that I don't want to go to Thailand. I'll have time to do those sorts of things during summer break from uni, and I really want to spend the time I have between now and next September here. I want to save some money and I want to just do nothing for a bit. So, I want to cancel my trip."

She'd held her breath, waited, seen her parents glance at each other and swap expressions, her mother taking the half frown in exchange for her half smile passed to Rufus.

"Are you sure, Kate?" Richenda had asked. "Has something happened to change your mind?" And Kate had thought of what has happened to her, not so much a change of mind as a transformation of body and heart. There's the tang of limes and the salt of sex that she feels herself emitting in great waves with every move and breath, the ache in her thighs and the feeling of fingernails moving across her lower back, not hard enough to mark her but hard enough to leave the sensation of themselves behind. There are only two places that Kate wants to be these days: the nest that they make for themselves at Butler's Pond in the good weather, or Michael's car, warmer but so much less comfortable, parked in the dark when it's cold and wet or when he's on his way to or from work, with no Pepper for an excuse.

And there's her heart, which seems to be stretched to vastness, taut and tense with love, vibrating at every thought of the man who is making the leaving of Throckton impossible. She wonders if Michael will ever understand the enormity of what she is doing; until they found each other, she was counting down the days until she could get away from her parents' constant bickering, the home made sad and cold by years of hopeless effort. Not yet.

"Not really." She had shrugged, remembering what Mike had told her once, that the best way to avoid an argument is to not engage with it at all: that if you give nothing, there's nothing to react to. Just the thought of him had sent out a twang that she couldn't understand her parents not hearing, or seeing, somehow.

Although the look in her mother's eyes had made her wonder whether she did know something.

But Richenda had said, "Well, it's your choice," and Rufus had nodded and added, "I thought for an awful minute that you were going to say you didn't want to go to university."

"No, Dad," she'd said, and she'd thought, *We'll cross that bridge when we come to it, if we have to.*

University Kate seemed like another person, in another world. Although, once, all she had to do to turn into that person was to keep putting one foot in front of the other, now, that other Kate seems hypothetical.

❁

The place they had found was in a hollow made by tree roots, well off the beaten track, well away from all of the other places couples with nowhere else to go went to. Mike had made Kate sit there, when they first found the spot, while he had curved a radius around her, checking to see whether they were visible.

"Probably best if we lie down," he'd said when he came back, pulling her down to him, and Kate had blushed, still not used to this frankness and frank enjoyment.

Her sexual experience had been limited, so far, to a classmate who had known as little as she had, and a university student intern of her father's who had been nice enough but couldn't wait to get away from her afterward—in retrospect, her bedroom at home while her parents were at work probably wasn't the best venue—and so Kate had been left with a mixture of guilt and "Is that it?" which had made her determined to wait for something better. She hadn't anticipated that "something better" would take the form that it had, but she knew that life's best love stories were unlikely. The usual form of things, as demonstrated by her parents, certainly wasn't anything to hold out for.

They had been lying on a blanket in their spot, later on the day when Kate had told her parents that she wasn't going to Thailand after all.

"What would we do," she had asked, sitting up, cross-legged, and reaching up inside the back of her T-shirt to refasten her bra, "if someone found out?"

"You'd be all right," Mike had said, smiling at her as she tugged down her T-shirt, raked her fingers through her hair, bound it into a ponytail again. "I'd be run out of town. But no one's going to find out."

"Eventually..." she'd said carefully.

His eyes, lazy in the dusk, had found hers then. "Kate," he'd said, "there's no eventually in this. In us. You'll go off to your turtles and some lucky boy will watch you in your bikini and—eventually— he'll pluck up the courage to ask you to come for a walk with him in the moonlight, and I'll be someone that you barely remember."

"I thought—" she'd begun.

"Sweetheart, don't think." He was tired. He said it kindly.

"Sweetheart" was his reassuring work word for sullen children, before he had learned their names. Kate didn't know this. She took those two syllables, wrapped them up tight, put them just behind her solar plexus for safe keeping. Used them to fend off that last sentence that, later, she would pick over again and again. *Boy* and *barely remember* would distress her the most.

"I'm not going," she'd said.

"Why not? What's happened?" He had sounded concerned, a bit scared. This conversation was not going the way that Kate had planned it. She had hoped for—expected—relief at this news, an admission of how much they had both dreaded parting, and finally, the thing she is waiting for more even than the next touch, a stuttering declaration of love. She had thought that this would be The Night. She had been wrong.

She had looked at him—he was sitting up too now, his eyes on hers, his mouth a line, his forehead a question, and for all that Kate's heart was twisting and shouting, her mouth managed to do the right thing.

"There weren't enough people," she said. "They canceled it."

"That's a shame," he said. Then carefully, cautiously, "You'll be looking for something else?" Inside, his heart is flapping, a tethered bird. Their jokes about turtles are so much a part of their conversation that he hadn't noticed, until now, how often he had thought about the end date of this—thing. (It's not an affair. He'd never do that to Elizabeth.)

❋

Later, walking back to the place where, by mutual consent, they parted, he had said, "Kate, you know there's no future in this, don't you?"

"Of course," she'd said.

"Good," he'd replied, "because I couldn't stand the thought of you throwing away your future because you thought there was more to me than there is. I never got much farther than Throckton, but I was happy to do that. I am happy." He thinks of adding "without you," decides against. "You—you could do anything. And you should. Don't think of me." He had remembered how he had wanted to help her, how, when they had first talked, he had encouraged her to talk about Thailand, about Oxford, asked questions about what she would learn, see, do. He knew when it had all changed: the lip gloss–mint kiss that never should have happened.

"Of course not. Don't worry about me," she'd said, and some tautness between what she was feeling and what she wanted him to see had meant that she'd smiled him a smile that was a perfect balance. Strength pulled it north, fear south; love sent it east, longing west. And so it flew a true path, and banged Michael right in his solar plexus, so he stood, half winded, for a moment or two before he composed himself and headed for home.

❧

After that Michael had tried harder. He had renewed his efforts to stay away from Kate. He had taken Elizabeth to a spa for a weekend, which had turned out to be a lousy idea. She'd spent most of both days having treatments that required either isolation or silence, so apart from half an hour in the Jacuzzi or a stroll around the grounds in the slot between Elizabeth's manicure and her massage, he was left to himself. He swam fifty lengths of the pool, he took a squash lesson, he ran a five-mile loop around the grounds in one direction, then the other. And all the time, he thought about Kate. About that smile. If the kiss had made his body sing, the smile could, very possibly, have done for his heart.

And yet. At dinner, Elizabeth had glowed with relaxation, good health, and gratitude. At night, she had slept the sleep of someone who has spent all day having the tension wrung out of them. Michael, sleepless, had watched the shadows of the night hours move across her face, and he had loved her. He had known that he loved her without end, that the years they had spent together had only made them more than they were to begin with, that nothing, nothing, not even Kate's magic, would take him from Elizabeth. A part of him still remembered the difference between love and infatuation; a part of him recognized his impulse as being different from his true wish.

And he lay there, not switching on his phone, not looking to see whether Kate had sent him something, a picture of her painted toenails accompanied by a question mark, a little "thinking of u," which was the most affection that she ever dared, and he wondered what it was that Elizabeth had been feeling, that day she sat on the floor with her head in her hands, that she had been unable to show him.

Mike,

I don't know why today was the day to sort out your clothes, but it was. It was the thing I'd dreaded most, and your mother and Mel had given up suggesting it. But now that there's something I dread more, I thought I would give it a try. Even though I like the smell of your things when I open the wardrobe door, and I like the way your clothes and mine are all squished up together.

First I looked at the colors, the grays and blues that, if you mixed them all together, would make the kind of sad sky that England does so well.

I started with the thing I thought would be the hardest: I pulled out your old leather coat that makes me think of winter walks. Especially my first January here, because I never put enough clothes on when we went out and you would wrap me in your coat when you said my ears had turned blue. Sex by the fire when we got home. My second winter, we bought me what your mother called "a proper coat" but I missed walking with the old leather one around my shoulders, your arm keeping it in place.

I sat on the bed and I held your coat and I realized what people mean when they talk about "sorting out" the clothes of a dead person. They mean decide which memories are really precious to you and which memories you can risk losing. The shirt we bought when we were meeting

Andy's girlfriend, and then neither of us liked her. The sweater that lived downstairs for most of the winter so that there was always something for one of us to put on when we took Pepper out. Your white dress shirt that you used to like me to wear in bed when we'd been somewhere dressed up, over my black bra and panties. The jeans with the tear in the knee from when you fell on our way down from Beau's Heights, and I thought it was funny until I saw how deep the cut was. I'm sitting here writing to you with all of these memories sprawled around me. I'm supposed to decide which ones I can throw away, manage without. Well, I can't manage without any of them. When I die, someone can throw away all of our clothes together.

If you were thinking of one day putting in a ghostly appearance, this would be a really good time. I don't think I've ever been so lonely.

E xxx

then

I T HAD BEEN A month after the seventh round of IVF failure, the fourth that they'd paid for, from their savings and from the money Elizabeth had inherited from her aunt and uncle and left, untouched, to pay for her children's university education, one day. When she thought of that former version of herself, so sure she would have the future that she planned, Elizabeth wanted to laugh, but couldn't, quite. Summer was coming.

Michael had hardly needed to look at Elizabeth's face to know that something was serious. She was sitting in the half-light of the kitchen, waiting for him, not doing anything, not putting food on the table for them, not looking at the crossword, not reading a book. No wine, no coffee at her elbow; no radio, no TV. Just Elizabeth, beautiful and calm and eerie in the evening. Michael had gone to switch the light on, but she'd said, "No." He'd looked at her then, looked for tears or pain in her face, now more afraid than concerned. "I think it might be easier to talk in the dark," she'd said.

"OK," he'd said, "then how about the garden? It's warm."

And she'd nodded, and then he had regretted his suggestion, because it meant talking about having a glass of wine, and finding the bottle opener, and Elizabeth going to get something to put on her feet, all of which had given Michael time to wonder what on earth this could be about.

He had been able to imagine a new test result, given with an apology about mixed-up lab samples, that meant that one of them was, in fact, properly infertile. Or something else the tests had shown: some medical condition that made being sterile the least of their worries. He had taken glasses from the dishwasher and thought about cystic fibrosis; about the heart problem that took his father; about Elizabeth's aunt with the aneurysm; her father, medical history unknown; her mother, who died before she had the chance to show where the weaknesses in her body were going to be. His stomach had been heavy. The skin around his eyes had pinched and ached.

Elizabeth had obviously been finding it difficult to look at him as they settled into their usual chairs by the garden gate, so Michael had poured wine and thought, *Even if it isn't medical, even if there's no bad news in that sense, she's gearing up to tell me something I'm not going to like.* He had listed the possibilities: *She wants to go back to Australia; she's going to leave me so she can find a man with a history of children, before it's too late for her; she doesn't love me anymore. All of the above.*

Elizabeth had been planning this conversation all day, and mulling it, in the quiet wakeful night hours, for weeks. It had been that morning when the thought struck her that she could no longer talk to Mike about what was in her heart, that all of this baby-making stuff had made them cautious, stepping through tall fields of fragile flowers when they spoke to each other, afraid that one day the stepping through might go wrong and then they would be facing each other, knee-deep in dead petals that their clumsiness had shimmered to the ground. And then—well, and then not having a baby would be the least of their worries. Once, they had had a joke about how, if they split up, Elizabeth would at least get to leave all of the terrible wedding presents behind on the grounds of air freight charges. They don't joke about that kind of thing anymore. Not because it feels as though their marriage will end; these months and years are binding them tighter, tighter, every day. But sometimes Elizabeth dreams of suffocation, sometimes of disintegration. She knows she needs to find some freedom, somewhere.

So she had taken a deep breath and flipped her hair back over her shoulders so that her whole face had faced her husband's, and she had said, "How would it be if we never had a baby?" The look on Mike's face had confirmed all that she had feared. She had watched as he thought, considered, opened his mouth, closed it, trying for words that wouldn't cause so much as a petal flutter.

"I would be sad," he had said, "because you—we—want to have a baby so much."

"Are you saying that because you know that that's the right answer?" Her tone had been sharper, more combative than she had meant it to be. Speaking the language of their love, she had touched his thigh, an apology.

He had put his hand, briefly, on hers, an acknowledgment.

"I mean," she'd said, "that I'm afraid we've stopped being honest about this, Mike. We're so busy trying to have a baby that we're forgetting things. Other things."

Michael had thought about the way it felt to come home these days. "I think we're paying a high price," he'd said. And then, remembering the sharp, good taste of undiluted honesty, "There are times when I dread coming home."

Elizabeth had bowed her head. "There are times when I dread waking up," she had said, and then she'd started to cry, and although Michael had thought that there couldn't be anything worse than dreading waking up, as she kept talking he had begun to understand that that was just the beginning of bad days. "I dread going to the hospital and I dread coming home. I dread my period but"—and her eyes, finding his, had looked wild where the moonlight was catching at the tears—"I dread being pregnant. What if I was, and then I miscarried? Or there was something wrong with the baby? What if I was a terrible mother? What if I died when the baby was small, smaller than I was when my mother died, and then it had to grow up without me?"

Michael had been on his knees in front of her, his first thought to be close enough to comfort, but, as he had listened, feeling his own list of what-ifs begin, he couldn't find a way to comfort her. Instead, he had sat with his back to Elizabeth, his shoulder blades at the outside of her knees, feeling her left hand on his left shoulder, knowing that her right hand was wiping away her tears as his right hand was wiping away his.

Elizabeth had said, "What if this just isn't meant to be, Mike?" and then, finally, she'd become quiet, still.

Michael, torn between truth and calm, had chosen truth. "What if it had something wrong with it?" he'd begun. "What if it grew up, and we were happy, and then our child died before we did? What if being an only child was too much for it? What if we missed all the years of just the two of us?"

And then, in the quiet of the night, he'd given voice to what had seemed, when it was nestled inside him in the dark, the worst thought of all: "What if all this isn't worth it?"

❋

That night they'd slept without moving, without dreaming, and in the morning when they'd woken they'd looked at each other with nervous eyes, afraid to confirm whether they'd really said the things they had the night before.

Michael had been the one to make the move. "I'm glad we talked," he'd said simply. "I feel much better."

And Elizabeth had smiled and said, "Yes. Yes."

Mike,

I'm making a patchwork quilt. I used to help Auntie Brenda do it, way back in the mists of time, when we didn't have a lot of money and we didn't have a lot to do. Auntie B used to save up worn-out clothes, curtains, sheets, and when she had enough she'd get out her hexagon templates and we'd start cutting out. You had to cut carefully around the hexagons so as not to waste anything.

Mel used to get bored fast, so she'd get the job of putting them in piles, which wasn't really a job at all, but she'd arrange all the hexagons into soft towers of different colors and that kept her happy.

Then we'd sew the hexagons onto smaller hexagon templates that were cut from old Christmas and birthday cards. Then we'd sew the hexagons together. If our stitches weren't neat enough Auntie B used to make us pull them out and start again. I think Mel pulled out more than she ever sewed, but I liked the precision of it, and I liked the fact that I was good at it, because most of the things we used to do—horse-riding and tree-climbing type things—Mel was always best at. She was cleverer at school too. But I was best at sewing.

Mel liked the part when you took the tacking stitches out and pulled the cardboard hexagons free, but Auntie B and I couldn't sew fast enough for her. You could make patterns of flowers or diamonds or stripes or diagonals, or you could make the patchwork completely random, but that was much harder than you thought it was going to be—there would always end up being a pattern, somehow. When the hexagons were all done and all sewn up, we made a sandwich with an old sheet on the bottom, some flannel in the middle, and the patchwork on top, and we sewed a knot where every point touched. We all liked that bit best, I think: the feeling of racing toward the end.

Like you said, the last mile of a marathon ought to be the worst, but it's brilliant, because you're nearly there.

I've decided to make a quilt out of your shirts.

I reckon it will take me three months.

By the time I'm done, everyone will have forgotten the stupid, malicious talk about that baby. And I won't have to get rid of your clothes, ever.

There will still be your shoes, with the shape and shadow of your feet in them.

Love, love, love,

E xxx

now

A s Richenda walks to the library, she lets her steps be slow and her breath weighty. Although she's not looking forward to what it is she is going to do, and she hasn't enjoyed what she's leaving behind, she can see no reason why she shouldn't make the most of this sweet space between.

It's Tuesday morning. For the first time in three days, no one is talking to her, glaring at her, sulking at her, or ignoring her. No one is weeping; no one is achingly inconsolable. No one is making demands about food and care that reveal what a horribly thin veneer of equality exists in their relationship.

Of course, Richenda understands why things have been the way they have been. Once the initial shock of Patricia's visit had worn off, Kate had spoken to her midwife, who (as far as Richenda could tell from Kate's end of the conversation) had made valiant attempts to reassure her over the phone, and then arranged to come around the following morning. Richenda and an unwilling Rufus had racked their brains and spoken to cousins and aunts they hadn't been in touch with for years, and been unable to find any evidence or anecdote of cystic fibrosis. "That doesn't mean anything," Kate had said, face ghoulish with the reflected light of the computer screen. "It's a double recessive. We could all carry it."

Denyse, the midwife, had sat with Kate and Richenda and gone through everything they needed to know. If both Kate and the baby's father were carriers of cystic fibrosis, there was a one in four chance that the baby would have it. Kate's breath became a moan, but Denyse had said, "Kate, you need to stay calm and listen. If neither of you are carriers, the chances are nearer one in a quarter of a million. Now, there is a good chance that the father is a carrier if his aunt was, but we're not going to panic, because even then, the odds are very much in your baby's favor." She had held eye contact with Kate as she'd counted off on her fingers. "There's no reason to think that you carry the faulty gene, there's been absolutely nothing in what we've seen of the baby on the scan to suggest that she has any problems at all, and we can do a simple test when baby is five days old, which will tell us for sure whether there's a problem."

"There's no test you can do now?" Richenda had asked, seeing Kate's stricken look, knowing that she was working out that that meant three months of waiting.

But no, Denyse had said, it was too late for the usual tests, which needed to happen much earlier in the pregnancy.

Kate was like a little girl again, weeping and following her mother, exhausted and afraid. "Why didn't you tell us about Michael?" Richenda had asked her, struggling to get her arms around her daughter, and Kate had said, simply, "I promised. I promised he could trust me."

Richenda had accepted this. Rufus had not.

"Did he force you?"

"No."

"Kate, you can tell us if he did." And Kate had tapped at her phone, passed it to Rufus, who'd held it out for Richenda to see. Michael and Kate, Michael with his arm around Kate's shoulders,

Kate smiling, Michael looking, Richenda thinks, a little bit embarrassed. No forcing.

Rufus's voice is unsure whether it's a shout or a sob. "So it happened more than once? It wasn't a—a—".

"A one-night stand? No, Dad, it wasn't. But I don't want to talk about it."

"I don't care what you want. I'm thinking about what I want. I'm sorry if you don't like it, Kate, but if I'm expected to have a hand in the upbringing and, presumably, financing of this dead man's bastard"—Kate had given a little mewl then, and although Richenda thought afterward that it must have been at the word *dead*, it seemed to come out just as Rufus said *bastard*—"and it is a bastard, Kate, you can dress it up however you like." Rufus had stopped, taken a breath, looked away as he tried to find where he'd taken his finger off the place.

Kate, undaunted, fierce at the insult to her baby, had offered, unrepentantly, "She's just a baby, Dad. I don't care what anyone thinks. I care that Mike isn't here and I care that there might be something wrong with her. I didn't want anyone to know, but now you do, so—"

"So?" Rufus had asked, voice low, trying to get Richenda to share his incredulous look. "So? Do you have any idea—"

"Yes, Dad," she'd said. "I know you think I've thrown my life away. I know you think it's the end of the world. I know you think Mike took advantage of me. You're wrong, but there's no way I can convince you of that. So you're just going to have to wait and see."

And just as Richenda was being impressed by her daughter's maturity, Kate walked away, up the stairs, and slammed her bedroom door behind her.

Rufus had said "See!" with triumph and malice, and Richenda

had truly wanted to hit him, one of only a few times in her whole life when violence had seemed like the best thing to do. Instead, she'd let him rage and snort and hypothesize at her, her mind on Kate and all that Kate would need. But Richenda had found the time too to take a vicious pleasure in not pointing out that all the things Rufus was raging over—Michael's duplicitousness, his finding someone younger, picking on someone vulnerable to his charm, the exploiting of his position—were things that Rufus himself could be accused of.

And then there had been Blake's visit, yesterday morning. He'd arrived when Richenda and Kate were upstairs, talking about the nursery—the only distraction for Kate seemed to be to think about preparing for her baby—and Richenda hadn't heard the knock at the door, so by the time the raised voices reached them, it was too late for her to do anything except go downstairs and watch and kick herself for forgetting that she'd arranged for Blake to be here now when under normal circumstances Rufus would be at work. Normal circumstances. As she heard the words in her head, Richenda felt as though she was listening to an excerpt from a long-dead language, words describing a concept that there was no need for in her world.

At the top of the stairs, she had heard Rufus telling Blake that they now knew that "your dead friend" was the father of Kate's baby. By the time she reached the bottom, Rufus was saying, "For the last few months we've all been asked to worship that man, who turns out to be nothing more than a grubby little cheat. How are we to know that he didn't push her in there himself?"

"Well," Richenda had said, knowing she was fanning flames but too tired to stop herself, "we don't, but as he went in as well, and as he got her out, we can assume it's unlikely. Kate might have pushed him in, for all we know. Hello, Blake."

At that, Blake had caught her eye, nodded a greeting. And in the warmth in his glance, the look that said, *Of course I don't understand what you are going through, but I do understand that it's wrecking your family and now I'm here I'll see if there's anything I can do to limit the wreckage,* Richenda had had the briefest of glimpses into an alternative universe, where it was a man like this who was steering into the eye of this storm, other storms too, with her.

Next to him Rufus looked mean, unkind. But Rufus really was just the outward manifestation of the shrew that was burrowing inside Richenda, resenting too the time she'd spent on guilt for Elizabeth's honorable husband, imagining how easy it would be to dazzle someone like Kate, so grown-up on the outside, so unsure and afraid that she'd canceled her gap year—oh. Richenda had felt life tilt a little further. The canceled gap year. Of course. She's always felt there was something Kate wasn't saying about that. She had shaken her head, wanting to clear it of questions that her daughter had no intention of answering.

Rufus had stopped berating for long enough to take a breath. He had looked small, next to Blake. Richenda had said, trying hard to keep her voice even, smooth, "Did you know, Blake? You worked with him. Did you know?"

At this new thought Rufus had glared afresh. Blake had said, "No. I had no idea at all until Rufus told me just now, although—"

"Although what?" Rufus had asked.

He'd shrugged. "Although police officers are trained to be suspicious, and they were in the same place at the same time. And a strange place at a strange time." As he had spoken Richenda had felt what he meant, felt the coldness of the air and the sucking of the water, felt how real all this was, how real it would continue to be.

"Has she told you? Is it certain?"

"Yes," Richenda had said. "Well, Patricia came here and told us that cystic fibrosis runs in her family. Kate's face told us the rest."

"Oh," Blake had said.

"And she has pictures of them. Not that it's any of your business," Rufus had added, "and it's not as though he's here to face the consequences. Presumably he'd have been disciplined?"

"Rufus, the man is dead. I think that's punishment enough even for you," Richenda had said, and Blake had half raised his arm, palm upward, in a gesture that said yes.

To Rufus he had said, quietly, carefully, "We don't really know what happened. But, assuming the relationship was consensual, and I don't think we've seen any signs that it wasn't—" He had paused. Richenda had nodded agreement with his assumption, saved him from the need to defend his friend from anything other than the kind of reckless stupidity that is a regular feature of life. "Then what he did wasn't actually illegal. It was certainly unwise—"

"Unwise?" Rufus had snapped straight again. Richenda had had water words ready to pour on the flames of what she had been sure would come next, but Rufus had just turned and banged out of the house.

The sound of Kate's tears had filled the silence. Blake had looked at Richenda, holding out his arms, and for a moment she had allowed herself the luxury of walking up to him and being folded into smells of soap and grass. She'd stood with her own arms by her sides as he'd wrapped her, not quite a friend, not quite a professional. Richenda had given herself a heartbeat, two, three, four, five, then stepped away, his embrace knowing exactly when to let her go so that she had, without awkwardness, been able to nod, touch his elbow, turn and go up the stairs toward the tears. Afterward, she'd thought that he had seemed to need that touch as much as she had.

And now, Richenda has reached the door of the library. She puts her hand on the smooth, hot metal plate, pushes, and then lets the cooler air move out so that she can move in.

❄

Patricia loves her work at the library. She loves the smell of the place, not dusty exactly—she makes sure there's no dust—but papery, which is a smell very close to dust. She loves the relentless order of it: letters, numbers, categories, a place for everything. She loves the sense of purpose that finds her every day as she puts her coat on the wooden hanger she brought in, checks the date on the milk in the fridge, and puts some lavender hand cream on before starting work. She loves being able to give a child their first library card, see the parade of familiar books loaned and returned, and—depending, of course, on whether and when the child decides it has better things to do than go to the library—following that child's progress as he or she makes their way through school, university, coming back with their own children and saying, "I remember this book." Sometimes, walking through Throckton, she will hear the words "Mrs. Gray from the library" drift after her and she'll feel proud of herself, and sorry that there's no one who'll understand if she tries to tell them how that feels.

She loves the sense that here, in this place where she spends her days, is written, somewhere, everything she knows, or is ever likely to want or need to know. She cannot see the point of typing a question into a machine when you can walk to a shelf, take down a book, and find the page where that very thing you want is waiting for you. Although Patricia has gamely learned how to use the computers they now have, although she will concede that they bring people in and they do have their uses, she still can see no greater miracle than a finger running down a page, stopping, finding what was needed.

But the most important thing of all is that here, there's always something to do. And on days like today, Patricia thinks as she heads off to reshelve Large Print, you need to be able to see where you've been. Here, toward the back of the library, she's less likely to be disturbed, and as the shelves become tidy and well-ordered under her hands, she finds herself becoming less agitated. The feeling of having an awful lot to think about becomes less, as she allows herself to think. The knowledge that she's done something that she's not especially proud of starts to find its proper place in Patricia. She remembers all the reasons why she did what she did, and if she thinks about the stricken look on that poor girl's face, well, she remembers that the girl would have had to find out sooner or later. Patricia hadn't frightened her; the thought of cystic fibrosis had frightened her. She could remember very well how that felt.

What the library can't solve for her, this morning, is the idea that people might misunderstand Michael, that they might think this whole thing, this baby, was his fault, his doing. That he was someone who made a habit of seducing young girls, when it's obvious to Patricia that it's the other way around. As far as she is concerned, Kate is one of the generation brought up to believe she is entitled to anything and everything she wants. Patricia was brought up to believe that what a man couldn't get at home he'd look for elsewhere.

Richenda's appearance around the end of the shelf makes her jump. Patricia notices how pale she is.

Richenda's words have the sound of the carefully rehearsed about them. "I wanted to thank you," she says, "for coming to see us. For—what you said."

Patricia nods.

"And I wondered if we could talk"—Richenda lowers her voice further, although there is no one near to hear—"grandmother to grandmother."

❀

The staff room is little more than a cupboard, really, but it has two chairs and a door that closes, and for now, that's all either of the women requires.

Richenda begins, "I don't think we'll ever know quite how we got here, but I think we need to find a way to move forward. For the sake of the baby."

Patricia reminds herself that this woman is the girl's mother, so there will always be things they won't agree on. She thinks about what Michael used to say, when he was talking about work, about sorting out problems and arguments and fights: you start by working on what there is in common. So that's what she does. She bites back her comment about having a fair idea of how they got here, and she says, "Yes. Yes we do."

Richenda says, "Kate will do her best, and so will I, but I think this baby will need all the love that we can give her. Am I right in thinking that you would like to be a part of that?"

"Her? A girl? They can tell? A girl?" It's as though a window has been thrown open somewhere in Patricia's world: light. The hypothetical baby has become a plump, pink granddaughter, creases where her wrists should be, seashell toes, and pale, soft hair.

Richenda smiles. "It's amazing what they can tell. Yes, she's a girl."

And from her handbag she pulls a photocopied sheet and hands it to Patricia, who realizes she is looking at the scan of her granddaughter. Bones. Lungs. Heart. Fingers. Michael's nose. Definitely Michael's nose.

If Patricia had known the phrase "I'm in" she'd have said it now. Instead she wipes an eye and says, "Of course, of course I will be a part of this little one's life. My granddaughter. Michael's baby."

Richenda is smiling, wiping a tear too, and Patricia, fearing a slide into something more than she can manage, adds abruptly, "Even though I'm not too keen on the way she came about."

"Well, me neither," Richenda says swiftly, taking a different road. "Kate is talking about calling her Kayla."

"Kayla?" Patricia repeats. "Is that even a name?"

"Well, quite," says Richenda. And suddenly the two women are laughing, quietly, cautiously, although Patricia stops when she thinks about the conversation she's going to need to have with Elizabeth, and Richenda stops as she thinks about Kate, already up when her mother came downstairs, reading websites about cystic fibrosis and making note after note.

"I can't believe she isn't perfect," Kate had said, "but I suppose she will be perfect to me, won't she?"

❁

Rufus does want to be a better man. He just doesn't want it enough, yet, to pass up the opportunity that life has thrown him for a little bit of revenge.

As he walks up the road, he remembers how he felt when he was last making this journey. How carefully he'd chosen the flowers, how much time he'd spent standing in the florist's while the bouquet was made up, that insufferable woman making snide remarks about how much Mrs. Micklethwaite would like these and how he must have done something very naughty indeed to merit such a gesture. In memory he smells the roses again, soft and sweet. In reality his shoulders knot and his hands clench. His thumb finds a hangnail on his little finger and works it back and forth until it hurts.

When he arrives, it's like history repeating itself. The sister is in the garden, smoking. She isn't wearing the red boots. She's barefoot, and her toenails are a deep ocean turquoise. She looks at Rufus with the same disdain. "Oh," she says, "it's you. No flowers today?"

"No. Is your sister here?"

"She's asleep," Mel says. "You'll have to make do with me, I'm afraid." Rufus recognizes that he's being played with, teased, and his sense of injustice grows.

"Wake her up."

"Don't be ridiculous, Rufus," Mel says, as though she had any right to say such a thing. She gets up and starts to move back toward the house. He takes her by the upper arm, and she looks at him properly, shocked, still a little amused, "That's still ridiculous."

He drops his hand. "I need to talk to your sister."

"I'm not going to wake her. Anyway, you're not exactly on the guest list around here."

"Very well," Rufus says. "Perhaps you'll give her a message for me."

"Of course."

"Please tell her from me that I now know that her late husband impregnated my daughter while, presumably, lying to her about the relationship. Please tell her that I regret every bit of credit and appreciation that I have given to that man. The thought of him being lauded as a hero makes me ill."

Mel is transfixed by the warp of his mouth as he speaks.

"I probably won't give her that message, actually," she says, "and you might like to consider that your daughter has passed the age of consent. All of the hero stuff was posthumous so I'm not sure that Michael got the chance to sign off on it, and I'm not sure he would have liked it much. He was a good guy. Good enough to get into a freezing cold lake and pull your daughter out. And if we're going to start believing every rumor that Throckton can think up, well, heaven help us all."

In her agitation Mel has lit up again—although it doesn't read to Rufus as agitation, more like provocation, the pause midsentence for the inhale a further insult—and now she's stuck outside, not wanting to put out her cigarette and show that she's rattled, banned from smoking indoors.

"Ah, then you're behind the curve," Rufus says, and the small, fat, bullied boy inside him is ecstatic, crowing at having a piece of news that others don't, loving being the center of everything. The man, he knows, worried and afraid for his daughter, is waiting to take over, but not yet. "That's not what his mother thinks."

"Rufus, I have no idea what you're talking about. Patricia talks a lot of crap, though, so if she's the source of your information, you might want to be careful."

This is Rufus's moment, and he savors it. "Michael's mother came to warn us that cystic fibrosis runs in the family, and Kate has taken her warning very seriously. In fact, Kate has told us that Michael is definitely the father of her baby. She has photographs of the two of them together. You might want to tell Elizabeth that too."

Mike,

I didn't know whether I'd like being back at work, but I do. There's nothing of it that's very spectacular, but there's always something to do, and that's what I like, I think: there's always someone who wants me to do something, right then, and they ask, and I do it. I don't have to decide things.

I don't look at a great long day and think, Well, if I put off having a shower until 10:30 a.m., then by the time I dry my hair that's most of the morning gone. I look at my watch and think, How can it be 3:30 already? And that has to be better, doesn't it? Today I booked the handyman to come and fix a tap, and I organized some flowers to go in the honeymoon suite on Saturday, and I arranged a refund for someone who'd been charged twice. I gave directions to the town square three separate times to three different sets of people, and I watched a baby while a woman nipped back to her room for something she'd forgotten. The baby didn't do much but I watched her all the same. I thought of—well. You know.

When I came home no one was here. Not even Pepper. It's funny how you know whether a house is empty or not as soon as you step into it. I used to feel as though you were still here. I don't anymore. Is that good or bad, do you think?

I've cut out nearly all the hexagon templates. Mel says we made enough quilts when we were kids to excuse us for the rest of this lifetime and at least five to come, but I like doing it. I like the way time goes by faster when I'm doing it. You wouldn't think fifteen hexagons cut from old cardboard means a whole hour gone, but it does.

Love, love, love,

E xxxx

between

WHEN MICHAEL AND ELIZABETH came back from the spa, Michael had done everything he could to stop seeing Kate. He didn't dare see her to tell her: just the thought of her made him unsettled, and he didn't trust himself in the flesh. So he cut himself off. It was kinder, better for both of them. That was what he had told himself, anyway.

He'd arranged to go dog walking with Blake and Hope, nodding brightly to Kate on the one occasion that they passed her on the way to Butler's Pond. "Pretty girl," Blake had said, and Michael had grunted what he hoped passed for casual agreement rather than permanent ache, amazed by how different she looked in the presence of another: younger, smaller, freshly beautiful. The fact that he couldn't touch her, acknowledge her, hurt him more than he'd anticipated.

She'd hidden her disappointment well. Michael's phone had remained silent, his walks with Blake or Elizabeth uninterrupted.

By day, he had congratulated himself on being free of her. Her silence only confirmed that he was doing the right thing. Walking past the place at Butler's Pond where they'd had sex, Michael had remembered only the seedy indignity of it, and wondered at his own idiocy. Finding a moon-silver hair in the car, he had a crashing realization of the damage he could have done to his beautiful Elizabeth, felt himself to be the man who had gotten off the train at the stop before the crash. He pretended that he hoped she had found a boyfriend.

But at night, his furtive feelings had stopped him from sleeping. He knew it wasn't love, because love was what he felt when he looked at Elizabeth. But he was having a hard time pretending it was nothing. It was just the sex, he told himself, it was just that watching her discover all that the body could do had reminded him of the possibility of it, made him forget the limitations. Looking in the mirror as he shaved, he recognized a fool: a supposed adult who was suffering over something that was never going to last, and so shouldn't have a lasting impact.

So he had started to run. Really run. He had thought if he was tired enough, he would sleep enough, and if he slept enough, he would stop thinking about Kate, who seemed to have vanished. She was never at Butler's Pond, never sauntering out of the end of her road when he was walking past, never nearby when he finished work. Michael had started to comprehend just how much effort must have gone into those casual sightings and meetings. Everything that Kate had done to be near him made him feel as though water was rising around him.

And if the running meant sleep and sleep meant that he stopped thinking about Kate—well, he would have stopped thinking about Kate. Mission accomplished.

He asked Elizabeth about signing up for the Marsham Marathon with him. It was the first they had run together, and so even when they weren't taking part they always went along and cheered. It was a marker in their lives, their love. It was exactly the thing, he thought, that would heal him, and bring them closer again. Not that they were distant, exactly, but there must have been a chink where Kate could get in.

Elizabeth declined. The thought of training through the winter was too much, she said. Michael, ever mindful of how he had taken her from her native land, of how he had asked so much of her and failed to give her the thing she wanted most, felt a new nerve twitch.

"I don't want to go out running with you," Elizabeth had said one evening, watching her husband as he stood, just inside the doorway, hands on knees, breath burning in and out, sweat gathering in a point on his nose, dripping. "But I miss seeing you." And she'd smiled in a way that said, *I offer this not as a criticism, but an example of my own flawed self.* She'd looked cool, eerie, in the kitchen as his eyes had adjusted to coming indoors. And he'd thought, *Oh God, another thing. Another tiny way in which this Kate business is hurting Elizabeth.*

❋

And the running didn't even work. It had been a Tuesday after-noon. Michael had stopped at the fallen tree to refasten his laces, have a drink, and wonder why he ever thought this was a good idea. His lungs blazed, sweat stung his eyes, his muscles sang with the promise of cramp to come, and still he was thinking of Kate. He was no longer sleepless, it was true, but in these nights he dreamed of her pale eyes, her soft skin, and found himself examining Elizabeth's face every morning with the fear of having breathed out the wrong name in the darkness. He came to be glad of the late shifts, the early shifts, which he had once resented for putting him out of step with his wife. However often he went over the last few months in his mind, he couldn't find the place where he lost control of himself, and he couldn't see where to get control back.

And then, as he had gotten ready to run another lap, Kate had
stepped through the grass toward him, her hair tied back so that
every clean remembered line of her face was open to him, her
eyes hurt, her body brave. She approached him like an equal, like
a lover, like a person to be taken seriously. Michael had felt, once
more, the water rising around him, chilling his chest.

"Mike," she had said, quietly, and sat down next to him. "I
thought we should talk."

"Yes." The neutrality of her tone made him ashamed, a
schoolboy caught in a lie. "I'm sorry, Kate. I didn't know how to
tell you that I thought we should stop."

"Oh, you told me all right."

Michael had been helpless in the face of such quiet hurt. He had
been prepared for this meeting to happen; he had been ready to
be comforting and strong, or calming and firm. But Kate's solemn
honesty had demanded solemn honesty back. "I felt as though I
was getting out of my depth," he had said. "I love my wife very
much, and I never meant—I didn't mean—"

"I know," she had said. "Me neither."

They had glanced at each other then, daring a look instead of
talking to the air in front of them. She had been the first to smile.
"You're not exactly what I had planned, you know, Mike."

He had been the first to risk a touch, his hot damp hand covering
her cool smooth one where it sat, demure, in her lap. She hadn't
responded, but she hadn't taken her hand away.

And, although he hadn't thought he would ever talk to anyone
about this, he had tried to explain to Kate how much more bound
he was to his wife than anyone else might be to theirs. Her commit-
ment in coming to live in Throckton, the baby that never was, the
way they had built a life together. He wanted her to understand
that he was happy; he wanted her to understand that he would

never leave Elizabeth. "I'll be honest, Kate," he had said. "I don't know what's happening to me. I never thought I would be..." He had faltered, and Kate had turned toward him, lifted her hand to his jaw, her thumb smooth as it stroked beneath the cleft in his chin.

"I know," she had said. "I know." And she'd turned her face away and told him how, when she had realized that he didn't want to see her, she had decided to go away to think, and forget him. She had been to Paris, to stay with a friend who was studying there. She had been angry, upset. "I don't think you understand," she'd said, "how much you mean to me. Unless you feel the same way. And I think you are a good man. I don't think you would use me."

Michael, who had his arm around her by then because he couldn't seem to find a way not to touch her, felt her voice move through his chest. He has always known that he is a good man.

※

Kate didn't tell him about the tears and the endless discussion of what she should, could do, the speculation about the future that the two of them might have, the ways in which that future might come about. She had gloried in the feeling that she only got when she was with Mike: the feeling of love, of happiness, of saturation, all combined into something that couldn't be wrong.

Nerve endings had danced in her hip where his hand sat.

She knew that she had to be gentle.

"I need you to know," she had said, "that I will never, ever tell anyone about us. I want you to know that I can keep a secret and I will keep this one, for—" She had been choosing between "forever" and "for as long as we need to" when he had interrupted her.

"Thank you," he had said. "Thank you." It had felt as though Elizabeth was safe again.

It was a very short distance from the eyes front to the eyes locked, the touch to the kiss. Kate, who had once been a holiday, was becoming a home.

When she had gotten her phone out and suggested that she take a picture of them, he'd agreed and smiled and held her for the camera, and thought, *Well, I'm really in this now.*

Mike,

There were times when I wondered how happy you were. Especially that bit after we decided not to have a baby—I say "bit" as though it was no time, but I think there were probably a good three months when we were finding our feet again. And you were so quiet. And you were so calm. And when I asked you about adoption, and said I felt as though I couldn't put us through any more baby waiting and baby stress, any more time being patient… You just said, sure, and the way you said it was the way you had agreed when I said I thought I would apple white to peach white for the paint color in the downstairs bathroom. It was as though it was all the same to you. And although I could understand that when it came to choosing between two shades of white to go in a tiny windowless room—a baby, Mike? A child?

I assumed, at the time, that you wanted to do what I wanted because you were looking after me, and so I didn't ever really think about it too hard. We were so tired, weren't we? Sometimes all this missing you feels a little bit familiar, and I realize that the pain is like the pain of knowing that you'll never be a mother. It's the certainty. I won't see you again. I won't have a baby. And for a moment or two those things are bearable. It's when you look up, look forward, that it gets terrible.

Sometimes I wonder whether not having a baby was a rehearsal for not having you. The universe breaking me in gently. The breaking part is definitely true. There's nothing gentle about this, though.

E xxx

now

As soon as Rufus has gone, Mel makes tea for Elizabeth, and tells her that she's taking Pepper for a walk. Then she heads off to Patricia's house. The fact that she knows it's Patricia's day off only makes her angrier with this mad, incestuous place.

"You're my cover story," she growls to Pepper, who tries to lick her hand as she attaches his lead, "so I'm going to have to take you. But it's not like my day isn't already ruined."

As she stalks through the streets she lets a call from Blake go to voice mail. She doesn't trust her own voice, and she doesn't want to give anyone the opportunity to suggest a more measured response to what she's just learned.

She thinks about what she will say, later, to Blake and Andy: that tact and diplomacy and quiet conversations and a whole load of dancing about have done nothing but cause pain and upset for all of them. Her heels are furious on the pavement.

Patricia answers the door in an apron, hands covered in flour. *As though butter wouldn't melt in your mean little mouth*, Mel thinks, as Patricia says, "Oh, Mel, I'm just baking."

"So I see."

"Well," Patricia says, "if you're coming in, would you mind taking your shoes off? And I'm not really set up for dogs."

Mel looks her full in the face, a look that feels like a blow, and says, slowly and quietly, so that the older woman has to lean closer to hear, blinking as the brightness of the day hits her, "Yes, Patricia, I would mind. So either you can let me in with my heels and this mop on a string, or we can talk about cystic fibrosis on your doorstep. You decide."

So Patricia steps back, into the hallway, where it is Mel's turn to blink and wait for her eyes to make sense of the different light, then into the living room, so full of photographs that it's like stepping onto a stage. Mostly the pictures are of Michael and Michael's father, the resemblance strong, although the father's shoulders are broader, the son's hair paler. Elizabeth and Patricia make the odd appearance too. Patricia, framed, stands camera shy and formal on her wedding day, then later, outside the same church in Throckton, holding a baby swaddled in a shawl. As time goes on, her pictures become a little more relaxed, the images of her most alive when she is trying to get Michael to do something: look at the camera, blow out candles, ride a bike.

Mel thinks of how Elizabeth is always lovely in photographs— she has often lamented to Mel that she looks so much better in photos than in real life, and Mel has always said that, if you take the long view, she has the better deal. Except the last time that they had talked about photographs, Elizabeth had just said, "Mel, I really don't care what I look like at all."

Patricia has wiped her hands on the corner of her apron and is turning away—"Well, I'll just put the kettle on"—when Mel moves in front of her.

"I do not want a cup of sodding tea," she says. "I want to talk to you about a visit I've just had from Rufus Micklethwaite. And if I hadn't been there, he'd have made his snide, nasty comments to Elizabeth. Sit down."

Patricia, part afraid, part ashamed, part affronted, sits and opens her mouth. She's not sure where she's going to start, but that doesn't matter, because she doesn't get the chance.

"No," Mel says. "I don't want to hear anything. I want you to answer my questions. Is it true? Did you go and tell Kate Micklethwaite that if it's Mike's baby it might have cystic fibrosis? Because if you did, you're a cruel, cruel woman, Patricia. You were cruel to that girl and you are being very cruel to my sister."

Patricia opens her mouth again, but Mel, still standing, with all the advantages of rightness and height and the thought of what havoc this news will bring, holds out an imperious, silencing hand. "Can't you see that Elizabeth is falling apart? Haven't you noticed that she barely speaks if she doesn't have to and she won't even eat your fucking chicken soup anymore? What do you think this will do to her? Hasn't she lost enough?"

Patricia waits, spine tense, heart thumping, but there doesn't seem to be any more to come. Mel is glaring, waiting, towering in her own righteousness, and out of the tumult Patricia has one lucid thought. *Whatever I've done, I can't have another conversation about how hard things are for Elizabeth. I just can't.*

She stands up suddenly, so Mel steps back, away, and in that moment of advantage she says quietly, "She's not the only person to have lost something here, Melissa, although no one seems to remember that. My son is dead. And if that baby is my son's child, the mother needs to know about the risks, so that baby can be cared for properly."

"Don't try to tell me you were doing the mother a favor," Mel says, scorn written from the arch of her eyebrows to the pitch of her chin.

"Well," Patricia said, "I had my own reasons. I'm not particularly proud of myself. But needs must, and I know now that that baby is Michael's child. When I thought I'd lost everything, it turns out that I have a grandchild. I'm sorry for Elizabeth. I am. But this is my flesh and blood."

"So much for your saint of a son then," Mel says.

"Yes, I know," Patricia says. She thinks about telling Mel how she's lain awake at night, wondering what he'd done, what Elizabeth had done, what she'd done or failed to do in all of Michael's fatherless years, to make this happen, decides against it. "But we don't really know what went on."

"You mean that you think Kate Micklethwaite seduced him with her wicked wiles, and he succumbed because my sister doesn't bake her own bloody bread, and he's as innocent as a married man who got a kid of nineteen pregnant can possibly be, which is not, actually, very innocent at all."

Patricia closes her eyes for a moment, opens them again. "Now who's being cruel?" she asks, but Mel isn't listening. She has turned away, shoulders shaking, and Patricia realizes that this willful, abrasive young woman, who a moment ago she had feared might hit her, or break things, or do who knew what, is crying.

And so she takes a step forward, and she touches Mel on the shoulder, and when there's no reaction she takes both shoulders, more firmly, and she brings Mel to sit on the sofa. Mel responds to Patricia's touch, goes where she is moved to, meek as milk. Sobs are jolting out of her now. She's like a little girl who's lost her teddy in a railway station. Patricia holds her, holds her tight, and she waits.

"This will break my sister," Mel gets out between sobs. "This will break her, and I don't know how to put her back together again this time. I put her back when he died and I put her back when she found that girl in the garden and I put her back when the rumors started. I don't know how to do it again."

Patricia's heart heaves in sympathy. She says, "We can all get used to terrible things. You know that. I expect you thought you'd never manage without your mother. When John died I was sure that it would be the end of me. Losing a son is the worst thing you can possibly imagine. I know about being broken. I just don't show it the way you do. The way Elizabeth does."

She thinks that she feels Mel nod, but it might be a sob. She is becoming quieter now, softer. Patricia holds on.

Mel says, "She says you're the closest thing to a mother that she's ever had. When I complain about you she says that you've looked after and loved her and done your best to help her and she hasn't always liked what you've done but you've always acted in her best interests. She says that while she and Mike should have had four parents, they only had one, and you did a great job of doing four people's jobs. And now she's losing that too. She'll be devastated, Patricia. She'll think you've let her down as well."

Patricia looks at the photographs all around her, and she remembers how John used to say that there are times for talking, whether you want to talk or not. So she keeps going, down this hard road, with a person she wouldn't have chosen as a companion.

"Mel," she says, and as she speaks she remembers how sometimes the things she says come out sharp when she intends them to be clement, so she does her best to make her voice match her intention. "Mel, have you considered that, perhaps, in time, Elizabeth will be glad to see that there's a little bit of Michael left in the world?"

Mel snorts, finds a tissue, blows her nose. "She's barely coming out of her room as it is."

"Well, maybe knowing that Michael wasn't the saint that we've all made him out to be will bring her out." Mel looks at Patricia now for the first time since she started crying. Her face is a mess of mascara and brooding. Her eyes are surprised at what she's heard, questioning, checking. "Oh, I'm not blind, Melissa, and I'm not stupid. I just want to think the best of my son."

"I don't feel as though I know how to do this," Mel says, and neither of them is quite sure how it happens, but a moment later they are embracing, and Patricia is saying, "Mel, none of us know."

❀

While Mel goes to the bathroom to wash her face, Patricia hesitates over whether to show her the scan picture or not. But she thinks about where secrets have gotten them, so when Mel comes downstairs, face bare and embarrassed, she says, "Richenda Micklethwaite came to see me. At the library. She wanted to talk grandmother to grandmother. She gave me a picture of the baby. A scan."

Mel sits down and looks at it, for a long time. Just as Patricia is trying to think of the right thing to say to make the silence stop, Mel traces the outline of the face with the tip of a fingernail, wishes that Elizabeth had been the one handing her a scan, showing her Michael Gray's baby. "Boy or girl?" she asks.

Patricia says, "Girl."

"Well, at least she can't call it Michael," Mel says, and then she glances at Patricia to see whether she needs to explain that all she means is that that's one thing Elizabeth won't have to contend with. Patricia smiles her understanding. "And what does the cystic fibrosis thing mean? Michael was all right, wasn't he?"

"It might not mean anything, the baby may be fine," Patricia says, "but it runs in my family, so I really did feel she should know."

"I can see that," Mel says.

Patricia thinks, *Well, that's as close to an apology as I'm going to get. As I deserve, probably.*

Mel stands, rouses Pepper from where he's sleeping in a nest of cushions in shades of brown and plum. "You're right. We're going to have to get used to it."

"You're doing a good job," Patricia says. "You're a good sister."

Mel feels the honor of a compliment from a woman not much given to compliments. But all she says is, "That's not what Elizabeth's going to say when I tell her about this."

Mike,

The trouble with the quilt plan is, I can't quite bring myself to cut up your shirts. I washed them all yesterday—they were all clean, but I just wanted not to have the smell of our wardrobe when I started this, not have the smell of our wardrobe wafting around me as I cut and sewed. (I'm not even sure if our wardrobe has a smell—I mean, I'm not sure whether those lavender bags and scented, padded coat hangers your mother was always giving us had any impact, but I wanted to be sure. I'm getting good at preempting and protecting myself from the things that I can see might hurt.) I'd told Mel what I was doing before I went to work, so she didn't think I was going crazy (crazier?) with the washing, and she said, "Sister, if this is what you need to do, I'm right with you."

And I suppose she decided she wanted to help, because when I came home from work, having half forgotten that I'd put the washing machine on at all, what should I be greeted with when I walked through the gate but a dozen of your shirts, waving at me from the line. And it really was greeting and waving, because despite all of Auntie Brenda's nagging (or maybe because of it), Mel never could hang a shirt on a washing line properly, and pegged them all by the shoulders, instead of the hems, as usual. So at first glance it was a chorus line of you.

I didn't see that one coming. I didn't protect myself from my sister's kindness and effort and support. I felt the way I feel when I pick up the post and there's a letter addressed to both of us: as though life has stuck out one of its nasty stinky feet and tripped me up again, when I'd only just staggered up after the last thing.

I've ironed the shirts, and folded them, and put them in a pile on the chair in the corner of our bedroom, with the bag of hexagons on top. If you were watching me bring them in from the line, you'd have seen me holding them to me as though you were inside them still.

We'll see.

E xxxxx

now

ELIZABETH IS WAITING WHEN Mel and Blake arrive. She has
something that she wants to say. There have been a lot of
casual mentions of her birthday, and Mel's birthday, and there
seems to have been more whispering in corners than usual. So
she has decided to tell them that there will be no celebration: no
candles, no singing, not even the plainest meal in the quietest
restaurant they can find.

What she wants, really, is to sleep through the whole of the
wretched day. In fact, she'd like to sleep through every festivity
between now and then, "then" being, as far as Elizabeth can
gather, the point at which she can find a way to live a normal life.
Andy, Blake, Mel, and Patricia never seem to tire of reassuring her
that this day will come. Andy leaves books about grief that say the
same, and which she refuses to look at since she flicked through
the contents section of the first one he brought and saw the word
"acceptance" in there. Elizabeth does not feel like moving toward
acceptance. She does not accept that she's in a process. She can see
that if she had a child, the way Patricia had had Mike when John
died, then there would be some point in birthdays and Christmases
and generally pretending that life was going on. But Elizabeth
doesn't feel that way. She's not trying to be maudlin; she's not

running toward the blackness. It's just there. It's just everywhere. So she's determined to make Mel understand that, to get her to see that, at the moment, with all that's going on, having even the smallest, meanest of birthday gatherings would be about as appropriate as putting on a bikini and a party hat and going to a funeral. Another funeral.

Pepper tumbles around Elizabeth's feet as Mel and Blake stand in the doorway. Elizabeth clears her throat and says, "I wanted to talk to Mel, but Blake, you may as well hear this too." As though she hasn't heard, Mel says, "I think I probably need to go first," and at this odd statement Elizabeth looks up, assuming she's misheard, sees the look on her sister's face, and takes a deep breath. *No, no, no,* her heart pleads. *No more. Not something else.* She sits.

Then Mel is kneeling in front of Elizabeth. She's nodding to Blake, who says he'll be in the kitchen, and she's remembering the advice he's just given her: *Tell her now, because you can control the way she hears it; tell her fast, because she'll know something is wrong and her imagination will be working overtime; tell her clearly, because every word you say will be a word she'll remember forever.* It had all seemed sound and sensible when they'd talked about doing it. Now that Mel is on the brink of it, it seems like the pits.

Mel takes Elizabeth's hands and looks into her wondering face. Knowing what she's about to do is the bloodiest feeling she's ever felt: a finger on a trigger at point-blank range.

"Did you know there's a history of cystic fibrosis in Mike's family?" she asks.

"Of course." Elizabeth's face is all bemusement. "We knew everything about each other. It was all part of the stuff we went through when we were trying to have a baby." She remembers how scary the words had sounded when she first heard them, how she had been amazed and furious at how matter-of-fact Mike had been about the whole thing.

"Well"—and the bullet flies out of the barrel—"Patricia took it upon herself to tell Kate Micklethwaite about it, and Kate freaked out and has said that Mike is definitely the father of the baby. Blake found out about all this this morning, from the Micklethwaites. Rufus came here to tell you. He told me and I went to ask Patricia about it. Kate has spoken to the midwife about the possibility of the baby having it. Having cystic fibrosis. From Michael."

But Elizabeth is more bulletproof than she looks. She shakes her head, squeezes Mel's hand as though she's the one who needs to be reassured, comforted. She is all big sister.

"That doesn't mean anything. Prove anything. She's told a lie and she's seeing the lie through, that's all. What are the chances that the baby will turn out not to have cystic fibrosis after all? It proves nothing, Mel. Nothing. You're all far too eager to believe her. I knew Mike better than anyone, and I know it's not true. You need to trust me."

Mel closes her eyes, but when she opens them again, nothing has changed. Elizabeth's mood, coming off her like a perfume, has high notes of anxiety, an afterglow of gloom. So Mel has no choice but to reload, take a breath, squeeze the trigger again. "There are pictures."

Elizabeth enters that space between knowing that something has hit her and not yet knowing what it is. She can't think what there might be pictures of: what cystic fibrosis would look like on a scan. She rummages through her memory. She did a lot of reading about it before the test showed she wasn't a carrier, so although Mike was, cystic fibrosis could go on the "we'll cross that bridge when we come to it" list. She can't think that anything would be obvious.

Then Mel says, "Pictures of Kate and Mike."

"Don't be ridiculous," Elizabeth says, but there's a space in her voice that lets Mel say more.

"I know," Mel says, "but I think it's time to face facts. Mike had some sort of thing with her, and we don't know what, but it does seem that there's a good chance this is his baby."

Elizabeth thinks of Kate, of how she stood in her garden, a pale angel, and how she had gone down on her knees and begged to be told more. How her head then could have been no more than a hand span from where Mike's child was starting to gird itself into growth and life.

She cannot feel her heart in her chest. She cannot feel her tongue in her mouth. As the bullet hits its mark Elizabeth's guts turn over, over, over, and her eyes burn at the pain of trying to stay open and look at Mel, who is crying now. She can see that Mel is speaking, see her lips moving and hear something, but her ears are too bewildered to assemble the words into sense.

The words that Elizabeth wants to say are all lined up in her head, all ready to march down to her throat and out through her mouth and make all of this stop, with their power and their truth and their good, clear sense.

"Mel, it will be nothing. Don't take it so seriously."

"Mel, remember, this is Throckton. Everything gets out of proportion and when you get to the bottom of it, 90 percent of what you'd hear if you listened is barely true."

"Mel, she's just a little bitch trying to cover up the fact that she fucked some idiot boy at a party. How much more glamorous to latch on to my handsome, dead husband than to confess to getting drunk and not bothering with a condom because you're nineteen and you still think the world is going to look after you?"

But Elizabeth's tongue won't work. She's surprised she is

breathing, because her heart is still and her lungs tight, her throat clenched. She looks at her sister, tearstained and pleading. And she stands, and she goes upstairs, and she sits on her bed, and she remembers her husband. His honest eyes. His clear smile. She remembers the days when he'd come home after difficult shifts—accidents, fights, domestic violence—and she would say, "But you could have been hurt." And he would smile and touch her hair, and his fingers would slide down the side of her face until they ended under her chin, and he would say, "Don't give it another thought, sweetheart."

Don't give it another thought. That's the only way.

❉

"Another day, another council of war," Mel says grimly twenty-four hours later as she, Blake, and Andy face one another around the table again. "I haven't seen her in twenty-four hours. I've spoken to her through the bedroom door. She's refused everything. She's called work and told them she won't be in for the foreseeable future."

"Is she eating?" Andy asks.

"There was a cereal bowl washed up when I came down this morning, so I assume so," Mel says, "but she's refused lunch and dinner and coffee. I've tried everything. I've tried taking stuff up to her, I've tried asking what she wants, I've pleaded with her to come out, I've offered to go out so she can come downstairs without having to talk to me."

"You haven't done anything wrong," Andy says.

"Guilt by association," Mel says.

"Have you actually seen her?"

"Yes, because I told her I was going to call you if she didn't come to the door and show me she was all right."

"And?"

"She opened the door, said, 'Leave me alone, Mel; I'm all right, but I just want to be on my own,' and shut the door again."

"How did she look?"

"Well, I'm not experienced, but pretty much like you'd expect a woman whose sister has just told her that her dead husband was screwing around to look."

Andy touches her lightly on the shoulder. "Sorry."

"No, I'm sorry, Andy." Mel traces the inside of each eye socket in turn with the tip of the first finger on her right hand.

Both men, trained to notice small things, see that her nail is ragged, the varnish chipped and pulled.

Mel takes a breath, tries again. "She looks like she did when he died. But more disappointed. I don't know if she's disappointed in him for doing it, or in the rest of us for thinking that he might have. Which would be worse?"

"Well, assuming that it's true, the longer she denies it, the worse it will be when…" Blake says.

"If nothing else happens," Mel begins hopefully.

"If nothing else happens," Blake says, "if things stay as they are, then by the time that baby is a month old all of Throckton will be in no doubt as to its paternity, because Patricia Gray will have a grandchild."

Andy says, "He's right."

Mel says, "I keep thinking that all I need to do is get her on a plane. Tell her we're taking a trip and take her home. She doesn't have to watch the bloody kid grow up."

"No," Andy says, "but she might need to." He and Lucy had talked this whole thing over last night, after Blake had been.

"If I was her, I'd leave," Andy had said.

"No, you wouldn't," his wife had answered. "If you were her, you couldn't if you tried. Don't forget, her husband is here, and she's not going to be able to leave him until she's sorted this out. Something is better than nothing."

Mel gets up, reaches for her cigarettes, and is about to head for the back door when the sound of Elizabeth's bedroom door opening, closing, her feet on the stairs transfixes them all.

"Elizabeth—" Andy begins, taking in the red of her eyes and the scrape of her hair, the way her hands tremble a little and the leg of her pajamas has a tear in it.

Elizabeth barely glances at him. "I'm not ill, Andy. I'm just really pissed off and I want to be on my own. Blake"—Blake has stood to greet her and reaches out to touch her arm, but she flinches at just the intention—"did you know about this? About this cystic fibrosis thing that everyone's run away with?"

Blake says, "No. I found out from Richenda at about the same time as Rufus came to see Mel."

Elizabeth nods, as though she's ticking something off a list. "And did you know before? When this was supposedly happening?"

"No. I had no idea at all."

"Exactly," Elizabeth says, with a sort of desperate triumph. "If none of us knew then—not his wife, not the colleague he'd worked with for years, not his best friend"—she tips her head at Andy, a question, and he shakes his head in return—"if it wasn't true then, why should it be true now?"

Blake sighs, glances around and sees it's his turn to try. "I agree that it's all circumstantial evidence, but there's more and more of it. I'm sorry, Elizabeth, because it hurts me to even say it and I can't imagine how much this is hurting you, but I think we have to entertain the possibility that this baby is Michael's baby. I'm so sorry."

For a minute it looks as though Elizabeth will hit him, but she doesn't. Instead she glares at the three of them, one after the other, and Mel moves forward from where she's standing and tries to take her arm.

Elizabeth pulls herself back, out of range, turns, leaves the room. As she goes, she calls back, "I want to see a photo. Blake, you're supposed to be liaising, so liaise me one of her crappy Photoshopped pictures so I can see how she did it, the little bitch."

❀

Blake and Andy stand together by the gate.

"I keep going through it," Blake says, "trying to think of what I missed. There must have been signs." He has been over and over it the past few months, looking for the moment when he could have said, done, something.

"Me too," Andy says. "Lucy noticed, when we all went for a drink after Bonfire Night, do you remember?" The Throckton Fireworks had been as good as washed out, and Michael, Elizabeth, and Blake had gone for a drink afterward, drawn to the promise of the open fire in the bar of the Red Dragon. Andy and Lucy had joined them after dropping the twins with their grandparents for an hour. It had been one of those evenings that had never quite gotten going. Michael, who could usually be relied upon to get a conversation started—even if it was about running—had been the quietest of all of them.

"Vaguely," Blake says. "I remember we were all wet through and we went home early."

"On the way back, Lucy asked what was wrong with Michael. I said I thought he hadn't been himself since the fire. She said if he walked into a burning building when he knew it wasn't safe, maybe the fire was the symptom, not the cause."

Blake gives a laugh-that-isn't. "She sounds like a better doctor than you."

"I know. I didn't think any more about it. I—" Andy seeks words that will explain the thrashing helplessness he's feeling, the way the muscles in his neck knot whenever he thinks of how all this could have been going on without his even wondering about it. How whatever he is feeling must be amplified beyond all bearing in Elizabeth.

"I know," Blake says. "I know." And he thinks of all the crimes that happen under people's noses, unnoticed because of their proximity, and the belief that someone so close would be incapable of doing such a thing.

"I wish we could do something more," Andy says. Which gets Blake thinking.

And Andy and Blake shake hands and part.

Mike,

You wouldn't believe what's going on here. It's stupid. I'm not going to insult you by even telling you about it. I've called their bluff. You used to say that about work: most times, you just call their bluff and it goes away. I do it at work sometimes, when people are horrible. If they threaten to go elsewhere, I smile and ask if they'd like me to call around some other hotels and find them a room. When that guy insisted his moussaka had given him food poisoning, even though thirty-five other people in the restaurant had eaten it with no problem, and said he was going to report us, I wrote down the number of our contact at environmental health for him and we never heard another thing.

So. I've called their bluff, "good and proper" as your mother would say. (I may never be able to bring myself to speak to your mother again.)

While I'm waiting for this all to go away, I thought I'd start on the quilt. But something went wrong with the cutting out, and now all I have is shreds and shards of fabric. And when they were your shirts, I loved them; now that they're material, they look broken and faded and frayed. Another plan awry.

I love you. I miss you. Every time I think I couldn't get lonelier, I do.

E xxxx

This time, Blake had taken the precaution of calling ahead to make sure that Rufus wasn't around. He hadn't asked directly, of course, but Richenda had said, "Rufus is off seeing a client today, so it will be just Kate and me if that's OK," and Blake had said, "That will be perfect," in a way that he thought afterward was a little too warm for the work he was about to do.

Richenda serves coffee in bowls today. "It's a habit we picked up when we lived in France for a while," she says and thinks as she says it of the lifestyle that that sentence implies: happy, carefree, part of a history of interesting adventures. Well, the adventure part could possibly be considered true, but their French year-and-a-bit she remembers as lonely and puzzling. She thinks of it now as the time when she could have, should have, gotten out; less than two years married, the certain knowledge of the great mistake she'd made becoming clearer every day. But then the thought of facing up to her disapproving mother and her disappointed father, a few uncomfortable months of living at home again and finding a new place in the world, had seemed worse than the prospect of muddling through another day with Rufus. So she'd stayed, and then there had been Kate, and then there was no point in regretting anything or wishing things were different.

"Richenda?" Blake's voice is gentle.

She shakes her head. "Miles away," she says. "I'm sorry. I assume this isn't a social call?"

"Afraid not," and he explains, probably in more detail than he needs to, certainly with more feeling than he realizes, what's happened.

"So, Elizabeth would like to see one of Kate's photographs of her with Michael?"

"Yes"—Blake's eyes say, *I'm floundering here*—"I think it might help her to accept things."

Richenda thinks of all the photographs of Caroline on Rufus's phone, his password so easy to guess that it's almost as though he wants her to look. "It will probably hurt her very much."

"Everything is hurting her at the moment." And Blake looks so bleak that as Richenda passes him to call Kate downstairs, she rests her hand on his shoulder. He sits very still, as though some rare and precious bird has come so close.

Kate comes slowly down the stairs. "I was in the rocking chair," she says. "I think if I rock Kayla in it when she's on the inside, then it will soothe her to be there once she's on the outside. It works on me. I was nearly asleep myself."

Blake stands. "Hello, Kate."

Kate half smiles, wary. "I still don't remember anything, you know. About the accident. When Mike died."

"It's not that, Kate," Richenda says and looks at Blake to see whether he will make the request or she should.

"Elizabeth is having a hard time accepting that your baby is Michael's," Blake begins.

"I'm not lying about it," Kate says. "Why would I lie?"

Blake thinks of Elizabeth's list of reasons. "I don't think

you're lying," he says. "I'm just telling you what's happening for Elizabeth."

"Elizabeth," Kate says, although she doesn't like to speak the name aloud, as it makes her remember how Michael used to say it, each syllable as soft and equal as the next, with the comfort and quality of a word said often. "I don't want to talk about Elizabeth. I'm just thinking about me and Kayla now."

Richenda looks at him. *Forgive her*, her eyes say. *She's young and she has no idea what she's saying.*

"Of course," Blake says. "I do understand that. I understand that Elizabeth trying to come to terms with this is not the most important thing for you now. But maybe for Michael? She was important to him for a long time, Kate, whatever happened in the end."

Blake can see by Richenda's face what a gamble he's just taken. He waits.

The ball scuttles: red, black, red, black, red. Kate remembers that Blake is the only person who congratulated her on her pregnancy. She remembers how Mike said he was someone he would trust with his life. Cautiously, Kate says, "What do you want?"

"I'd like you to text me one of your photos of you and Michael. Then I can show it to Elizabeth. Then I'll delete it. That's all."

Blake is searching his pockets for his card with his cell phone number on it, so her "no" catches him off guard.

When he looks at her, she's sitting up very straight, hands on her stomach, eyes on his. "I don't have to prove anything to her. She doesn't have any right to see anything of mine. I don't belong to her; my photos don't belong to her just because her husband's in them."

"OK," Blake says, "but, Kate, she's really struggling. This might help her."

"Why do I have to help her?"

Richenda says, "Kate—" just as Blake says, "You don't." Richenda leans back in her seat, knowing that all the things she's on the brink of saying, about marriage and death and grace and life being about more than just you and what you want, aren't the right things to be said.

"You don't have to help her. But if we only helped when we had to, where would we be? You have your baby. Elizabeth has nothing left of Mike except the fact that he's not the man she thought he was." To Kate, he sounds a bit like Mike. It's not that his voice is the same, but it's the sort of thing that Mike would say. She remembers standing in Elizabeth's garden; the pleading, the conviction that Elizabeth was the only person entitled to grieve for Mike as she was grieving.

"All right," Kate says. "She can see the photos. But she has to see me too. I'll show them to her. She's not pretending that I don't exist anymore. You can tell her that and see what she says."

❄

Elizabeth says yes. Well, she says, "Bloody little cow. All right. Get her around here. She can sit in Mike's house and my house and see how she likes that," which Blake translates into "Yes" and passes on to Richenda in a conversation where both express their misgivings.

Richenda says, "I think it best that we keep things as calm as possible," with a question mark at the end, and Blake, whose translation skills are coming into their own at the moment, realizes that she doesn't plan to tell Rufus until this is over and says, "Yes, I agree."

And so, on a sunny day in the middle of August, Richenda and

Kate walk up to Elizabeth and Michael's front door, and Kate rings the bell. Her face could be made of wax. Mel opens the door.

"You're a bit early," she says, not unpleasantly, "but ten minutes isn't going to make this any easier for anyone, I suppose." And she steps back, and Kate walks into the house that she's walked past and wondered about so many times.

Three steps and she's in a living room that feels like a home. Above the fireplace there's a framed wedding photo. Mike has a white shirt on, and he's laughing. He looks younger. So does she: younger, prettier, longer hair. Kate looks at the shelf of travel books, the lamp with the twisted wooden base she thinks must be from Australia, the alcove where the Christmas tree goes.

She wishes she hadn't come.

Blake is already here. He's standing, to the side of the fireplace. Mel indicates the sofa, and Richenda sits at one end, Kate in the middle.

Blake smiles bravery toward Richenda, smiles it again to Mel, who says, "I'm dispensing with the traditional offer of tea. I hope that's OK."

Richenda nods.

And then Elizabeth comes down the stairs and into the room. Her hair is damp and she wears jeans and a white shirt with a hole in the elbow. Her feet are bare. So is her face. She nods to Richenda, who nods back.

Mel opens her mouth to say something, but Elizabeth says, "It's fine, Mel."

The room holds its breath.

And then Elizabeth looks at Kate.

And Kate looks at Elizabeth.

Elizabeth sees blossom. She sees bloom. Everything about Kate is rounding, orbing outward as though the baby she carries is filling every space in her with its presence and intention. *I'm coming, and when I come, I'll change your life.* Her hair is glossy and her eyes are bright, and even the sharpness she is holding in them can't contain the cornered, afraid child she is.

Kate sees tiredness. She sees sadness. She sees the contents of her own heart—love, grief, loss—carved onto someone else's body. Elizabeth's toenails are unpainted and her hands don't rest. There's a cut on her fingertip. She works her wedding ring around and around on her finger, with her thumb. Her engagement ring, a diamond solitaire clasped in yellow gold, sags from her finger a little. Kate finds herself wondering whether Mike chose it or whether they had bought it together. She sees the ring on Elizabeth's thumb, too big too. Recognizes it. Remembers the time she tried to take it off, half playful, and he'd pulled his hand from hers and said, no. Just that one word.

The room needs to breathe.

Elizabeth says, "Thank you for coming, Kate. I hope you're well." She sits down, next to Kate but careful to be far enough away to make sure that their bodies can't accidentally touch. At eight months pregnant, Kate is taking up a lot of room. Elizabeth holds on to the arm of the sofa with her left hand, to keep her anchored at a safe distance.

Kate, scrabbling for purchase as she realizes that Mike is smiling out from every picture frame in the room, says, "Do you?"

Richenda says, "Kate."

Elizabeth says, "It's much easier to think unkind thoughts about someone when they're not sitting next to you. And there's no way your baby is Mike's child. So yes, I hope you're well. My husband died because you're walking around, so it would be a shame if you weren't well."

Kate can't work out if Elizabeth is being bitchy or not, decides that she isn't, that she doesn't have the right sort of eyes. And her mother, who is now holding her hand so very tightly, has promised to step in if need be.

But then Richenda says, "Kate, you don't have to do this if you don't want to."

Mel opens her mouth, but Elizabeth, who seems to be watching herself from out of her own wedding photograph on the wall, says, "I'm sure you appreciate that this is difficult for me."

"Yes," Richenda says in the voice Kate recognizes as the one reserved for people in shops who are rude and Dad when he comes home too late and too flushed. "It's actually rather difficult for everyone, so let's get on with it, shall we?"

And Kate takes her phone from her pocket.

Mel is next to Elizabeth, perched on the arm of the sofa, her hand on her sister's shoulder.

Kate passes the phone to Elizabeth.

She isn't as shocked as she thought she was going to be. She is hurt, more hurt than she has been since she sat in the funeral home and thought about how Mike had left her when he promised he never would. But not shocked. The sound of Mel crying is more shocking than the photograph, which just makes Elizabeth think, *Well, there's Mike. What's he doing with his arm around that girl?*

Elizabeth starts to scroll forward through the photographs. He looks uncomfortable. They both look cold. Really cold. In most of the photos they're both looking straight at the camera, but in one Mike's head is turned toward Kate, his mouth caught in the blur of a word.

Elizabeth, hungry for detail, asks Kate, "What's he saying?"

Kate leans over, half smiles, and says, "He was saying that Pepper doesn't like the flash."

And that's when it happens. The others watch and see the darkness dawning. Inside, Elizabeth is bellowing, wailing, clawing. Screaming. Screaming, "You know my dog. You fucked my husband, and you call my dog—our dog—by his name, as though you have the right to. As though you're part of the family. Which you're not, and you never will be."

But her body has turned to marble and her heart to the kind of sharp, hot dust that whirls in every passing gust and scratches its way across your eyes.

She says, "Blake, will you let Pepper out, please? I think he wants to go into the garden." And Blake obeys, even though Pepper is passed out in his basket. And then Elizabeth musters her best shot, which isn't much of one, and says to Kate, "Those pictures were all taken in one go. You could have been leaving a party. He could have been humoring you. They prove nothing."

Elizabeth is twisting the ring around her finger again. Kate has taken her phone back, has her eyes down, face hidden by her hair.

Richenda and Mel are both looking at Blake, who says gently, "Elizabeth, I know this is hard, but we agreed that Kate would come here and show you the pictures, and that's what she's doing." He catches Mel looking glistening daggers at him. "Mel, we can't go on like this."

"I agree," Mel says, "but that's not to say we should be trying to make things worse."

Richenda makes to stand, but Kate resists. She hands her phone back to Elizabeth, who finds herself looking at a text message from Mike's number, from the previous July. "Dog walking tonight." She scrolls past what seems like hundreds of messages that say "Dog walking" or "Running" or occasionally "No dog walking," which is somehow worse. Elizabeth's face goes from pale to paler to peaked, and she starts to shake.

Mel takes the phone, glances at it, hands it back to Kate, and says, "Thank you for coming. I think you can go now."

Richenda helps Kate up, a hand under her daughter's arm, and they are almost at the door, Elizabeth crying in a sad defeated keening, when Mel says, "Actually, one more question."

Richenda, who has tears clawing at her own throat, would have kept Kate moving, but Mel's voice is quiet, pleading, and so it seems safe to turn around.

"Is that everything? I think we need to know whether that's the lot. We don't have the resources for any more revelations."

Kate says, "That's everything. That's all I have of him," and it's an easy lie, because what she is still keeping to herself is so buried, so ugly and ignored, that she couldn't immediately put words to it if she wanted to. But as she watches Mel and Blake go to Elizabeth, it kicks a few words out. "So I don't know why everyone feels so sorry for her."

Elizabeth is on her feet before she knows it. Mel sees a flash of the sister she used to know, who couldn't bear life on a farm in the middle of rural Australia anymore, who raged to be free. This time there are words, ready and biting at one another in their eagerness to get out. "Because I was his wife and he and I could not have a child of our own. Because, whatever you think, he loved me and he loved our life together. Because within two years you'll be off-loading your baby onto your poor mother every evening and screwing your way around Throckton in the hope of finding someone to love you."

Richenda takes a step forward, Elizabeth one back, but she doesn't stop talking, couldn't if she wanted to, but she doesn't want to because for as long as she's talking she can't listen to the terrible things that her soul is screaming, "And by the time you're twenty-five you'll be scraggy and stupid and you won't have a thing to look forward to."

Richenda is turning, trying to turn Kate, but Kate isn't going anywhere until she's said, "I'll have nothing to look forward to, except my baby growing up."

"If it grows up," Elizabeth says.

The room inhales, a sharp, shocked breath.

Kate, tears jumping from her eyes, is movable again.

Richenda has a novel feeling of wishing her husband was here. This would be the perfect place for all the unpleasant, unkind rants about Michael Gray that she's had to endure lately. She says, "That really is enough, Elizabeth. I'm sorry for your loss, and for your pain, but that's enough. Kate, come on."

Elizabeth nods.

Kate leaves, followed by her mother.

Mel says halfheartedly, "Well said, Sister. I couldn't have put it better myself." And then to Blake, "Text messages. From Mike. Before you ask, no, nobody wants tea. I want a cigarette and when I come back in I'm bringing whiskey." She gives him the look that says, *You look after her for a minute*—it's a look that she's passed, caught, passed, caught more often than she wants to think about in the last few months, dropped only once or twice when Elizabeth has intercepted with a "For heaven's sake, you lot, I'm not about to throw myself under a bus"—and she goes.

Elizabeth looks as though someone has not only switched out her light but removed the bulb and the fuse. Blake guides her back to the sofa, sits her down, sits next to her. Waits. He doesn't have to wait for long.

"He did it, Blake," she says, turning stamped-on eyes to him. "Mike did it. He did it with a girl just over half his age. He did it over and over again. He did it in the dark and the cold at Butler's Pond. He did it in the place we walked the dog together. He did it with the dog there. He did it with her and then he came home and did it with me." Her voice is growing softer and softer. "He did it, presumably, without a condom. He did it and he made a baby."

Blake thinks of the man he knew. "But he loved you," he says. "You can't doubt that he loved you."

"I can doubt what I damn well like," Elizabeth says, and she gets up and heads for the stairs.

Mike,

I don't know why I'm writing to you because you're dead, you bastard, DEAD. And anyway there are no words for this. No words. Just colors. Spikes of colors when I close my eyes, echoes of them when I open them. Blood red and filthy orange and shades of mud and earth and the winter water that you drowned in.

I think what I'm angriest about is the fact that you're not here so I can't scream and shout at you. I can't take the fists that my hands make whenever I'm not doing anything else with them and beat them against your stupid cheating chest. I can't hold your face and make you look at me so you can see exactly what it is that you've done to me. I can't have you sitting there while I cry my heart out, again, over some stupid fuckwitted thing that you've done, again, the fire then the dying and now the—this. I don't get to push you out of the door and slam it behind you and listen to you pleading to be let back in.

I can't ask you questions. Well, I can ask, but you'll never be able to tell me the answers. And I wouldn't, couldn't, ask her, and she wouldn't tell me, and even if she did, I wouldn't believe her.

How did it happen? Where did you meet her? Who kissed who first? Did you plan it or did it sneak up on you? Was it sex or did you love her? Did you ever bring her here? Did you drive her anywhere in our car?

What, in the name of all that's holy, did you think you were doing screwing a kid? I mean, I know she's technically an adult, but she's just left school, for Christ's sake. All she's ever done is go to school. What did you talk about? Pythagoras?

What was wrong with me? Did you think I was too old? Was I starting to get fat? Too sterile, too familiar, too demanding? Why wasn't I enough for you?

If you were here I'd be telling you that I never wanted to see you again. I haven't even got the satisfaction of doing that.

You bastard. You cheating, lying, unfeeling, bastard. You dead bastard.

E

between

NOVEMBER HAD ALWAYS BEEN a hard month for Michael. Midmonth saw the anniversary of the day when, at the age of nine, he had come home from school to find his mother refusing to let him into the living room where his father had collapsed of a heart attack. Michael could remember, still, the sight of the boots, the table turned over, that he'd glimpsed through the doorway and then immediately wished he hadn't. Patricia had screamed at him—up until then, she'd been the woman he'd never known to raise her voice—screamed at him to wait outside for the ambulance so that it would know where to go.

In the first few years after his father's death, Remembrance Day came to mark the beginning of his mother being withdrawn and silent, which was horrible, except when she was weeping, which was worse. They always put the Christmas tree up on the weekend before Christmas, the two of them dragging it valiantly home on a tarpaulin because they didn't have a car and Patricia refused to pay to have it delivered, and that was the beginning of the return to normality. Michael would put the star on top; Patricia would switch on the lights and step back and say, "Your father loved Christmas. He used to say that if you couldn't enjoy Christmas then there must be something wrong with you," and that was their permission to smile again.

Even more than a quarter of a century later, Michael still felt the anniversary squatting like a hungry demon in the middle of the month. Although his mother claimed to be pragmatic, she always became gaunt and quiet and looked at her son with tears in her eyes.

Elizabeth, who had made a point of refusing to mark the anniversary of her mother's death—"It was spring," was all she would ever say; "there were lambs when we moved to the farm"—had never understood quite how important, how pervasive, this time was for Mike and Patricia. She was preoccupied anyway with remembering what the damp and dark of an English winter was like: remembering, it seemed to her husband, as thoroughly and willfully as she had forgotten it through summer and early autumn.

Without having noticed that he was doing it, Michael had brought his lackluster November mood to his time with Kate. Meeting her, during faked overtime, at the waterside, kissing her and listening to her, appearing by her side as she walked home from a shift at the restaurant, spending, if anything, more time than he had yet with her, he was nevertheless vague, unavailable.

Kate had had a lot of theories about this; she had kept Bella posted ever since her time in Paris with her friend. They spent late nights and long afternoons messaging each other about it. The only thing Kate wouldn't say was who it was. "No one you know," she would type. "Older, involved, that's all you need to know. And that it's love." On good days, she was sure that he was brooding over how much he loved her and how he wanted to be with her. "Has he said he loves you?" Bella, with all of her newfound Parisian wisdom, had asked, and Kate had replied, "No, but he sees me twice a week, sometimes. If people found out he'd never hear the end of it." "Maybe that's what he's thinking about," Bella had said.

On the grayer days—the days when he had said almost nothing, held her hips too tightly, kept his eyes closed, nodded a good-bye—Kate had wondered whether this was the beginning of the end. But that was unthinkable. They seemed bound so tightly together. Each body had learned the geography and geometry of the other; the thought that their hearts might not understand so well had made no sense to Kate.

In the end, she decided that this was just the place in their relationship when they were getting into a routine. She had thought about tiredness, coldness, stress at work: all of the things that were masked in the early days, but showed through sooner or later, like a scuffed heel painted over with nail polish. She had tried to make things more comfortable, bringing blankets, a hot water bottle, whiskey pilfered from her father's hoard, making a nest with them. Bella had suggested that she try making things "more exciting," and so, late one afternoon as the gloaming was beginning, she'd asked, snaking a finger down the middle of his chest in a way she considered unmistakable, if there was anything he'd like to do. Mike, lying on his back with his hands behind his head and his eyes closed, had said, "Have a really good night's sleep."

And Kate, her need to keep from showing her disappointment distracting her from watching her tongue, had said, "When you come to stay with me in Oxford we can lie in." Michael affects not to hear, but there's a moment when his body tenses, and her body feels it.

"All I meant," she says, "is that when I'm at Oxford, if you were to come to stay, we would have a bed to sleep in."

In her mind, the room was furnished in much greater detail. Wooden furniture. A desk under a mullioned window. A framed photograph of the two of them on the sill. A drawer where Mike could leave some clothes so he didn't have to bring a big bag every time. A bottle of wine on the floor, a plan for dinner later, and then maybe a drink with friends who accepted them as a couple and thought nothing of the two of them being together.

When Michael gets home, Patricia is sitting in the kitchen, granite faced, while Elizabeth looks up from slicing carrots to smile brightly at him.

"You hadn't gotten back to your mum about what you wanted to do tonight, so she's brought a pie around, and we thought we could all eat here."

Patricia adds, "I called the station and they said you'd finished work for the day. I went to your father's grave but you weren't there."

"I went for a run," Michael had said. "I hadn't forgotten that the anniversary was today." It had seemed an easier lie than, *I've thought of little except my father and what he would think of me over the last couple of weeks, but all of my days and nights seem to be running into one, so I truly don't know what day it is most of the time.* "I thought I'd rung you, Mum."

Elizabeth had chipped in, "He's always like this the week after night shift."

He had kissed his mother, who had said, "You smell as though you've been dragged through a hedge," and his wife, who had whispered, "I'm on your side," and then he'd gone upstairs to have a shower and he had stood under too-hot water, scrubbing himself too hard, until he felt something close to clean.

That night, curled around Elizabeth, he slept without moving, his arm heavy across her waist. He slept the sleep of a man coming out of the other side of a fever.

The next day, he had arranged to meet Kate, and he held her hand, and he looked straight at her, and he had said, "I'm sorry,

Kate, I can't do this anymore. I can't see you. I never should have started this. It has to end."

She had been quiet for a long time, watching their hands as though there was something secret, or maybe sacred, in the places where their skin touched.

And then she had taken a deep breath, and he had braced himself, but all she'd said was, "I promised you I wouldn't tell anyone about us, and I won't."

Mike had opened his mouth to reply, but she'd pulled her hand from his then, and said, in a voice that belonged to someone younger, more afraid than she had ever shown herself to be, "Please don't say any more. Please don't try to make it better."

And she'd walked away. And Mike hadn't known whether she looked back or not, because his head was in his hands as he sat, overwhelmed by relief, sure that in his wife and his work he had everything he needed, after all.

Mike,

I have questions for me too. Why couldn't I tell? Why didn't I know? What did I miss? What did I forget to do for you, show you, tell you that meant it was OK for you to do this to me? Why can she be pregnant and not me? How can I go on, not knowing the answers?

I was your wife. Your wife, Mike. We didn't have any children. We were everything to each other. And yet.

I'm staying in my room. I hear Mel and Blake and Andy talking. Sometimes I go down and make tea when they're all there, because it makes them stop talking about me, because if I think I can show them that I can walk and talk and drink—I can't eat, everything makes me sick— they might just let me be.

Andy told me that if I'm not coping we can try "other approaches." I said, "Andy, right now, I just feel like lying down and dying. Can you blame me?" "No, not really," he said.

I still hate you.

E

now

PATRICIA HAS HAD THE briefest of briefings from Blake.

"Kate has been to see Elizabeth, and it's all out in the open."
Patricia, mostly relieved, had said that that was good.

"Yes," Blake had replied, in a tone in direct odds to the word,
"but I'd give her a bit of space for a while if I were you, Patricia.
She's not really coming out of her room."

So Patricia has busied herself with other things. Matinee jackets,
mostly, although she has bought the ingredients to make a cake
for Elizabeth's birthday too. Nothing too celebratory, just the
chocolate cake that she likes. Just so she knows that Patricia won't
forget her.

After the hairdresser, she goes to see Kate, who answers the
door with a smile that makes Patricia overlook, for a minute, that
this girl is difficult, this relationship is difficult, that the baby means
that she's going to have a lot of sideways looks and awkward questions for a while. Kate's wearing a T-shirt, stretched tight: they
don't hide their pregnancies the way they used to.

"Come in," she says. "Mum and I have just been finishing
Kayla's room."

Rufus rises when Patricia enters, and although he shakes her
hand, his eyes are cold.

"I didn't know you were coming," he says, "but I'm very often the last to know anything in this house." Patricia is still trying to formulate a reply when he excuses himself and goes out.

"Ignore him," Richenda says. "He's not adapting very well."

"It's not easy," Patricia concedes, remembering the last time she was here, the tears and the panic. Kate looks bigger, more tired, but happier too. "How are you? How is the baby?"

"I'm fine," Kate says. "Fat, but fine. And the baby—we're going to have a checkup and a scan the day after tomorrow. At the hospital."

"That's good."

"Yes." Kate stops, rubs her belly, a clockwise motion, looks down as though her body will speak to her. "I just keep thinking, well, the first scan was fine, and everything she's doing is everything the books say she should be doing, kicking and elbowing and hiccupping. So. I think it will be all right." She looks to her mother, to Patricia, for confirmation.

It's on the tip of Patricia's tongue to say, that's because you want it to be all right. She remembers her own days of carrying Michael, when there was nothing to go on but the look on the midwife's face as she wielded her tape measure and used an ear trumpet to listen for a heartbeat. "Things have come a long way in nearly forty years," she says instead.

Kate looks a little shy as she asks, "Would you like me to ring you and let you know what they say?"

"Yes." Patricia nods. "Yes, please." And then she passes a bag that she's brought to Kate.

Kate takes out jackets, hats, bonnets, bootees, in pinks, peaches, purples, white. She holds each garment up to the light.

"Did you make these?" she asks.

"Yes," Patricia says.

"We've only got onesies," Kate says, "but these are so pretty. Vintage."

Patricia and Richenda look at each other, smile.

"I'm glad you like them," Patricia says. She looks away so that she can hide her face, her feelings, for a moment. She remembers talking to Elizabeth, cautiously, about babies, and Elizabeth saying, tightly, "I'm not sure babies are going to be our thing, Patricia. I wouldn't get your knitting needles out just yet."

"But they're so tiny," Kate says.

"Some of them will probably be too big," Richenda says.

Kate looks at her stomach and says, "Whatever's in here is huge, Mum."

And then this disparate almost-family makes its way upstairs to take a look at the nursery. On the door, wooden letters spell out *KAYLA*, and Patricia looks at the word and thinks, *Well, I think perhaps I can learn to live with that, after all.* Kate sees her looking and says, "I haven't decided on a middle name yet."

The room is peach, with cream curtains. It's pale, plain, beautiful. There's a rocking chair in the corner, a chest of drawers, a crib. It's all ready, except that there's a framed Beatles poster propped against the wall, unhung. It seems an odd choice to Patricia. who is planning a trip to Marsham to buy a sampler kit this weekend. Richenda catches her look.

"This was in here when it was the spare room," she says. "Kate thinks she might keep it in here."

Patricia says, "When I was born, my parents put me in a drawer filled with blankets to sleep. That's what it was like for them. You might not feel it, but you're very lucky."

Kate says, "Mum's been brilliant. I'm going to stay here for the first year, and we're going to see how it goes. And so long as Kayla is all right, I'll think I'm the luckiest person there's ever been."

Then, made bold by Patricia's first unguarded smile, asks, "Where did Mike sleep? When he was a baby?"

"Oh, his dad made him a cradle," Patricia says, thinking how only this girl and Elizabeth have ever been allowed to shorten his name to Mike. "His dad was good with his hands. I kept it next to my side of the bed. You can have it, if you want it. If you're not putting her straight into the crib."

"Really?" Kate says, as though Patricia has just offered her the very earth and skies.

"That's very kind," Richenda adds.

"Of course," Patricia says. "No one else is going to use it." And then she remembers that Michael was the one who always went up into the attic when she needed anything. She doesn't know how she'll get it down. She'll have to ask Blake, or Andy, or the neighbor's son she doesn't much like, for help. And her loss crushes her, quietly, again, the way it finds a thousand tiny quiet ways to crush her every day.

"Do you want to go and make some tea, Kate?" says Richenda, who has been watching everything with a cat's attention. And Kate does, and brings it to Patricia, who's grateful for it, even though it's in a mug. *But,* she thinks, *that's the young for you.*

Mike,

I've worked out that I need to have twenty minutes of sensible conversation with Mel and ten with either Blake or Andy every day to keep them from doing anything more than look worried.

But I can't sleep and I can't eat and I feel weirder and weirder with every day. The days are merging because I'm not opening the curtains and I'm not getting dressed. My mind is working overtime. I keep thinking about things. Stupid things. Like, you can't call a baby Michaela Micklethwaite but if you were wanting to get a Michael in there you could call it Kayla. (Mel told me about the name. She thinks it's stupid. So do I. More importantly, I think you would have thought it was stupid, you with your endless suggestions of Camellia, Daisy, Poppy.)

And then, there's Beatle. I asked Blake how it's spelled, and he said, like the band. So now I'm thinking, Pepper. Sgt. Pepper's Lonely Hearts Club Band. But she's too young to know about the Beatles and you didn't like them, so I suppose that, at least, is a coincidence. A paranoid coincidence. That's what happens when you think too much, when your brain churns and churns around the same horrible, muddy, stony, uphill loop. When you can't talk to the person you need to talk to, even though you can't bear the thought of seeing their face. Even though, at the same time, you want nothing more in the world than to see their face again.

Tomorrow is my birthday. I used to love how much we made of birthdays. On the first of my birthdays when we were together, I was in Australia still, and you sent flowers in the morning, which I thought was sweet, and then you turned up in the afternoon, which I thought was a kind of madness, especially when most of my birthdays growing up had been a new bell for my bike and a joint party with Mel, and so I'd never bothered much. I remember saying to you, "You've set the bar high now," and you said, "There's no day more important than the day you arrived in the world." And so one of our traditions was made. I suppose it would have changed, if we'd had a baby's birthday to celebrate.

Last year, when you took me to Venice, I thought it was because you adored me, but it turns out you were just making it up to me for something I hadn't found out about yet. Love in the bank. Well, it doesn't work like that.

This year my birthday is all down to me and I can do what I like so what I am going to do is this. I am going to bed in a minute, and I'm going to take a couple of sleeping pills and wash them down with a whiskey. Every time I wake up, I'll do the same thing again. Just until my birthday's over.

E

ANDY ARRIVES AT ELEVEN on Elizabeth's birthday with flowers. Friendly flowers, muted flowers. Mel takes one look at them and asks, "Have you been talking to Rufus Micklethwaite?"

"Lucy chose them." Andy is looking for Elizabeth, with the expression of hope and trepidation that Mel feels is a reflection of the way her own face looks most of the time.

"Nothing. She hasn't woken up yet. I took some tea up at ten, but she was dead to the world."

"Probably best," Andy says. "I'll come back this afternoon on my way home. I'm concerned by how much she's sleeping, though."

Mel shrugs. "She's been like this since Kate came around with her I'm-coming-to-fuck-you-tonight text messages from beyond the grave."

"Tough times," Andy says. "I'll see you at about three."

Mel nods.

❊

Three is when Elizabeth surfaces again. There's a mug of tea, cold, by her bed, but she thinks it's different from the one that was there earlier, when she took her last lot of pills. She wonders whether she can face at least a bit of the day.

But the plan has been so strong in her mind: take the pills, wake up when the day is over. Take the pills, wake up tomorrow. So this swallowing of tiny white pills is the obvious, the logical thing. And then she hears the voices in the garden. Mel, talking to Patricia.

That decides it. Elizabeth reaches for the pills again, gulps at the tea. As soon as she's taken them, things start to feel very strange.

The mug slips from her hand and the tea arcs itself across the space in front of her and onto the floor, landing in a wet strip.

The mug itself bounces on the corner of the bedside table, the vibration throwing the pill bottle off to land upside down on the rug. Elizabeth reaches for it, but her hand is in kaleidoscope.

The world has turned peculiar. Not scary, exactly.

Undulating.

Echoing with silence.

Calm.

A little nauseous.

Then very, very black.

❁

Patricia is saying, "I brought her a cake, and a present, and a card, but—" Her hands move in the air, grasping for a way to say, *I don't know whether it's the right thing, or if there is a right thing, but I'm trying.*

Mel says, "I know. It's hard. You've just missed Blake. He left her something. An envelope. He says not to give it to her until he's been back to explain. He was quite agitated."

"They always made such a fuss about their birthdays, the two of them." Although Patricia has determined that she has nothing to feel guilty about in getting involved with the Micklethwaites and her granddaughter-to-be, she can feel herself gabbling, anxious, faced with Mel's tired eyes and reproachful, sad smoking. "But it's hard to know what to do."

"Tell me about it."

But Patricia is spared any more, because Andy arrives, and Mel says, "Patricia put the kettle on, that cake isn't going to eat itself, and she can't possibly claim that four people is a party. I'll go and get her." And two minutes later, there's the scream.

❋

Andy calls the ambulance and puts Elizabeth in the recovery position. He says to Mel, "She's breathing. She's been sick. These are good things," although his hands are shaking. The bedroom smells of acid, tea, whiskey.

Patricia collects clean pajamas, a flannel, a towel, toothbrush, toothpaste, one of the guest soaps she gave Elizabeth at Christmas that's still in a box in the bathroom. She puts them in a bag with Elizabeth's phone, purse, book, and she puts the bag at Mel's feet.

"You go with her," she says. "I'll take Pepper and I'll lock up here."

Mel nods.

"Do you think it was deliberate?"

"I don't know, Patricia," Mel says. "All I know is that she didn't want a birthday. Could we really blame her if it was?"

Dear Mike,

Blake brought me a book about grief and one of the things it says is that you should write a letter to the person who has died and tell them how you feel. I thought that was a good idea. I've never written more than a thank-you note and I had to borrow the paper from Mum, because writing on paper from the printer or in a notebook didn't seem quite right.

I feel sad. And at the same time I try to think how lucky I am. Kayla is like a door opening, except I didn't know the door was there before. I'm going to have a completely different life from the life I had planned, but the more I think about it, the more I realize I wasn't really the one who had planned it. Exams, gap year, Oxford... It was all assumed somewhere, way back, because I'm bright and my parents are well off. That was going to be my life. I was sleepwalking.

Now I'm awake. I'm wide awake. Although my body's getting tired, I think being pregnant makes everything sharper and sweeter. I hear Dad muttering about my life being thrown away and I can't find the words to tell him that, really, it's just finding the right way.

At the same time as feeling lucky I feel sad. There are times when it feels unbearable not to be able to see you and touch you. I felt that way when you were alive too. I used to lie in bed at night and miss you and wish you were with me. I used to pretend that there was no Elizabeth. That day she found me in your garden, and I realized that she was wearing your dressing gown, was the first time that I really started to understand that she was a real person, that you had a real relationship.

Because we never lay in a bed together, when I lie in bed on my own it's easy to forget the real reason that you're not here, just for a moment or two. Then I remember, and it's like I'm thrashing about in that horrible water again.

The things I think about most are:

—I didn't get to tell you about the baby.

—I don't know what you would want to call her.

—We never went out for a meal together. When I was waitressing, I used to watch people in love with each other. The way they chose food, ate food, took their time, was different from any meal I've ever eaten. And I won't be able to say to Kayla, "Your dad and I came here" or "When we went to this restaurant your dad always ordered that."

—I don't know whether you ever would have come back to me, or loved me, or been a family with us. I hope you would have. I think you did love me. I think you probably loved her too. When you were here, I couldn't see that. Now that you've gone, and everything's complicated, I can understand better, I think. Especially because I broke a promise that I made to you. I'm sorry. That got complicated too.

Today Kayla and I go to the hospital to see the midwife and have a scan and talk about cystic fibrosis some more. In my heart I'm sure she's all right. In my head, I know we won't know anything for certain until she's born. But my head is swimming with questions and worries and the horrible thing Elizabeth said. Mum says any mum is worried, whether there's a risk to the baby or not. Mum says there's no reason to think that Kayla will have anything wrong with her at all: I'm well, Mike was well, his mother is well, and I should remember those things. I know she's right. She's right about a lot more than I used to think she was.

Writing this has been a bit weird. I don't know whether it's good or not. But I don't know how to end it.

between

K ATE HAD SPENT THE autumn full of an unwavering certainty
that Mike would change his mind. It wasn't as though he
hadn't done this before: avoided her, kept away from her, ignored
her. Come back for more. And Kate knew what made him come
back, so she kept out of his eye line. She watched him run but she
stayed well behind. She petted Pepper outside shops but she was
gone by the time he came out, newspaper under his arm, asking
Pepper what on earth he was eating this time. She worked double
shifts in the restaurant, a place she knew he would never come to,
and she read books in front of the fire on her days off, although
she probably couldn't have told you anything about them once she
finished them and put them aside. She helped her mother with a
work project and she answered the phone in Rufus's office for a
week when his receptionist left without giving notice.

And her feelings boiled and rolled like a solstice sea. She longed
for Mike. She missed him, she ached for him. She let herself cry at
night, late, when the rest of the house was sleeping, but most of the
time she presented a pale, serene face to the world.

And she waited.

Weeks passed, then a month. Almost another. These seven
weeks had felt like a lifetime. The only thing that kept Kate's little

ship of hope afloat was the fact that Mike didn't seem to have been doing much. There were no signs of him reembracing married life: no trips, no hand-in-hands through the streets of Throckton or around the shores of Butler's Pond. Mike seemed to be doing, mostly, solitary dog walking. Sometimes he was with the other policeman who had a greyhound, and Pepper scuttled along around the taller dog's legs. Once, she saw him with Elizabeth, arm in arm, but that was at Beau's Heights, and Kate thought this proof positive that she was not forgotten, that Mike, loyal, would not take his wife to the place that was so special to the two of them.

Christmas had threatened, then loomed. Kate had accepted invitations to parties and drinks from her friends who were coming home from their travels for a week or two. She had even made some halfhearted plans to join Bella for a fortnight in Morocco in the spring, but she knew that, if Mike had come back to her by then, she wouldn't be able to leave him, and if he hadn't, she wouldn't be able to leave Throckton in case he did.

Her world was transcribing a smaller and smaller orbit in the sky. She didn't mind, because her aim was to make a world smaller still. Just her and Mike.

And so came the ritual of the buying of the Christmas tree. It was the one thing that the Micklethwaites had always done together: come hell or high water, spitting rows or furious silences, on the second Saturday before Christmas, the three of them would get in the car and go to the garden center. There was an unspoken agreement between Richenda and Rufus. They both knew that a perfect Christmas was out of the question, that depending on where they were in the biorhythms of their marriage, either Richenda would be sulky and Rufus sneaky, or one or both of them would be noisily disappointed in the other for something, or both of them would be exhausted from the effort of trying to make things good. But a perfect Christmas tree was within their reach. It must be bushy and thick at the bottom, and arrow straight at the top, and the tree must be exactly seven feet tall, with the single top branch long enough to be striking but not so long as to be stringy. Richenda would ask the garden center staff to take off the netting in order that she could check the trees they had short-listed. They wouldn't like it, muttering about how busy they were, but Kate's mother would smile, and they would do it, and then Rufus and Richenda would stand with their heads together, as close as Kate ever saw them, earnest as owls, deciding. And Kate, watching, would wait for the moment when her blessing would be sought, and then the three of them would pay for the tree, arrange for delivery, and go out for lunch. It was the only time in the year when Kate could see why her parents might, once, have loved each other, seen enough in each other to attempt a life together.

This year, she'd left them to it. With her parents' marital relations frostier than the winter air this Christmas, the decision was clearly going to take some time, so Kate wandered through the rows of trees, thinking how different this year was from last. Last year she had had to be persuaded away from her books, focused as she was on doing well, doing better than well, getting away from this place and off, up, away in the world. This year, she was in possession of her four meaningless As at exams, no turtles nurtured, no foreign adventures apart from a fortnight sniveling in a shared house in Paris, and none of it mattered. All that mattered was where Mike was, what he was doing, what he was thinking. Whether he was thinking of her.

And then she'd seen them.

Mike and Elizabeth were holding hands. She had an ugly coat on, the sort that Richenda sometimes wore for bedding down the garden in the autumn, when she'd catch her daughter's look and say, "Kate, I don't care what I look like so long as I'm warm." Mike was wearing the leather coat, the one he and Kate had sometimes lain on. In all the people and the trees, with her head down and her hood up, Kate had been able to get close enough to hear what they were saying.

Elizabeth's eyes had been bright. Kate hadn't known that the brightness was to do with the terrible feeling Elizabeth always had in places like this. Christmas trees meant Christmas, which meant children. Children at every stage. Elizabeth always felt as though she was walking through an illustration of everything that she would miss: maneuvering a buggy up and down steps and through doorways; walking around, high with tiredness, a baby squalling on your chest; holding a little mittened hand; hoisting someone onto your shoulders so they could inspect the top of a tree. Watching sons tumble and race like Labrador pups, their ears and feet too big for them. Refereeing arguments. Marshaling the overexcited, calming the tired. Trying to get an unwilling adolescent to take their earphones out for long enough to contribute to the discussion. It had been all around Elizabeth, as usual, making her feverish with disappointment, beaming with determined love for the life that she does have.

But all Kate had seen was someone confident and happy, someone that she wanted to be, or at least, someone who was in the place that she wanted to be her place.

As she watched, Elizabeth had stood on tiptoe and reached up with her hands. She had dropped Mike's hand, as though the holding of it was nothing, and she'd said, "We have this conversation every year, Mike; you always say the ceiling of the alcove is higher than it is and we always buy a tree that's too tall and then we have to hack bits of it off. So I measured it, and it's this big."

He had laughed.

She had said, "Don't laugh. You know this morning, when you came back with Pepper and you were asking what I was doing, and I said I would tell you later? I was seeing if I could touch the ceiling, because I knew we would be having this conversation. And now here we are, having this conversation."

As Kate had watched, Elizabeth had pouted, and Mike had caught her around the waist and kissed her, such a kiss, as though the two of them were in love. And he'd whispered something, and she'd laughed, and he'd laughed, and Kate, who had been skewered to the spot by the sound of Elizabeth's voice, had found that she could move again.

She'd come up behind them where they stood, still entwined, and bumped Elizabeth's arm as she passed.

Elizabeth had turned and Kate had been able to say, "I'm sorry, I didn't see you there" clearly and smilingly, and there'd been that second's space when she'd been able to look at Mike, her eyes flicking to him and away, just for a blink, before she had walked on, past, to the place where her parents were still wondering between trees, and it was as though she'd never stepped away from them.

What Mike had understood in that moment was simple—he'd hurt Kate, and he'd hurt her very, very badly. He'd hardly given her a second thought since the day he'd told her that things had to stop. It was as though Elizabeth whispering that she was on his side had brought him home, and if he did think about Kate, it was in the way that he thought about a trip once it was over: within three days of being back into the routine of your usual life, it feels like another world.

He had turned back to Elizabeth, who was watching a mother cradling a scrap of a baby, the baby's cry hardly making an impact on the air, and he had thought about what an easy thing it was to hurt someone, how much less simple to save them.

❄

When the tree was decorated, Elizabeth had opened some wine, and she had said, without preamble, "I think you ought to tell me what's wrong, Mike."

They'd been sitting opposite the tree, the room lit only by its lights. It was the right height for the alcove, for once, something that Elizabeth had delighted in pointing out when they brought it in. When Patricia had popped around to "check the arrangements for Christmas Day"—as though they would dare to spend it anywhere but with her—and commented on what a good fit it was, Elizabeth had winked, and Michael had thought that the knock he had taken from seeing Kate had gone unnoticed.

But then Elizabeth had asked her question, and oddly enough, that moment when all was right in their world was the moment when he could have told her everything. Kate's pale eyes, the way she was there every time he turned around, until she seemed like a part of his life, the taste of mints and the smell of lip gloss, the way he thought it wouldn't, couldn't last, but it kept on lasting. (Sometimes he tells himself that, in the scheme of things, four months from Throckton Fair to the definite end was nothing compared to more than a decade with Elizabeth.) How every time, he had thought it would be the last, had understood that it was all wrong, but then she would be there again, and somehow disappointing her would have been worse than walking away, because she was there to be disappointed while Elizabeth didn't know. The curious addictiveness of secrets, for him who had never had any. That had been the moment when he could have told her everything; that had been the moment when she could have forgiven him, or started to, and the constant nagging thought that Kate might turn up at his door with one of those stupid pictures that she took would have been gone for good.

He had almost told her.

Then Elizabeth had said, "This all started just after the fire. Whatever it is, it started after the fire."

Michael had thought of the fire, a series of memories making a storyboard. First, the initial catch of the smoke in his face, the hot choking, the solidity of the heat he was pushing through. Then the terror on the mother's face when he found her, guided to her, it seemed, by the force of her need. The sight of the baby, who seemed already to have life threading out of him, wisping away. Pushing them through the smoke and out, back into the day, safe. The cold air as shocking as the hot had been not two minutes before. The paramedics, quick and professional until the baby cried, when their spines relaxed with relief and, just for a moment, they sought another eye to say, wordlessly, "I thought we were on a loser there."

Elizabeth's face at the hospital, horrified and pale. Kate's face at the summer fete, sun in her hair, another sort of pale.

He had said, "Yes, it started after the fire."

"Why did you do it?" she had asked. "I know I asked you at the time and I know you said you didn't know. But now…" And she had looked at him, as if to say, *Now you can talk, now I can listen. Now the shock is over and the world is coming back to being the way it should be. Now we can make some sense.*

He had sighed, blowing the last of the moment to talk about Kate out of him. "It was the thought of that baby," he had said, his words slow as they stretched to make themselves fit the things that there were no words for. "It was the thought of that baby. I thought about you saying how getting pregnant was only the first thing, then you had to keep the baby safe and help it grow and anything could happen to it, any time." Without looking at her, he had known that she was crying, although she wasn't making a sound.

"I see," she had said, and he had felt as though there could be an end of it, just as, a few moments ago, there had been a moment for Kate.

But he had kept talking, finding truth as the words came out, as though saying them was the only way to discover what he meant. "I couldn't bear the thought of that. I thought, what if those people were like us? What if it took them five years to have a baby? And now the baby is dying. I couldn't stand there."

Elizabeth nods. "I can understand that."

"And then, afterward, everyone was angry, and I could see why, but I felt—I felt disconnected from it. From all of you."

"Did you ever think that you might die? Because that was what I thought." She had said this before, at the time, but then it had been an accusation, and Michael had had to defend himself against it. As a statement of fact now, it was different, harder to hear.

"I don't think so," he had said, wishing for more words, better words. "I was just...lost. In the moment. Not thinking about anything. And that's a strange feeling. Hard to shake." He corrects himself, striving for some sort of accuracy. "It's been hard for me to shake, I think." Now Kate seems like a part of his recovery, the thing that's brought him back to his wife.

Elizabeth had nodded, and her body, taut as a rower's in the last strokes of a race, had relaxed and sunk toward his. "Have you shaken it now?"

"Yes," Michael had said, pulling her to him with arms full of everything he couldn't find words for. "I have." And he had been almost completely certain that it was true.

now

ELIZABETH IS NEITHER AWAKE nor asleep. She's lying in a clean white bed in a clean white room and, tempted as she is to think of herself as dead, she's fairly sure that heaven would smell better than disinfectant, and hell worse. Also, her head is banging, and she can feel the stiffness in her hand where she thinks a drip must be. Her stomach aches. She thinks someone might be sitting next to her. Keeping her eyes closed, she feels around her memory for clues, gently, so as not to make the headache roar. She finds: sleeping pills, whiskey, birthday; Mike, Kate, baby. She feels like a fool. She feels like a failure.

Dear Mel,

If you are reading this, then the worst has happened and I've done the thing I promised that I would never do. I've left you alone in the world. You probably don't remember. The two of us were sitting in the back of that social worker's car, and they were driving us to Uncle Al and Auntie Brenda's farm, and neither of us had really grasped that Mum was gone, but I think it was starting to sink in because you were crying. Not sobbing, but a sort of ongoing low-level snivel that was a much more truthful reflection of what the two of us were feeling, and what we would keep feeling for a long time. Motherlessness was a shock at first, but the worst of it has been that it never stops. At my wedding, I remember watching Mike's mother struggling down the sand in her heels and that hat, and how we looked at each other and tried not to laugh, but I think we were also trying not to cry because it's hard to have a wedding without a mother. It's hard to have a baby, or not have a baby, without a mother. It's hard to be here now, grieving and fuming, broken beyond all mending, without a mother.

And although we had no idea, on the day we sat in the back of that car, with the windows open but still the faint smell of other children's carsickness, of quite how it was going to be, I think my nine-year-old self had some sort of sense of it. So I took your hand and I told you I would never, ever leave you. And you looked at me and said, I know, as though it was the most obvious thing in the world, as though the fact that our mother had just been wiped off the face of the earth thanks to a blown-out back tire hadn't altered your world view a bit.

I'm writing this two days before my birthday, four days before yours. I'm writing it when everything is dark and frightening and I find myself wishing for a central reservation hurtling toward me, cold English water pulling me down. I keep thinking of how much I wish I could talk to Mike again, how, although we all understand that death is final, you don't completely get how final until it's too late.

Just after we got married, Mike made us write down everything we wanted to happen after our deaths: what happened to our bodies, who got what of our possessions, funeral songs, all that sort of thing. (Do you remember you wanted "The Birdie Song" for Mum? Because we all used to dance around to it when it came on the radio, and so you were sure it was her favorite song. I wish they'd listened to you. It would have been so much more fitting than anything about that horrible funeral. Although we did get "All Things Bright and Beautiful." I remember you leaning over to me during the eulogy and asking who the vicar was talking about.) After we'd done it, I kept thinking I would write a letter to him, that he could open after I died. I thought it would be comforting. Now I really wish we'd both done it, for each other.

So, here I am, writing to you, to say I'm sorry. I'm sorry I'm not here anymore. Whether you're reading this when you're thirty-two or when you're eighty, I promised to look after you, and if you're reading this, I've broken that promise.

As I write this, you're the one who's been doing most of the looking after. But I hope that it balanced out somewhere between me writing this and the rest of my life. I hope I got to be strong and helpful again, although at the moment...

KATE HASN'T SLEPT MUCH. She gives up and gets up at 6:00 a.m. and sits downstairs in the darkness, wondering how often she will be here when Kayla is born. She thinks about how everyone says she'll be really tired, but she can't imagine how she'll ever be more tired than she is now. Her body is starting to resist any sort of movement, wanting stillness and rest, but at the same time unable to find comfort, full of aches and twinges that make nights feel like marathons run.

And Kate's heart is unquiet. It carries the memory of Elizabeth two weeks ago, her pain and her fear. She keeps thinking about the conversation that she'd had with her mother, on the night they returned from seeing her and showing her the photographs. Kate had been distraught, and Richenda quiet, until Kate had said, "She had no right to speak to me like that," and waited for her mother's unstinting agreement. Instead, Richenda had sat down next to her, and said, "Kate, that woman has done nothing wrong. Even if they were unhappily married, she did nothing wrong. And she's done nothing to you. She trusted her husband and he betrayed that trust—"

"But—"

"But nothing, Kate. All of the times he was with you, he had told his wife he was somewhere else, or let her think that he was. She clearly had no idea what was going on—"

"But isn't that her fault?"

"Well, if trusting someone who loves you is a fault, then yes, I suppose it is."

Kate had made to get up, uncomfortable in almost every way it was possible to be uncomfortable, but Richenda had said, "I haven't finished." Kate had rearranged cushions behind her as she waited.

Richenda's mind had gone back to Rufus's first affair, in France, when they were newly married, his second while she was pregnant with Kate. She has thought that there have been several women since; she suspects that Rufus is lining the next one up now, but part of her clings to the lack of any real evidence. The new shirts, the late showers; it's all circumstantial, when it comes down to it. And she had to admit that the fear of being alone had kept her here: the possibility that life with Rufus might not quite be the most difficult way to live. She had thought of how her fiftieth birthday wasn't too many years away and had known that she'd waited too long to leave him. Perhaps, she had thought as her daughter waited for her to speak, if she had known then how much it would still hurt now, she would have done things differently.

"Can you imagine, just for a moment, how it must feel for Elizabeth, who had no idea her husband was unfaithful to her, no idea that he had fathered a child, and no way to understand it because she can't ask him?"

It's on the tip of Kate's tongue to say yes, she can understand perfectly well, because she is in the same position, but the wiser self that she will one day be intervenes and keeps her silent.

Richenda had said, "Elizabeth was unkind to you, and she said things that she shouldn't have. But Elizabeth is suffering in a way that neither you nor I can understand. If you want people to extend compassion and understanding to you—and you are probably going to need them to, if your life with your baby is going to be something good—then you need to think about doing the same for other people." And Kate had said nothing, and gone to bed, and tried to pick the seeds her mother had sown out of her heart.

But now, in the dark morning, it seems that she didn't get them all. She wonders what Elizabeth is doing, whether she is awake too.

Rufus clatters down the stairs, and when Kate says, "Morning, Dad," he jumps. Jumps again when he looks over to her, still unused to the unexpected body below the face he's adored ever since he watched it take its first scrunchy blink, more than nineteen years ago. He makes himself smile.

"Tea?"

"Yes, please."

"Toast? Or maybe some coal?"

"Very funny, Dad."

They sit, by unspoken consent, in the half dark. Kate balances her plate on her bump, and Rufus says, without thinking, "Your mother used to do that when she was expecting you." Kate thinks, *Two references to pregnancy in one morning. Maybe we're getting somewhere.*

She asks, "Are you disappointed, Dad?" and although in her head it was a strong, matter-of-fact, it's-time-we-addressed-this question, when it comes out, it's spoken by a little girl.

And perhaps that's why Rufus can answer it. "I'm disappointed for you, Kate," he says. "I hoped for so much for you, and although I know you think that you can manage it all still, and perhaps you will, it won't be the same. It won't be as—as carefree. It will be harder than you think it is, whether the baby is ill or not, and

I don't want that for you. I want you to have a wonderful life, not…" He pauses while he tries to think of a better phrase than "saddled with a baby," and in that space, Kate hauls herself up and over to him and sits next to him.

"She's kicking," she says, and she takes her father's unwilling hand and puts it on the place, and he can't help but smile. "And I know, Dad, that this isn't what you wanted, and it's not exactly what I planned either, but it's what I've got, so I'm going to do my best with it."

Rufus thinks of all that he wants to say. About how watching Richenda love Kate had been the best thing that he'd ever seen, as well as the thing that had made him feel most superfluous. About how, although it looks as if he cannot bear the thought of this baby, what he really cannot bear is the thought of his daughter being trapped, unhappy, unable to move, in the way that he and Richenda have been. But he takes a good look at Kate, who is looking down at her own body in wonder, her hand following the baby as it moves. Her filled-out face reminds him of her at six, with pigtails and a bike she fell off more than she ever rode, although it didn't stop her trying.

And he says nothing, until Kate turns to him and says, "Dad, will you go through my questions for the midwife with me, and see if there's anything I've missed?"

And he says, "Yes, Kate, of course I will."

❁

Elizabeth's world starts to fade. The hospital smell gets fainter and the rattle of voices around her stops, a tambourine put down on the floor. She feels a breath sigh out of her, and she is empty, then she is filled again with nothingness.

For the first time since Mike died, Elizabeth remembers what peaceful is like. She has the feeling she gets when she steps off the plane and sees the blue of an Australian sky. She tries to breathe without making a noise. She thinks she must be sleeping. Then she smells limes, hot fresh sweat. In her head, she asks, *Mike, is that you?*

Hello, he says.

She knows that it isn't him, of course it isn't. But it also sort of is, for as long as she keeps her eyes closed.

I'm so sorry, maybe-dream-Mike says. *So sorry.*

I know, her heart says. *I know you are. But I don't know why you did it. We were happy, weren't we? We were good. I go over it and over it and I can't see why you did it. We loved each other.*

The air moves as it does when someone shrugs, shifting the smells around. Elizabeth breathes in more limes. Mike's voice again: *I don't know why I did it either, except she seemed to need me.*

She keeps her eyes closed. She knows that she mustn't try to look at him; she mustn't try to touch where she is sure he is. If she does, he'll vanish, like her shadow when she switches out the light. *I needed you*, she thinks.

I know, Mike says. *I can see that now.* It's as though there's a cobweb thread between them. His voice comes again. *You were always so capable, so strong. Even about the baby, you could cope in a way that I couldn't.*

Did you really think that? Elizabeth asks. *It broke my heart. Breaks my heart. When it isn't breaking over you.*

Mike is getting quieter. *I think I needed someone to help*, he says. *You didn't seem to need me, Elizabeth.*

In this peaceful place she smiles. *If you were alive, I'd kill you for saying that, Mike. Shagging teenagers isn't helping anyone. And anyway, I was only capable because you were there. You were my stepping stones, and you've gone. You could see when I was sad before I did, and you found a way to distract me from the sadness. You came to collect me from work when it was raining. When we were running, you matched your pace to mine, even though you could have gone faster. Sometimes, I was sad, and just the sound of you at the door was enough to make me happy. I can't go on without you. I'll drown. I'm drowning. Right now.*

You can do this, Mike says, and Elizabeth can hear him breathing. She wants him to touch her. The tears are starting, the noise of the hospital coming back. He says, *I promise you, Elizabeth, you can do this.*

I wish you'd tell me what happened that night, she says. Her hands are gripping the blanket now, and so there's a pain where a needle goes into the back of her hand and she's stretching the skin around it, but it's not so much the pain as the sense of returning that makes her flinch. She tries to push the feeling of her body away, but her throat is adamant in its dryness, her headache pressing in. And there are tears, tears.

"Mike," she says out loud.

"Mel," comes the reply, as gruff as her own. "Welcome back, Sis."

And then there are people in the room, and painkillers, and questions, and Elizabeth cries when she understands what she's done, or nearly done. She tries to explain that all she was trying to do was sleep through her birthday, but the words don't seem to make sense to anyone except her. And then sleep comes again.

❊

The next time Elizabeth wakes, she feels better. Andy is by her bed this time.

"Hello," he says. "You've been asleep for a long time, but you're fine, Elizabeth."

"Hello," she says, and then she lies quietly for a while. Then: "I thought I was talking to Mike. It wasn't a dream." Her lips feel gummy, her throat furred. She struggles to sit up. Her head hurts but her mind feels clearer, a stirred pond allowed to settle. Andy hands her water, which is warmish with a metal tang. She doesn't mind.

"I'm so sorry about all this, Elizabeth," Andy says. "I should have seen the signs. I should have done more. I didn't know you were so—"

She closes her eyes. "I was trying to sleep through my birthday."

"Well, maybe," he says, "but you've had such a terrible time, Elizabeth, and I could have done more. We all could have done more."

"Well," Mel says, coming in with water, a bag of chocolate limes, magazines, a newspaper, "I think we could all agree that Mike could have done less."

Andy looks at her. Elizabeth tries out a laugh, just a small one. "There's no need for a doctor face, Andy," she says. "I'm OK." And as she says it, it sounds true.

"Well, you look like shit, Sister," Mel says.

"I feel like I've got a dozen hangovers."

"That's understandable," Andy says.

"You deserve them."

"I know. I'm going to pull myself together. I promise."

"Good," Andy says. Mel doesn't say anything until he leaves. Then: "I went back to get some sleep. Andy made me. And I found your suicide note."

Elizabeth says, for what feels like the fiftieth time and she still has the psychiatric assessment to go, "I only wanted to sleep through my birthday. That was all. I didn't leave a note."

Mel says, "Well, I found that letter you were writing me, that not-suicide note in which you wrote to me as though you were dead and I was alive."

"It wasn't—" Elizabeth feels all the disadvantage of the pajama-clad against the dressed, and gives up.

"Whatever it was," Mel says, "we need to stop thinking about dying all the time. Mike's dead. You're not. That needs to be our starting point now."

"Yes," Elizabeth says. "Yes." She wonders, if she put a little greenhouse in the sunniest corner of the garden, whether limes would grow.

❋

Richenda and Kate are leaving the hospital when they meet Patricia coming in. "Oh, I was just about to call you," Kate says, although actually she'd all but forgotten her promise, as she was so busy promising God or Mike or whoever it is who looks after these things that if Kayla is all right she'll be the best mother, the best person, she can be. To compensate for the almost-forgetting, she launches into a word-for-word recitation of her consultation, telling Patricia about the tests that the baby will have when she is five days old, the likelihood of her being all right, all of the things that can be done to help her if she isn't. Richenda, watching the conversation, can't help feeling that for a woman who's knitting enough baby blankets to fill a Red Cross helicopter, Patricia doesn't seem to be paying a lot of attention.

"Is everything all right?" Richenda asks.

"No, not really," Patricia says, agitation vibrating around her words. "Elizabeth took an overdose. She's awake now, she's all right, but, well, it's given me a bit of a fright."

They all stand, absorbing.

"I'm not sure where she is," Patricia says, looking around the atrium at the signs and corridors.

"This place is a bit of a maze," Richenda says, seeing what she can do to help, and as Kayla's two grandmothers consult the hospital map on the wall, Kate feels as though Mike is tapping her on the shoulder, he's so clearly there. She can hear him, telling her what to do. As soon as he says it, Kate knows that it's right, that it's time to get it all sorted. That there's Kayla to think about.

When Richenda and Patricia turn back, she says, "Do you think she'll see me?"

❁

When Patricia walks into the hospital room, she's overcome by pity and sadness for Elizabeth, who looks like the sorrowful, lost woman she's felt herself to be so many times, although she's never shown it. She feels tears beginning. Then Mel is at her elbow; Elizabeth reaches out a hand. For a moment, there's a real understanding.

When Patricia has gotten hold of her feelings—when she's stroked Elizabeth's head, her cheek, thought of how she could have lost this sweet girl too, closed her eyes and wished for something different for all of them—she realizes that it's going to be more difficult than she thought to do what she's just promised to do. But she does it. She holds Elizabeth's hand, and she says, as gently as she knows how, that she's just bumped into Kate, who is waiting outside and wondering if she could possibly come in and talk to Elizabeth. Mel swells to about twice her normal size.

"No, she fucking well can't, and she has no business asking, and neither have you."

Patricia does what Elizabeth and Michael would have rated as a seven on the shocked-face scale they had for his mother. They'd only managed a ten once, one Christmas, when Mike had suggested that he and Elizabeth were going to spend Christmas away, alone together, a plan that they hadn't dared see through.

"Well!" Patricia says. "I only asked."

Mel raises her voice so it can be heard outside, in the corridor. "Get that little cow away from here before I get hold of her."

But then Elizabeth says to Patricia, "Yes, she can come in," and to Mel, "She and I are just going to have to find a way."

She's rewarded with two faces that hit nine and a half on the shocked-face scale. "Can you both go outside please and ask Kate to come in?" She doesn't know whether it's the drugs or the sleep or the not-quite-dream about Mike, but she feels calm now, as though maybe she can get through.

Kate does a shocked face too—Elizabeth seems so ashen, diminished under the too-bright hospital light. Elizabeth smiles, a sad smile but a real one, that makes Kate realize how many pretend smiles were coming her way at the moment, and says, "I know, I look terrible, even for me. Sit down, Kate. It was brave of you to come in here."

So Kate sits. She hasn't been sure how she will start. Mike had seemed to vanish as suddenly as he had come, before he could say anything useful. So she just says, "I thought I should tell you what happened that night. I feel as though I should now. I didn't, before. I'm sorry."

"It was wrong of me to try to make you," Elizabeth says, "but I would like to know. I'd like to know it all, from the start, if you wouldn't mind telling me."

And once Kate starts, it won't stop coming. It isn't easy exactly, but Elizabeth's eyes are on her, and she feels as though what she is doing is making the most important speech she'll ever make. Kayla is hushed inside her, as though she understands that what she's experiencing is a piece of her own history being made.

Sometimes Elizabeth winces, sometimes she cries, but she doesn't stop looking and she doesn't speak. Somewhere in the middle, she takes Kate's hand. At the end, they are both crying.

Hello, my darling Elizabeth.

Sometimes I wonder what it would have been like if there hadn't been email when I came to Australia, and when I went home again. I know we would have called each other, but I wonder whether we would have written too. I remember, as a kid, being sent to the post office to buy those blue fold-up letters for my mum, when she used to write to her friends in Canada. I think we would have written letters, and I think because they were going to travel halfway around the world, we would have thought really carefully about what we wrote. Our instantaneous emails were lovely because they were so easy and inconsequential. But now I wish we'd written, because I think I could have done with the practice.

Because if you are reading this, my sweet, lovely Elizabeth, I am a very long way away again. When I've finished it, I'm going to seal it and give it to Blake and ask him to keep it to give to you if you ever need it. It's not a "sorry I died" letter, because if I was going to write one of those, I would have put it in the drawer with our other papers. (I hope you faced down my mother and stuck with my choice of "Spirit in the Sky," by the way.) It's a letter for you, for if ever you get to the point where you doubt me, or doubt my love for you, or feel as though things couldn't be any worse, then Blake will give it to you.

It's nearly Christmas. Today we bought the tree, and we talked about me walking into that fire, and I was overwhelmed by the feeling of how much I love you. I know we haven't had the life that we planned, that it's gone off the tracks here and there, and been hard. But whatever has happened, whatever I've done, I don't want you to think for a moment that I don't love you, heart and body and soul.

I'm writing this in the kitchen, and you're asleep in the bedroom, so really only about six feet away. I know you're sleeping because I can hear you snoring. I know that you'll stop when I get into bed, because you'll roll off your back and curl yourself into me, and suddenly you'll be as serene as can be. We have always been like that: serene together. Even in our first weeks and months, when we were fizzing with excitement and newness, there was something very still and calm at the center of us, like the water that you see when you look down a well. The trouble with a well is it makes you want to throw a stone into it. I'm sorry for the times I threw stones, and for the ripples.

If you're reading this, my darling Elizabeth, I'm sorry that things have gotten so bad. I could never imagine living without you. There was no imagined future for me where we weren't together. I promise. Nothing could be truer.

If you're reading this, I'm sorry I left you. I don't know whether this letter will make things better or worse. When I sat down to write it, I was wondering how I would manage to say all that I wanted to, but now it seems quite simple. Elizabeth, I might have been able to do a better job of loving you, but I couldn't have loved you more. Whatever this dark place is, it will end, and I promise you'll be happy again, and you'll be free of it.

Mike xxxx

I LIKE IT WHEN IT all goes back to normal," Elizabeth had said on the ninth of January, settling in with the crossword and a hot chocolate, nape damp from her bath still, while Mike had clipped on Pepper's lead and chucked her chin in passing.

"You love Christmas," he'd said.

"Yes," Elizabeth had said, "I love Christmas, but I also love the bit when it all goes back to normal. That's why I'm such a delight to be married to. I'm so easy to please. Christmas, not Christmas, I'm happy."

Mike had grinned, said, "See you later." And then he was gone.

❄

Michael has grown careless in his walking. It's more than four weeks since he had seen Kate in the garden center when they were buying their Christmas tree, and there'd been a moment when he'd wondered what she might do. But her promise of silence had been fervent and there was something in her that he had always trusted: trusted enough for nakedness, for text messages, for something that he didn't understand but that made him vulnerable.

All the same, he has avoided the usual spots, until tonight.

The moon is nearing fullness and when he sees her, a haze of moonlight and cold-air mist around her, he stops and looks, the way he would if he had come across a deer. Those eyes. She hasn't seen him, and so he keeps looking. He can see, so clearly, the woman that she almost is. He hopes that, in the future, if she thinks of him at all, she will think well of him. Any other possibility is unbearable, in this dangerous moonlight.

And then Pepper bounces over to her, and her face lights, and she searches Mike out and feels every bit as elated as she had known she would when he came back to her. She hasn't gone to the usual place every night but often enough, she has thought, for him to find her when he is ready to. And there's something else, something like the moment before exam results: the feeling that her life is about to change.

Unwillingness is watermarked into him as he sits down next to her. "Kate—" he says, but she's faster.

"I'm sorry about the Christmas tree thing. It wasn't very mature. I was just—I was surprised."

"You have nothing to apologize for," he says. "All of this is my fault."

"Well," Kate says, so, so aware that this could be her last shot, that he could be about to tell her again that they can't see each other anymore, so, so determined to do what she needs to. "I'm glad I've seen you, because I've got your Christmas present."

"I don't think—"

"Please," she says. Her voice is made magnetic with the memory of the day she bought it: a jeweler in Marsham, someone who didn't know her, so when they had asked if it was for her boyfriend she'd said yes, as though she were half of the most acknowledged couple there had ever been. "Our hands are the same size," she'd added, "although Mike's knuckles are bigger," loving the saying of his name.

He unwraps it. It's a ring. His heart sinks. "It's lovely," he says, "and very thoughtful, but you know I can't take it. You know I can't wear it."

Perhaps if Kate weeps, or screams, or threatens, or protests, it will work out differently. But she doesn't. She recognizes the hopelessness of the situation. She sees the look in his eyes, the way he is measuring the distance between where he is with her, and the life, the wife, he wants, and she thinks, *OK then.* And the hope goes out of her, and she takes the box back out of his hands.

And Mike feels hopelessness, and love, and acceptance pass through her—in this place that is the closest they have to a home, they are as alive to each other as a mouse and a cat—and he says, "Why don't you wear it for me?"

But his voice is too full of their scant past to make the words sound the way they should sound. They come out as softly as starlight. And so Kate, knowing that she's playing but knowing how true this is too, takes the ring and puts it on the third finger of her left hand, and she kisses him, and he is lost once more, lost even though he had promised himself he would never take this winding road again.

❀

They are walking along the path that will lead them back to the main road when Michael stops, and starts to throw stones into the water. He picks big ones, the size of a child's fist, and he hurls them as though he is trying to break windows.

Kate steps forward, puts her hand on his arm. "What is it? Mike?"

And he stops throwing, and turns, and looks at her.

Perhaps if he hadn't—if he'd kept facing away, if his words had lost some of their force without his eyes to vouch for them—things would have worked out differently.

"Kate," he says, "I shouldn't have done that. I'm sorry. I love my wife. You're lovely, lovely, but—I'm going to stay away from you. You're special, but you're not my wife. I don't love you. I love her. I'm sorry."

Kate's bra is uncomfortable because she hasn't done it up properly. Her thigh has a damp, cold trickle running down it. She says, "I don't understand."

"You do," Michael says. "You do."

And Kate, who cannot believe that her world can be changing so fast, tick and tock and tick again, moves to take off the ring, only silver because she couldn't afford gold, unengraved because she had thought there was more chance of him wearing it that way, and sees Mike checking his watch.

If he hadn't, things might have worked out differently.

Kate, who had been about to ask him to keep the ring, even if he never wore it, never thought about it, turns instead and throws it into the water.

And she slips.

Falls.

Mike grabs for her but only reaches her bag.

And so Kate is in the water, gulping for breath, shocked by the biting cold, feeling for the bottom of the lake that isn't there, reaching for the bank, which she can't get to.

She's cold. Colder than she would have thought she could be, so quickly. She hears Mike shouting at her to get hold of something—she sees he is holding something out to her—but her arm can't find it. Her legs can't work against the cold and the weight.

And then Mike is next to her. As soon as he'd seen her eyes lose focus, as soon as she'd gone quiet, he'd realized he had no chance of getting her from the bank, and he'd gone in.

With her clothes, she weighs a ton. She passes out as soon as he touches her. It's as though she knows she is safe.

He lifts her onto the bank, lays her down, and he sees her chest rise and fall, and he wills those moon eyes to open.

He is dragging himself out of the water, although the water is doing its best to hold on to his freezing clothes, when Pepper, who has a dog's instinct for a crisis and a dog's capability for planning, hurls himself in to help.

Mike curses, reaches for him, misses, reaches again, and then he loses his footing and he's over and under before he knows it. He breaks the surface with a great shout, not so much as a word as a plea for things to start going right, right now, and he frightens Pepper into going farther away from the bank.

And he goes after him, even though he knows he shouldn't.

Of course he does.

Mike,

It's almost a month since I last wrote you a letter.

After Kate came to see me at the hospital I felt a sort of relief. I cried and cried and Mel and all of the nurses and doctors were doing worried faces at one another, but I kept on telling them I was all right. And I did feel better than I had done since you died, in a funny way. Kate brought me the bits of you that were missing, and when I had them, the picture was whole. I didn't like the whole picture, of course—I never will—but having it meant that I knew what I was dealing with. I had the answers I needed.

Before I was allowed to come home I was assessed by a psychiatrist. She listened to the almost-full story—everything except for you coming to see me at the hospital, I'm not ready to let that go yet. And she said, "I think what's happening to you is very simple, Elizabeth. Your husband let you down by dying and he let you down again by fathering a child with someone else. You're grieving. There's nothing more human than that. It would be more worrying if you weren't sad and upset. I don't think you made a serious suicide attempt, but I do think you need some help, to cope with it all."

And it all seemed so straightforward when she put it like that.

So now I see a counselor twice a week and, after eight sessions, I feel *a bit less angry and a lot more sad, but it's part of a process. The biggest thing is understanding that I am in a process that will lead to me being all right again. For the last nine months I've been fighting to stay at the bottom of the pond.*

Kate and I have met, twice. Once she waddled her way around here—by prior arrangement, as our two households are like warring nations trying to figure out a truce—to see if I was all right. I think the talk we had at the hospital made her realize that I was a real person who loved you, so we have a peculiar bond forming. I don't think I was very nice to her. I wasn't horrible, just too sad to make an effort. I refused to talk about the baby. We sat in the garden—you know that corner where the bench is, where, in autumn, the heat sometimes gathers? We sat there. I asked her why she brought the flowers here. She said, "I used to walk past your house and think about him being inside. I still did it when he had died. It felt like the closest I could get." I said, "That makes sense. Well, about as much sense as me thinking Mike was leaving the flowers." Mel brought some tea out and asked Kate how many stretch marks she had. I told her off, afterward.

Then I went to see Kate. I'd been going through our papers, sorting things out, shredding, filing, and I found the papers and letters and reports from the fertility clinic. Everything that our blood and genes said, none of which helped us, in the end. I thought of what a waste of time it had all been, and then I thought about how Kate would know none of it. So I went around and I told her everything the reports said about you, including being a cystic fibrosis carrier. I didn't know whether it was the right thing to do—I checked my heart, so carefully, for malice before I went, and if I'd found any I wouldn't have gone—but I think she was relieved. And if there are problems with the baby, the more she knows, the better.

I met Patricia going in as I was leaving. (The Micklethwaites have now been added to her jam distribution list.) She looked caught out. I smiled and said, "Doesn't Kate look well," which was a mighty effort, but your mother is the only family I have here, so I was prepared to make it. And it's true: Kate is round and fat, like a big shiny apple.

I've asked Mel to go home and promised to go out there and stay with her for Christmas. We were booking flights this morning, when Richenda rang to let me know that Kate had gone into labor during the night and they were heading to the hospital. She didn't give me any more details. I'm not sure I wanted any more details anyway. I knew the important thing: your baby was on her way. Kate texted me a little smiley face. (I feel so old, sometimes. Texting during labor? Really?) I texted back "Thinking of you." It was the best I could manage. And it's true. I am thinking of her.

I had a plan ready for this. Blake and Andy and the counselor all say it's great that I feel I'm ready to start building a new life without you, but I need strategies. Apparently, hoping that it will all be all right somehow doesn't count as strategy. (I can hear you saying that too.) So I left my phone on the kitchen table, and I took my bag from the door where it's been packed and waiting for the last week, and I rattled Pepper's lead until he woke up. I promised Mel that I wasn't going to throw myself in. Then our funny little dog and I walked down to Butler's Pond, to the place where you did the decent thing, or at least a decent thing, in getting Kate out of the water. I'm starting to think that all of the decent things you did during your life, added up, might outweigh the indecent thing. (Like the letter. The letter was good. Thank you. So was Kate being brave enough to tell me what happened in the end.) I haven't finally decided on that, though, so you're not out of the heavenly dog house just yet.

I miss you still, so terribly. My jaw hurts when I wake up in the morning, because I've been grinding my teeth in the night, all through my furious dreams. You're such an ache of absence. If I look very far ahead, I get overwhelmed, and feel tiny and weak and as though it's not worth trying to be anything except tiny and weak.

I tried sitting by the water and reading for a bit, but my mind wouldn't *settle, so I stowed my rucksack and ran a couple of laps around the lake. (I'm doing the London Marathon for us, by the way, for the Cystic Fibrosis Trust.) Then a couple more. Pepper was tired, so I sat on that fallen tree and looked at the water, and wondered how often we'd sat watching a sun start to set. Probably very often. Certainly not often enough.*

Your mother and I had a long talk on the day after we'd met at the Micklethwaites'. It wasn't easy, but it was easier than the way we've been avoiding confronting any of this. She said that this baby is not to blame for how she came to be, and should be welcomed and loved like any other baby. I said yes, and I meant it. I told her I wasn't sure how good I would be at it. She said, "Elizabeth, none of us know that."

I stayed at Butler's Pond until the sun went down. I had some crackers in my bag and I shared them with Pepper. Blake came past with Hope but I waved them away. And when I felt, as certainly as it's possible to feel without being faced with the reality of it, that I could do my bit of the baby blessing, I walked home. I walked home very slowly, and I felt sad and lonely, but I always feel that way when I remember that I'm going to put my key in the door and you won't be on the other side, waiting for me.

There was a message, though, delivered by your mother in her special talking-to-an-answering-machine voice. (I switched it back on and changed the recording on it last week, so it's my voice now.) Mel held my hand as I listened to it. The baby is here. She was born at 7:07 p.m., weighing 7 lb. 2 oz., and she is safe and sound. So is her mother. The birth was smooth and calm, in the birthing pool with the lights dimmed.

Her name is Daisy Gray Micklethwaite.

Congratulations, Daddy.

And, I think, good-bye.

E xxx

reading
group guide

1. Several of the characters are harboring devastating secrets. Are secrets always bad things? Has there been a time in your life when you kept a secret from someone you loved? How did it turn out?

2. Elizabeth and Mel see themselves as orphans, with only each other in the world. How has this belief shaped the way they behave?

3. Think about the marriages in the book. Which of them are healthy? Do love and marriage always go together?

4. How do Elizabeth's and Kate's ideas of what love is change during the course of the book?

5. Do you think Elizabeth really wanted to die?

6. Do you understand why Mike behaved the way he did? If you were Elizabeth, would you have understood?

7. The life events of having a baby, or not having a baby, are

important to the story. If Elizabeth's infertility treatment was successful, do you think that would have changed her and Mike's outcome?

8. Patricia and Elizabeth grieve very differently. Have you had experience with someone in your life who grieves in a way you thought was odd or inappropriate? What does how we grieve say about us?

9. To what extent is Kate responsible for her own actions? Do you sympathize with her?

10. The image of water is significant throughout the book. What are some possible reasons the author chose this as a theme?

11. Is there one single point in *The Secrets We Keep* where it all goes wrong, or is it tough to pinpoint where everything begins to unravel? Can you look back on your own life and identify pivotal moments where things changed for you?

12. What do you think the characters will be doing five years after the end of the book?

a conversation
with the author

How old were you when you wrote your first story? What was it about?

Goodness, that's a tricky one! I remember doing a lesson on descriptive writing at school—I was probably about eight or nine—and the following Sunday at my grandmother's, writing a description of her living room in the tall, narrow notebook she had for making shopping lists. She kept it for years, and whenever I did well or won prizes for English at school, she would talk about it. It obviously made an impression on her!

What do you love most about writing?

I love the possibility of a perfect world. Not perfect in the sense of everything being shiny and delightful—that would be the world's dullest book—but perfection in the sense of a balanced world of cause and effect, action and reaction, the stars aligning at a single point and making someone's world alter beyond recognition. The fact that that someone is made-up is neither here nor there.

What inspires you the most as a writer?

I get inspired by possibility, by the million directions every small step we make could take us.

Who are some of your favorite authors? Why are they your favorites?

I love books by John Updike, Margaret Atwood, and Jane Austen. They all have a knack for making characters who aren't always likable but who you root for all the same. Updike's Rabbit and Austen's Elinor Dashwood are two of my favorite characters ever.

When do you know the story is finished?

When I think of a change and go back to make it to find that I'd already thought of it, or that the change I had in mind won't make things better, only different. But that's not to say that some sound editorial advice won't mean that I make more changes. And I think any story is written from the place where you are in your life. If I wrote Elizabeth's story a decade from now, it would be different, for sure.

What advice would you give to aspiring writers?

Write. It sounds ridiculous, but I would say that 90 percent of the people I meet who say they want to be a writer haven't written a word. Find the time of day that suits you best, and write five hundred words every day, regardless of whether you feel like it, whether you're inspired. In six months, you'll have a first draft. It will probably be awful, because that's what first drafts are for. But at least then you have something to work on.

What is one thing you know now that you wish you knew when you started your writing career?

That it's the writing that gives the most pleasure, and I had that from the beginning. Don't get me wrong: meeting readers is brilliant and holding your book in your hand is a thrill like nothing else. But the very best bit, for me, is when it's just me and my tea and my screen and my words. If I'd known that at the start, I'd have worried less about being published and understood that I already had everything I wanted.

Did you always want to be a writer, or did you start off in a different career?

I always wanted to be a writer. I studied English at university, and for as long as I can remember, if I have a book in my hand, I'm happy. But I have another career too—I train organizations all over the world on creativity and thinking skills. I've been doing it for more than a decade, and I love it. And it brings me into contact with other worlds, other stories.

If you could spend one day with an author, dead or alive, who would it be and why?

George Eliot. Her writing is brilliant, and her breadth and depth of knowledge fascinates me. She was thinking and writing about things women weren't supposed to be dabbling in. I'd want to talk to her and understand more about what motivated her—and what she thought she would do if she wasn't constrained by the social mores of the time.

What are your favorite genres to read?

I like good writing that takes me along and doesn't jar. So I read across almost all genres—literary fiction, science fiction, nonfiction, historical romance. Basically, I'll try anything (except horror). I give a book fifty pages, and if I'm not engaged, I give up. There are too many books in the world to persevere with the ones that don't work for me!

How would you describe your writing style in one word?

Emotionally intelligent. (Okay, that's two. I cheated.)

What is the most challenging part of being a writer?

Sitting in bookshops at signings, being surrounded by books that, as the hours wear on, you become convinced are all a million times better than yours so that, in the end, you want to dissuade everyone who comes to your table from buying your book and recommend Jane Austen instead.

What research or preparation did you engage in before writing this book?

I talked to police officers about procedures, doctors and parents about medical issues that occur in the book, and a GP about how GPs operate in their communities. I quizzed Australian friends about being an expat and talked genetics, architecture, and running with anyone who was willing. I like to get details right, even if it is about what shoes you would wear for a marathon. I'm constantly amazed by how generous people are when it comes to helping me out with what must seem like really foolish, basic questions.

Which character do you feel most closely connected to?

I'm afraid they are all my book children, and I love them all equally (although I don't always love their behavior). And that's all I'm saying. (Oh, all right then. Maybe Elizabeth, because she has such a good heart. Or Kate, because she had no idea where that pumpkin jam was going to take her.)

Are any of your characters inspired by the people around you?

Yes and no. There's no one I've taken from Real Life

wholesale. But I borrowed Kate's moon hair from a woman on a train and Blake's compassion from a student doctor I met in the hospital. Patricia's trying forbearance was the stock-in-trade of a friend of my maternal grandmother. I suppose what I do is Notice Things, and then, when I'm creating a character, I go to my store and see what's in there that feels like a match. I saw a young man on the train with his shoes laced incorrectly, and a whole character in a forthcoming book has come from that. Oh, and Mel comes from a lot of the things I would say if I were able to think of something witty in time, instead of three days later.

acknowledgments

I'm very grateful to Alan Butland, Jude Evans, Emily Medland, and Susan Young, who have read every word of this book in all its incarnations and been both honest and encouraging, which is quite a difficult trick to pull off. Thanks too to early readers Anne Booth, Camille Johnson, Claire Marriott, Alison Morton, and Ned Tilbrook.

Claire Malcolm at New Writing North gave me the key to unlocking the story I really wanted to tell. Joy Tilbrook insisted that I put a dog in, and that was immensely helpful to the story too. (She also loaned her dog, Hope, to Blake.) Charles Armstrong came up with the original title (*Surrounded by Water*) fifteen years ago, when we were very drunk indeed. Thank you all.

Sharon Birch and Karl Weston talked to me about police and legal matters. Dr. Jane Stewart gave up an afternoon to talk fertility treatments and cystic fibrosis, and Dr. Becky Haines gave great insights into the life of a GP. Alison Morton told me about being a translator. Diane Mulholland answered my questions about being an Australian expat in the UK; Sara Lancaster, about what it's like to be an architect. Chris Schorah and Lyndsey-Jane Copeman talked genetics with me. Gemma Ravenscroft answered my first questions about cystic fibrosis with great patience and understanding.

Michael Breeze, Peter Hepworth, Philippa Moore, and Jo Sullivan shared their experience of marathon running. Denyse Kirby and Kirsty Burfot helped me out with the midwifery side of things. Twitter named the twins. I appreciate all of your help.

My fabulous agent, Oliver Munson at A. M. Heath, is unfailingly supportive and insightful. Emma Buckley at Transworld in the UK did great work with bringing early versions of this book on. The team at Sourcebooks in the United States has been patient, professional, and a joy to work with. Thank you all.

For nonspecific but immensely valuable love and support, I am grateful to my family and friends: Alan, Ned, Joy, Mum, Dad, Auntie Susan, Lou, Jude, Rebecca, Scarlet, Nathalie, Emily, Kym—I don't know what I'd do without you.

about the author

Stephanie Butland lives in Northumberland, in the northeast of England, with her family. This is her first novel. She has written two previous books about her dance with cancer.

You can follow Stephanie on Twitter @under_blue_sky and find her on Facebook. Her website is www.stephaniebutland.com.